D1253485

THE THREE
MUSTANGEERS

Donated by
the Will James
Society

The three rode out of town for wild horse country.

THE THREE MUSTANGEERS

By Will James

Illustrated by the Author

MOUNTAIN PRESS PUBLISHING COMPANY
Missoula, Montana
1999

First Printing, May 1999

Library of Congress Cataloging-in-Publication Data

James, Will, 1892–1942

The three mustangeers / by Will James ; illustrated by the author.

p. cm. –(Tumbleweed series)

ISBN 0-87842-400-8 (alk. paper). – ISBN 0-87842-401-6 (alk. paper)

I. Title. II. Series: James, Will, 1892–1942. Tumbleweed series.

PS3519.A5298T48 1999

813'.52–dc21   99-13722

                                             CIP

PRINTED IN THE UNITED STATES OF AMERICA

Mountain Press Publishing Company

P. O. Box 2399 • 1301 S. Third Street W.

Missoula, MT 59806

TO CHARLIE SCRIBNER

BOOKS BY WILL JAMES

PUBLISHER'S NOTE

Will James's books represent an American treasure. His writings and drawings introduced generations of captivated readers to the lifestyle and spirit of the American cowboy and the West. Following James's death in 1942, the reputation of this remarkable artist and writer languished, and nearly all of his twenty-four books went out of print. But in recent years, interest in James's work has surged, due in part to the publication of several biographies and film documentaries, public exhibitions of James's art, and the formation of the Will James Society.

Now, in conjunction with the Will James Art Company of Billings, Montana, Mountain Press Publishing Company is reprinting each of Will James's classic books in handsome cloth and paperback editions. The new editions contain all the original artwork and text, feature an attractive new design, and are printed on acid-free paper to ensure many years of reading pleasure. They will be republished under the name the Tumbleweed Series.

The republication of Will James's books would not have been possible without the help and support of the many fans of Will James. Because all James's books and artwork remain under copyright protection, the Will James Art Company has been instrumental in providing the necessary permissions and furnishing artwork. Special care has been taken to keep each volume in the Tumbleweed Series faithful to the original vision of Will James.

Mountain Press is pleased to make Will James's books available again. Read and enjoy!

The Will James Society was formed in 1992 as a nonprofit organization dedicated to preserving the memory and works of Will James. The society is one of the primary catalysts behind a growing interest in not only Will James and his work, but also the life and heritage of the working cowboy. For more information on the society, contact:

Will James Society • c/o Will James Art Company
2237 Rosewyn Lane • Billings, Montana 59102

ILLUSTRATIONS

PREFACE

Most Humans, like most animals, grow up in mind and body and learning to fit with their surroundings. The city man will wear his stiff collar and spend his life between four walls in as contended a way as the barn-raised horse will with his halter on his head and box stall around him. The cowboy will take the heat of the sun, the cold of the "Norther" and sleep on the ground, and his horse would kick a box stall and stable to pieces to be running on the range. Neither of the two breeds of men or horse would or could trade places.

With the three men in this story, the surroundings of their raising was in outlaw country and amongst outlaw men and they growed with that as natural as a hawk grows with wings. They're not outlaws because they're bad or want to be bad. There's no more desperate or vicious thoughts about their outlaw doings than there would be with a fox robbing a chicken coop. It's the only life they know, riding is their work, and outsmarting stockmen and sheriffs while stealing cattle and horses is their pleasure.

The story of course is fiction, but I done my best to make it true of the average of the range outlaw.

THE THREE
MUSTANGEERS

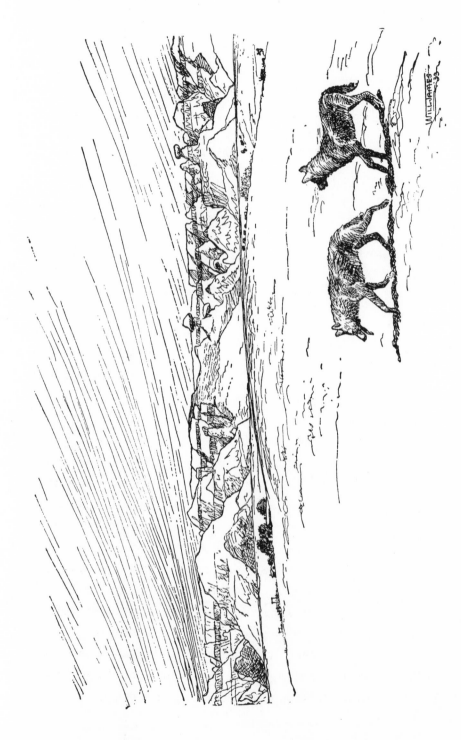

Andy Thomas' dad had took some land and went on to build a ranch to within a couple of miles of the badland strip.

CHAPTER ONE

ANDY THOMAS WOULD OF MOST LIKELY BEEN a plain average and just a hard-riding cowboy if he'd been brought up where such kind of men rode. There was such men in the country but there was more of the other kind, the bad kind. The country itself was bad and rough, mighty rough and the ridges of it was mighty tricky. Few stock roamed in it, only during winters when the ground was froze, and the name which had been fitted on that hundred-mile strip by the first white man who'd come to it fitted it mighty well. It had been called the Mad Lands.

Indian war parties had rode around it, and that had been a good thing for some white men of them days because they could dodge and hide in the twisted jungle of earth till the warriors went by, but, then again, the buffalo had never went in there either, only for shelter in the hardest of winters and that made it bad for who might be hiding if he was short of meat.

Andy Thomas' dad had took some land and went on to build a ranch to within a couple of miles of the badland strip. There was plenty of alkali and wire grass on his land and enough good water, then in the badlands his stock could winter in shelter and feed on the few bunches of grass that'd took a footing around the bends of deep and narrow washes. He'd never have to go in there after his cattle when thaws come, they'd all come out of their own accord and what few didn't he left 'em be.

He done well in that country, a lot better than any body did or could suspect, and it wasn't till young Andy Thomas got big enough to be useful and understand some that he got an inkling why his dad done so well.

The ranch being located close to the badlands, and being there was no other ranches along them badlands to within thirty miles each way made the Thomas ranch a mighty handy place for outlaws of different kinds to hit for if they was being crowded too close and wanted to hide right quick. They'd found that they could get some grub in a hurry from Old Thomas, and a fresh horse if they needed it and then they could ride their way into the deep of the badlands. They'd also learned what a fox Old Thomas was at putting any pursuers off and on the wrong trail. There'd be a sort of pious look about Old Thomas' face and strong feeling for law if a sheriff dropped in on him. He'd feed him his best and offer him a horse, remarking that he hadn't seen anybody for so long that he'd got to wondering if there was any other human beings besides them at his ranch.

The sheriffs, or deputies, or posses would most always leave without even asking if he'd seen the party or parties they was out after. And there they was lost because they'd figure that anybody they was after sure wouldn't go to hiding in them badlands without grub. Old Thomas sure hadn't seen anybody to give any to, they thought, and it was seldom that any outlaw ever cached any grub before committing his crime. If he had, and he did get in the badlands they figured Old Thomas would somehow know about it and tell them, so they went to investigating in other parts of the strip. All of that strip was bad, dry rough and made up of twisted pinnacles. It was a dangerous country to ride. In some places sometimes a horse could easy drop out of sight from under a rider, then there was boxed narrow washes that narrowed sudden and the rider would have to turn back, the ridges would come to narrow, knife edge tips too. The earth had no bottom where it looked hard and dry in places, then there was some clear springs that was poisonous to drink from and slimy look-ing water out of some others that was good, sometimes.

It was a country that a man had to know, where you had to ride all day to make five miles in a straight course and where once a stranger got far enough in it he was mighty lucky to ever find his way out.

The officers from the neighboring countries all knowed of that bad-lands strip and none of 'em cared to go winding thru it unless it was for a man that was plum bad thru and thru and had a big bounty on his head that was for getting him dead or alive. Even the outlaws them-selves dodged that country, they'd most all take to the rocky timbered mountains, and there's where many would get caught.

But for some hundreds of miles around there was many who knowed of the safety of Old Thomas' badlands and come on the high lope to him whenever the law was on their trail. That place was a secret to them, and after they'd stayed in their hideout till things sort of blowed over and then rode out again for new territories to where they wasn't known they'd just sort of close their eyes at the thought they'd ever seen the camp they'd hid so well in, they might soon be needing it again, and drunk or sober none of 'em would ever tell where it was.

The way the outlaws got to know of the Thomas ranch dated back to the time he first started to build it, some ten years before, and by the time any outlaw rider spotted the place and rode up to it he was many more miles from some place where things had been ticklish for him, he'd most always be out of the little grub he could pack and mighty hungry, and his horse would be most all in, too. All that would sort of make a rider take a chance, and when noticing the scattering of buildings and corrals in the distance that rider would be mighty pleased at the sight and head his tired horse for it.

The first few riders got sort of cool receptions from Old Thomas, but he took care of 'em and fed 'em. He was hospitable and asked no questions. He'd give 'em a fresh horse in the place of the one they was

The brand was the main thing.

riding because most of them boys was riding fine horses, only tired and ganted up and leg-weary, but that all could be cured with a few weeks rest. He never worried if the horses was stolen, for he was an artist at altering a brand and being if anybody come on the trail of the outlaws and seen the horses they'd be officers and not owners of the horses. The officers wouldn't have no way of identifying the horses only by brands, color, and markings. The brand was the main thing, Old Thomas would take care of that first.

But what few officers trailed their men to his ranch wasn't worried about the horses they rode, they was wanting the men that rode 'em. Then Old Thomas would point some direction towards the worst of the badlands, away from his territory.

With the first few outlaws that come his way for grub and help, Old Thomas got to thinking it sure wasn't a bad idea to have his place be a sort of home light for the bad gentry. For after them first few had hid where he told 'em, him furnishing 'em grub for a month or so and turning officers the wrong way they came back to him with solid gold money which all well paid many times for his trouble and grub.

Old Thomas had a raw ranch to improve and build up, he had to stock it up with cattle too. That sure took money, and then he had a wife he wanted to build a good ranch home for. He'd have to hire a ranch hand or two to help him do that and he sure didn't have much money to start with, so, whatever he got from the bad boys he helped sure helped him, and when tired dubious acting strangers rode in on him he wasn't exactly like a father to 'em but he sure gave 'em the protection they wanted, and that was all they wanted.

Some couldn't pay for their keep in the badlands. Far as that went, Old Thomas never asked none to pay, he didn't have to, but the most of them that didn't pay was because they had nothing to pay with. Some was too lowdown in mind to appreciate too, but many of them that didn't pay sometimes rode back and paid, and with mighty good interest. It might of took 'em a year or two and with covering a heap of territory, taking a lot of chances with doing more against the law, hiding in other countries and all, it would take a little time for them to make their circle and get back to Old Thomas' territory. The outlaws figured they might be needing his help again, and need it mighty bad.

Old Thomas got to know his badlands mighty well, so well that he could hide an outlaw, with grazing for his horse, ten miles or so inside of 'em and he felt sure that no strange rider could of trailed or found him within ten days' time, and then the strange rider would have to have an idea to within a few miles of where the outlaw was hid if he did find him in that time.

There was quite a few such places that Old Thomas had spotted, and quite a few outlaws got to know of them places thru him. They was safe places, not like amongst mountains, because no matter how rough a mountain is, how thick the trees and how many places there is to hide away in 'em there's always the chances of some trapper, prospector, or ranger running onto the feller on the dodge, and as news of bad deeds and descriptions of the men who do 'em seem to travel on air everywhere it sure don't pay for a feller hiding out to meet any stranger no time. Any of them strangers might be wearing a star too, for them star wearers will go any place any outlaw will and go thru as much hardships getting him as the outlaw will in trying to get away, and what turned the officers at the Mad Lands wasn't that they was afraid to take the chances to go in there, it was that they didn't think a man would be fool enough to try and hide in that poisonous and treacherous land. A man would have to have food, there wasn't a speck of game in that country and they believed so in Old Thomas' pious look and words that they couldn't think of him helping any man who'd do the least bit wrong. His was the only place were they could get help, and believing in him as they did, the officers rode the way he pointed and left his territory pretty well alone.

One outlaw brought on another till there was times when Old Thomas was taking care of three and four of them sheriff dodgers at once. All was going fine. He built his home, had his little ranch stocked up, and to make things finer here comes this squawking infant one day that him and his wife decided to call Andy.

Andy's first ride had been on a stolen horse that an outlaw had traded to Old Thomas for a fresh one, and as Andy growed up he was pretty well riding them kind of horses all the time. He'd got to watching his dad change the brands on them stolen horses with no more feeling that there was any more wrong to it than if he was hoeing potatoes. He had the same feeling about the outlaws that come and went, they was fellers to hide and protect and to keep quiet about. There'd been nothing said to him that whatever they'd done was wrong, they'd just done something

Any of them strangers might be wearing a star too.

that other people didn't like for 'em to do and they had to hide for a spell on that account.

The first breed of outlaws that Andy remembered was mostly "road agents" (stage robbers), train and bank robbers and gun fighters. There was very few of the range riding outlaws like the cattle and horse thief. Andy liked the range outlaw the best because he understood and could talk to them better. Most of the other kind of outlaws seemed kind of lost out there in the badlands. Of course that's what they wanted, but Andy was still mighty little when he seen it was a good thing his dad hid and took care of 'em because they'd sure been caught.

One would ride in once in a while that was wounded bad and delirious. Old Thomas would hide him in the house and with the help of the close mouthed squaw that worked around the house he would pull him thru, most always. Andy talked to them as much as he could while they recuperated. He lived on their stories and that took the place of book reading for him.

But while his mother lived he didn't get much chance to talk to any of the bad gentry. She didn't believe in bad men and in helping them, and her and her husband had many a talk on that subject, to which he'd come back at her that none of these fellers was bad at heart, just took the wrong trail and most any of 'em would give their life for him. They'd do bad wether he helped 'em or not, and he didn't see nothing wrong in helping 'em when they was afoot and hungry and wanted to hide.

He hid outlaws that he could of turned over to officers and collected many thousands of dollars in reward for 'em. Them outlaws knowed it, and the way they'd sometimes return the favor Old Thomas had done 'em would sort of confuse him all over in accepting. It didn't bother him that what he accepted had been stole, it was good unmarked gold, the outlaws had staked their lives to getting it and he accepted what they offered knowing it'd make their heart feel good.

CHAPTER ONE

Andy was only eight years old when his mother died, and missing and yearning for her as he did he took to the company of whatever outlaw showed up all he could. Old Thomas didn't stop him at that because he figured the boy would sure be getting first hand information which would most likely learn him aplenty, give him a bellyful of the life and keep him from ever wanting to lead one like it.

Later on, Andy got to riding towards the Bad Lands a-looking for outlaw hideouts, just so he could talk and visit with 'em. His company would of sure been welcome because hiding out is sure mighty lonesome and hard on the nerves, and all that keeps the outlaw in hiding is the one scary thought or visions of years behind the bars, or maybe a hang rope.

Andy never could find any of the outlaws' hiding places. He sure tried hard enough, and one day his dad rode onto him a few miles inside the bad lands.

"I been wondering who's been making all these tracks around here," says Old Thomas, looking hard at Andy. "Don't you know, Son," he says, "that these tracks you're making make this country look pretty popular? . . . A sheriff would think so and wonder who could be riding in this forsaken country and why, unless it was somebody on the dodge. He'd be apt to get mighty curious and do a heap of investigating all around, and by accident he might run acrost one of the boys' hideouts. That'd queer this whole country, Son, and besides, the boys not recognizing you from a distance, you're taking chances of getting your bonnet perforated fooling around here."

Heavy rains come and washed out all of Andy's tracks, then one day, while the earth was still boggy, a feller rode in on a horse that was as wore out as he was himself. But he couldn't stop, two officers was right on his trail, and he had to have a fresh horse and hit for the badlands, and hide where he could sleep and sleep some more. He felt like he hadn't closed an eye for a week of nights, he hadn't had a chance to, for the officers had been hot on his trail. There was a two thousand dollar reward on his head, wether it was brought in in one piece or not, and he wanted to keep that head.

Old Thomas gave him a fresh horse and tied a parcel of grub behind his saddle. Then as he looked at the fresh tracks the outlaw had made riding in he got sort of worried. Them horse tracks in the soggy earth stuck up as plain as a sore thumb, and would stay plain for some days to come. They'd show even plainer in the badlands, and for that reason he asked the outlaw not to ride towards the badlands and his old hideout on account that the officers could sure trail him there now, and not only get him but also learn about some of the hiding places of that territory. Old Thomas advised him to ride along the valley till he come to a gravel bottom wash that was still running water from the last rains, to follow that wash till he come to the salt grassy flat and then, if he worked right and made use of the other washes that was still running water, sort of criss cross up one and down the other he would be leaving mighty little trail for the officers to follow, and what there would be of it would be mighty confusing.

But, as right as that seemed to be and as much as he wanted to keep his head the outlaw couldn't use that head of his much right then, all that head wanted to do was to be layed down and close its eyes. It couldn't think no further than the safety and rest there'd been at the hideout in the badlands. It just nodded at Old Thomas, and it worked only long enough to guide the horse to the badlands and the old hideout.

The sun was high and hot the next day when an officer rode out of the badlands leading two horses. On each one of the horses a dead man was tied, one was the outlaw and the other was the other officer.

As the living officer told it to Old Thomas there'd been quite a fight. The outlaw's horse had nickered at the sight of the officers' horses and woke him up, he'd come up a shooting and, well, the evidence was on the horses to show what happened.

As the living officer told it to Old Thomas there'd been quite a fight.

Little Andy was a witness to all the talk as the bodies was shifted from the horses' backs to a buckboard. He took it all as a happening that could be expected. Somebody had sit at a game and lost. "And if you don't want to play the game don't sit in it." That's what some outlaws had preached to him. Far as the dead officer was concerned he'd been playing his game too.

Old Thomas took it very different, for he knowed now that suspicion was on his territory, that it'd be looked into, got acquainted with and that no outlaw would ever feel safe in it any more, not even with Old Thomas' pious lies to the officers, nor with his pointing some other way.

And sure enough, Old Thomas' badlands got invaded by one sheriff after another. Many outlaws who didn't know that their hiding grounds had been learned about came to it to rest and found handcuffs. One whole posse came in there and crippled up a whole gang of road agents. When the gun smoke cleared there wasn't half enough of the road agents left to make half a gang. They'd been surrounded while they thought they was safe and by four times their number. Only two got away.

Old Thomas done his best to warn the boys that the territory had been found out but many had hit for it without seeing him. They'd been in too big a hurry, and some of 'em having enough grub on their saddles to last 'em for a day or so had figured on resting up first and come to see Old Thomas and get the grub afterwards.

That hideout territory was now as well known to the officers as it'd been unknown to 'em before. They knowed every crack and hole in it for twenty five miles around, they'd rode and walked and slid and crawled all over it and it got such a reputation, on account of the many hunted men that'd been caught there that if there was any kind of a crime committed to within five hundred miles of that territory there'd be officers riding straight for it and combing it all over again for the outlaw that was wanted.

CHAPTER ONE

Come a time when Old Thomas was feeding and swapping horses altogether with officers and none at all with outlaws, there was no profit to that. What outlaws was left in that neighboring country figured any place safer than Old Thomas' territory and they took to every other hiding place but there.

Consequences was that territory got as lonesome as it was before the white man come. Even the officers got to quit coming there when looking for a man because all the outlaws had got wise and circled around that badland the same as a wolf would circle around a sighted trap.

All was mighty quiet and no visitors, good or bad, showed up at the Thomas ranch for a few years. Then, as elections come and new officers took the place of the old hands the outlaw gentry got to feeling safe again in coming back to their old hiding territory. It was sort of forgotten by then, and the new officers didn't know that country. But what outlaws came back didn't nowheres number what had been there before, not enough to stir up the suspicions of the officers towards that perticular territory, and what few officers come to Old Thomas was again easy turned by that old boy's same pious actions and words.

As election after election came and went and one new officer relayed on the other, Old Thomas managed to keep his territory known as "poison to the outlaws" to them, and the few outlaws that came there kept a feeling secure in their old hideouts. By then the mixture of outlaws had got to change quite a bit, there got to be fewer road agents and train and bank robbers and more and more of a mixture between them and the range outlaw, cattle and horse thief. Then there was the breed of straight range outlaw, the man who didn't hold up stages or banks or trains but done his outlaw work with branding iron and rope, the cattle rustler. But most of that last breed that sometimes came to hide at Old Thomas' territory was riders that didn't bother with changing brands. They was fellers that'd just make away with a fair sized bunch of cattle or horses, drive 'em a couple of hundred miles and turn 'em over to a "ready buyer" who'd take care of shipping 'em out of the country. That was quicker cash than rustling, but a feller had to work quicker, take more chances and sometimes have to make a getaway and find a hiding place a whole lot quicker too.

Old Thomas didn't get much gold from the straight out and out horse and cattle thief, but skirting along the edge of the badlands was a scattering of cattle that'd been missed in round ups and naturally got pretty wild on account of not getting a glimpse of a rider over more than once a year. Them cattle had been in the habit of hitting for the thick of the badlands any time they would get a glimpse of a rider and it was seldom that any of them could be turned and headed back towards the flats. So, as it was, many of them cattle went unbranded, and being that Old Thomas had a few of his own cattle roaming along the rims of the badlands it couldn't of easy been proved that any of the unbranded cattle belonging to other outfits around couldn't as well be his.

And that's how the hiding cattle and horse thief sort of repaid Old Thomas. While hiding and just sort of moseying around a bit they'd sometimes run acrost some unbranded stuff of the size that anybody who put their iron on 'em first could claim, and wanting to keep their rope arm in shape a bit they'd rope some big unbranded critter or two once in a while, run Old Thomas' iron on 'em, knock their horns off so they'd take a sudden dislike for the badlands and send 'em a scooting out for open country and towards where Old Thomas or Andy could gather 'em in sometime.

The outlaw cowboys had no use for the unbranded stuff they branded and sent Old Thomas' way, they wanted theirs in big bunches, get rid of 'em quick, have the fun with the money they received and then get another bunch. The most of 'em would keep that up till they got shot or hung by the hard riding stockmen that would be on their trail, or, if lucky, get to court and behind bars.

These boys in Old Thomas' territory was lucky, because they was still in hiding and free. Pretty soon they'd be lining out again, making a long ride to some new country they'd have in mind, and gather and trail another good bunch of horses or cattle into their picked shipping point. In the meantime, to break the monotony of hiding on account of being too careless the last time, them boys welcomed the sight of horned stuff that was also wild and in hiding, and it more than pleased 'em to tame 'em and make 'em Old Thomas' property.

As summers and winters went by and the boys that was lucky enough to get back to their hideouts kept a stretching their ropes and shoving good cattle down Old Thomas' way that herd of his got to accumulating a considerable and some of the shipments he made kind of got a few stockyard inspectors to wondering, for they was powerful big shipments for the size herd they knowed he had. But they couldn't find no flaw in the ownership of the stock no time, so they kept their mouths shut, and their eyes open.

This was about the time when Andy had got to where he was beginning to wonder if he ought to shave the fuzz that was coming on his face or let it go another day or so. He was a pretty good size boy by then, tall enough, plenty wiry and not far from his twenties. It was about ten years now since his mother had said her last words to him, and that was for him to be a good boy always. Andy had been good, but his ideas of being good was to be good at the game and never to be caught, and in the last few years he'd been sitting at a pretty ticklish game.

To begin with, Andy had got to be a powerful rider, powerful in skill and grace in all he done with any good or bad horse. Bad horses had been his choice, he had plenty of 'em to pick from and his dad never interfered as to him picking on such. He'd only said, "It'll take many of them to teach you what you will have to know so as to teach the others you'll be riding."

But Andy wasn't trying to teach anything, he let the bad horses be as bad as they wanted to and when one got tired he rode him back to the ranch and changed to another that was just as bad. But he done his work with most every one of 'em before he'd come back to the ranch, and that work was the following of a hankering not to never leave any good size critter stay unbranded, wether he had a right to that critter or not.

With the kind of horses he was riding, the kind that wouldn't let you spit without he had a dozen cat fits and then go to bucking the second you reached for your rope, Andy naturally had to be a whole lot of a cowboy to do his work or he'd of found himself afoot and talking to himself. Andy did find himself scratched up and bruised a few times but he never even knowed about the bruises and he wouldn't knowed about the scratches either if it hadn't been for the fuzz that was cropping up on his face and him looking in a mirror and wondering if he hadn't ought to start shaving some day. Sometimes that fuzz was pretty well caked with hardpan dirt.

Nobody but the person that's done it knows what it means to take a bad half-broke range horse and go to roping a good sized range critter with him. The roping is not the only thing, there's the dangers of mix-ups between man and rope, horse and critter. The critter had to be busted and layed down and tied for branding too or there's no use in roping it, and that I think takes a heap of ability when a cowboy is riding an ornery range horse. Such ponies do more than just lay their ears back and kick, and when mixed up with one of them and a rope and a critter as something goes wrong it's safe to say that landing in a den of lions and tigers is a little bit safer.

An athlete trains for whatever game he's in, he puts everything he has in him while training so as to win, but after the event is over he'll most likely rest and maybe gobble up a few too many things he shouldn't eat or drink. It was different with Andy, he was in steady training without his mind being hard set on it, nor without even any thought of training. He gobbled up the same amount of beef and coffee most every day. Some days he was too far away from home or any place to get to gobble

Nobody but the person that's done it knows what it means to take a bad half-broke range horse and go to roping a good sized range critter with him.

anything, but, like a wolf, he'd make up for it when the chances come. He'd lived like a wolf ever since his mother went. The moon or dark of cloudy nights was just as apt to find him curled up amongst granite boulders as between the solid walls of home.

He'd been only twelve years old when he come up missing for the first time. That was for two days and Old Thomas liked to tore the whole country upside down for fifty miles around a looking for him, and all the explaining Andy had to give when he came back was that he'd been chasing a bunch of wild horses for a long ways and hadn't been able to turn 'em.

When he come up missing time and time again after that, Old Thomas didn't worry much more about him. There was no holding him home, and he was no good around home anyhow. He wouldn't even set up a post if it fell on him and he wouldn't do a thing only while on a horse. But he was mighty good there and he sure saved his dad the hiring of a rider to keep count and handle his scattered cattle, and even tho the count was sometimes away over what he figured, Old Thomas never suspected Andy of branding any outside stuff for him. He credited all of that work to the boys hiding in the badlands.

It took an awful rough day to keep Andy out of the saddle, and on one horse and then another he'd be on the go most of the time, not just riding around but always with his eye to locating the stock, for anything unbranded, and if there was anything he liked to do that was to run wild horses. There was plenty of them in the country, and if any rider seen a long string of dust a soaring acrost the big flats they knowed for sure that it was Andy who was in it and fogging after a bunch of wild ones.

As an athlete's body develops to fit his game, Andy's sure done the same to fit his. There was a nice bow in his legs, his feet had growed to fit and hold a stirrup and his back was as straight as a lodge pole pine. He was active as a cat around a striking or kicking horse, and an athlete in another game would of got pawed down while Andy seemed to barely move, but Andy couldn't of jumped over a two foot pole.

His training come from outlaw country, outlaw horses and outlaw men, and such kind sure don't make no pet out of no man. He never got to sit on no school bench, and that way there'd been no break in his training. His school bench had been his saddle. His mother had teached him how to read and write but he didn't do no more of that after she went, and when sometimes he sort of hankered to put some of his feelings in writing he most always found himself where the only things he could make signs with was a twig of sage and hardpan earth, and then there'd be a rope and bridle reins in his hands.

Road agents kept a dwindling and thinning down in numbers in the badlands. Word would come to Old Thomas that one had been caught, one shot and another hung. Few was lucky enough to get out on bail, and Old Thomas sometimes stood for the bail without anybody but the outlaw knowing for sure who furnished it. The range outlaw was now taking a holt where the gambling train and bank robber was leaving off.

CHAPTER TWO

ANDY HAD GOT TO KNOW the badlands pretty well by then, near as well as his dad did. He'd never closed an eye on the changes of the kind of outlaws that come and went, he'd heard outlaw and sheriff talk and sort of keeping an eye on the trail of both was some more of his training. He wasn't much interested in gold bullion. He'd seen bars of it hid away and to him they was just rusty earth.

But when riders come that fingered ropes instead of gold his ears perked up, and he layed one ear on many a coil of rope, many a time and talked with them that handled the hemp.

If officers had crawled up on him and the hemp-men at any of them times he'd of been just one of them, in hideouts and looking no different than the others. He'd of fought the same as them too for along with his training he'd also learned how to manipulate the shooting iron mighty well. He'd shoot at rabbits, sometimes they wasn't there, just imagining, and if they had been there there'd be hardly any fur showing that they had. Wolves and cayotes kept their

WJ.

He wasn't much interested in gold bullion.

20

distances but he got a few of them too, not caring to kill them but just to test his aim on moving objects.

With the steady moving in of the range outlaws, Andy got to make his home pretty well in the badlands, and along about then there come another change a creeping on the range outlaws. Some of them had got mighty ambitious and to figuring that stealing cattle and horses was too slow a work, too much work, taking too many chances and not getting enough in returns. They went to try their hand at stopping coaches and trains and making themselves to home with the banks. What they didn't know about that game made things mighty interesting for 'em, but what they did know about range and how to ride and get away made them also mighty interesting and slippery for officers who took up their trail.

Andy couldn't very well understand how good cowboys, them that knowed all the tricks of cattle and horse stealing should turn to be plain road agents and bad men. He of course knowed it was for the quicker and maybe more money, but money wasn't anything to Andy, it was only gadjets that you trade for other gadjets when you're in town. Andy had never went to town, never cared for gold or gadjets and it was a puzzle to him why a feller should throw a good rope arm away to using a gun with it.

All Andy cared for was a good mean horse, mean horses gave him the action he craved. Then, with his saddle and a good rope he was happy. The six-shooter he toted with him was the last in his affections, he just toted it in case something needed to be stopped.

He seldom swapped words with the gentry that'd got to where they'd use their good rope arm to handling a gun. They could tell of many stories about what happened here and there, how they made their getaways and how much they got, how they'd been too fast for the law, and so on, but them was the live ones talking, and there was many dead ones who couldn't chip in on the talk.

There was still many of the riders who kept to straight cattle and horse stealing, and them is the kind that Andy pitched camp with.

Some of them had got mighty ambitious and to figuring
that stealing cattle and horses was too slow a work.

Andy had got to shaving by now. The fuzz on his face had turned to black wires and his dad was beginning to cuss him for ruining his razor.

"What do you want to shave for?" he'd said. "Horses and cattle don't care wether you wear whiskers or not!"

"I know that," Andy would answer, "but I have the same hankering of getting rid of my whiskers, Dad, as you have of keeping that mustache of yours."

The straight razors kept a getting dulled, and while they was, Andy's mind kept a getting sharp. He'd took in enough of the outlaw game by now to know if he wanted to be one or not, and what kind to sit in on and play. He didn't care so much to be an outlaw, but the whole country and the folks around was outlaw and he didn't know nothing else. He picked his choice on what kind to be, and that was the kind with a good mean horse, a good saddle and a good rope.

Amongst the badlands that bordered his home he got to knowing the kind that had the same sentiments, they was the straight cattle and horse thieves and them is the ones that Andy pitched camp with. He got to knowing many of them, and with the many of all kinds of riders that come and went there was two who stood above all the others to his liking. Them two always rode and "worked" together, always on fine horses and they made their raids on cattle and horses mighty fast, and with a knowledge at the game that made the work very near safe.

One of them boys was stringing along to his thirties, looked tall on a horse and short on the ground. That was on account of the way he could set up in his saddle, he had a long back and short legs, and his right name was Stub O'leary. Stub had dark hair and whiskers. He liked red cattle and bay horses, and his failing after a shipment had been made was to meet up with somebody with long red hair who didn't give a doggone as to what he would talk about. Then Stub would rave on about a fine ranch he claimed he had and didn't have but which he figured he sure would have some day, some way, somewhere. It seemed that Stub had always wanted such a spread as he'd so often describe, and keeping his eyes open for such a location he'd went against the law to try and rush in the money that'd be necessary to get and hold such a spread he'd so long hankered for.

Stub's partner in cattle and horse stealing was a tall light man, light hair and whiskers and ornery as they make 'em. His constitution had been ruined by one time, when he was still a kid, holding two horses for strangers who'd rode in town and didn't make their getaway at holding up a bank. The boy had been took in as one of the bandits and it wasn't till after he'd served a few years in the penitentiary that it was decided he was innocent. From the time he got out he took it onto himself to get even with the world. He was a town raised kid but the town was surrounded with cow country, and when he got free he changed his name from Hugh Stanley to many other names he thought of. While he went to work to make a hand of himself with horse and rope he learned the cattle and horse stealing game. The cow country was good to him, or maybe it was that he was naturally good in it, for with all he'd done in that country that was against the law he'd managed to keep enough yards ahead of it so that any of the good shots would had to be awful good to get him stopped.

Of course, Hugh found plenty of big countries too small for him and he'd have to change his name again and move on to another. It was while moving on to another and him shoving a good bunch of cattle along that he run acrost Stub. They met at night. Stub was shoving a bunch of stolen cattle too, both riders was sort of mighty lonesome and when one seen the blur of one another and the cattle in the dark of one night they both left their cattle and met halfways between the herds. They was both for swapping a few words because they was going the same way with their cattle and on account of the way the country run into a long narrow draw right there there was only one thing to do, that was

They was both for swapping a few words.

to let the cattle mix all the way out or one man hold his cattle back while the other went ahead.

But the two riders, already suspicioning what the other was, and learning that they was headed for the same shipping point, still a hundred miles away, and that they was to deliver to the same buyer let their bunches mix into one herd and went the rest of the way together.

Both Stub and Hugh had kept shy of taking on any pardner in playing their game, they'd figured that with a pardner there'd be apt to be trouble some time and one might get the other in bad and in jail, meaning to or not. For that and other reasons the both had been playing a lone hand. But when Stub and Hugh met and throwed together them two got pretty well acquainted and took a mighty big liking to one another by the time the long hundred miles to the railroad was made. They found that even tho their sentiments with things in general was different they had the same ideas and ways in their game of handling stolen stock, and what decided 'em the most to become pardners was the confidence that'd come to develop between 'em for one another, a trust for each other would stand any test any time or place.

That had proved true in the couple of years they'd rode together, and even tho they disagreed sometimes it was only when talking on things in general but never with or about their work, for there they was both alike as any good pair of spurs and one knowed exactly what the other feller would do.

To Andy, there was only one thing he could find against Stub and Hugh and that was that they didn't come to the badlands often enough, sometimes not more than once a year. That was because they was very seldom seen with any stolen stock and nothing could be blamed to them, so they didn't have to hide. But when they would run into unexpected happenings and have to rush back to the badlands, Andy sure did make camp right with 'em. He often wished as he made camp with 'em and words was swapped all around that they'd sometime hint for him to go along with 'em on their next ride, and even tho Andy knowed more about the tricks of the outlaw game than they did and they liked him mighty well, neither Stub nor Hugh seemed to want to take on another pardner.

Andy kept on riding his bad horses, handling his rope and branding somebody else's cattle for his dad. He didn't care about the cattle. His fun come in getting 'em and they didn't mean anything to him after owning 'em, his great satisfaction was in outsmarting the wise cowmen of that outlaw country. Most of them was also mighty free in helping themselves with somebody else's stock but they sure didn't want anybody else to bother theirs. They was forced to that in order to hold their own herds to what they would be if there'd been no thieves, and them cowmen made it mighty tough for any rider they found meddling with their cattle. They'd usually raise him up a tree with a rope around his neck or riddle him with 30–30 slugs.

Andy wouldn't of been no exception. He'd long ago been suspected of being mighty free with his rope, and a few times, if he hadn't been riding a mighty fast horse, he wouldn't of got away. So far, the only way he'd been identified was by the fact that whatever horse he'd be riding always bucked or fought when he started him into a run.

There was many times long before Andy got to be twenty five when he hankered to ride away from the home territory and badlands and get to see other countries, other folks and maybe a town, but the thought that held him back always was that he'd be mighty lost amongst other folks than the kind he'd been brought up with. From the way Stub and Hugh talked about them once in awhile he felt that at the sight of him them folks would do to him what they'd done to the hunted outlaws that hadn't been able to make it to the safety of the badlands.

It was different with Stub and Hugh, he thought. They've rode in many states, had the experience of getting around dangerous places and knowed the tricks for a getaway if they did. They'd been in town and around places where he would sure be lost if he tried it alone. He'd liked to've stirred up a nice bunch of cattle and made his way to a shipping point with 'em, but when he'd got to the shipping point he wouldn't knowed what to do. He'd seen trains a few times, while outside his home territory, he'd be up on some tall pinnacle and the trains would be thirty miles or more away.

So, with all he knowed of the outlaw game and outlaw country he knowed very little of the law abiding country and how to work there. If he could go along with such men as Stub and Hugh all would be fine. He would of liked to go with some good honest cowboy just as well, but he hadn't got to meet any of them long enough to know 'em.

Then come a time, as herds for hundreds of miles around kept a dwindling and the thieves kept a disappearing so quick and mysterious that the eyes of the law begin to center on the badlands again. Officers got to searching in that cut-up country and cussed every foot of it, all excepting that strip of Old Thomas', for that old boy was still on the job and brought on more pious talk to make it known that his strip was sacred, that he wouldn't tolerate no outlaws, and being, as he said, that he rode in it often he would know if there was any hiding there and he would sure be the first to inform the authorities.

But there was still a couple of old hands of the law in office who remembered the gang of road agents and gun men that'd been found hiding in Old Thomas' territory after that old boy had said that such couldn't be.

Them two old hands and a few other officers rode in on Old Thomas late one evening, stayed at his place and figured on hitting for the badlands before daybreak the next day. They kept an eye on Old Thomas and wouldn't let him out of their sight for fear he'd ride away and warn every outlaw he could. But they hadn't reckoned on Andy who had been in the dark of his room, seen the officers come in and heard their talk.

As luck would have it, Stub and Hugh was hiding in the badlands right then. Andy's first thought was to get out of the window and warn them, but there was a screen on it and it was nailed. If he made the noise of cutting thru it the officers would hear, so he had to wait till they all scattered to their sleeping places and in the meantime he done a heap of worrying that his dad would let one of the officers bed down in his room.

But Old Thomas was wise, he sort of depended on Andy, that that boy would have plenty of sense to hit out and warn the outlaws soon as he heard the officers come in, and he manouvered to keep them out of his room.

It wasn't long after Andy heard the first few snores of the tired and sleeping officers when he ripped a hole in the screen with his knife, crawled thru and hit for the corrals. He saddled up a gentle horse that night for he didn't want to stir no noise saddling up a fighting one, and in a short while he was winding his way amongst the crooked bends of the badlands.

When the officers rode in there at sun up the next morning, they found many hiding places with plenty of fresh signs in 'em and it sure left 'em wondering how come they didn't find a man. They rode and searched all day and made camp in the thick of the badlands that night. They went and combed more and more of the country, and then they gave it up. They hadn't found a man.

By that time the few outlaws that'd been stirred out of their hiding places by Andy's warnings had scattered fast and well, and all was more than a hundred miles away, and still riding.

Andy was riding too, and right alongside of Stub and Hugh. Nothing had been said about taking him as a pardner with 'em, but as they was riding together on the second day from the badlands and Stub and Hugh begin talking of their plans and including Andy along with them plans that was better than handshaking over a lot of words about being pardners. He was now one of them and they was sure with him.

With the plans they made as they rode they come to decide for sure on one thing and that was that for a few hundred miles all around the badlands strip was too close a country for 'em, for Stub and Hugh. The only thing to do now was hit out for new territory where they wasn't known and folks would believe the new name they'd give 'em. Another thing was they was getting tired of being on the dodge and decided to lead honest lives in a new country they was hitting for.

That new country they was hitting for was near a thousand miles away. Stub had been in that country before, many years before, there was hundreds of wild horses there, he said, and he could get contracts from the big outfits to catch them. The big outfits wanted to rid the range of the wild horses on account they was eating a lot of grass that was needed for their stock, and many of them would furnish good mustang runners with grub, pasture for the horses they caught and then give the horses to the men who caught 'em to do as they pleased, so long as he took 'em out of the country.

At that time there was good markets for any kind of horses. Stub said that the horses in the one perticular country he wanted to hit for was most all good size horses. They would bring good money, and the fun of catching 'em would be as much fun as stealing 'em, only difference would be that a feller wouldn't have to dodge and hide afterwards.

"That's fine," Hugh had said to that, "but we can't run wild horses with only one saddle horse apiece. We'd ought to have at least six or eight good ones to each of us."

"You haven't turned honest so sudden," Stub had answered, "that you've lost your art of picking up good horses as we go along, have you?— we'll have to get us a string together before we get too far out of this territory because when we get to the other end we got to keep our new names good. Besides we want to do a little so this territory will remember us some after we leave. I know they'll miss us."

With all the tricks of the horse stealing trade that Andy knowed he got to learn some more as he rode along with Stub and Hugh. Instead of hitting straight out of the territory where their names was bad they bordered it. They'd take one day where range horses was aplenty and ride thru one bunch after another looking for horses that was likely. They wanted sound horses with saddle marks on their backs, many of them running on the range are often spoiled outlaws, but if they was sound and built right they'd rather take a chance on them than a fine looking unbroke gelding. The unbroke horse has to be educated, that takes time and he won't be able to stand half the ride that a good spoiled horse will, for even tho the spoiled horse might fight like a wolf at the first few sittings he'll be wise to the rein and he'll know how to pack a man, even tho he'll try to unpack him. A few hard days' riding will settle him down, he's usually good for some mighty long rides too and after that he's usually a mighty good horse, providing a feller can ride him from the start and rides him often after that.

Either Stub or Hugh or Andy could sit on any spoilt horse. They didn't perticularly care about a spoiled horse, but if he was sound and didn't wear himself out fighting he was just another good horse to 'em.

As they'd go thru bunch after bunch of horses during the one day they'd look for saddle marks on sound backs and legs, make a count of how many there might be in each bunch and if there was enough in any one bunch to make it worth their while they'd spot the location of that bunch, take a chance on 'em not grazing or roaming too far away and ride on to the next bunch.

In their riding they'd also keep their eyes open for any riders, and if any had bobbed up and got inquisitive enough to want to meet 'em they wouldn't of bothered with any horses on that range, not on that day. For any inquisitive riders would of set many other and peeved riders on their trail if any horses was moved that day or night. And while watching for riders and spotting good horses with saddle marks on 'em they'd also keep their eyes open for something else, that was for some kind of corral, box canyon or deep wash where they could hold the horses they'd gather and cut out the ones they didn't want. A bunch of cattle can be held in the open and any one or ten head can be cut out of the main bunch at a time, but that can't be done with range horses. They'll hold and run together. A feller can sometimes cut one horse out of the bunch, but if it's a good horse that horse will make a fast dodging circle and beat him back to the bunch.

Their first "one day" of gathering a string was pretty fair. Amongst the many bunches of horses they went thru they spotted four and got their location. Then they had the good luck of finding an old decrepit corral. It was on a big flat and in plain sight of the world, but night would make it hid, and before night come, all the while watching for riders, they'd picked up the scattered poles and mended the old corral so it'd do.

The four bunches of horses that'd been spotted didn't roam nor graze very far when dark come and the boys had very little trouble finding 'em, running 'em all in one bunch and into the old corral.

Nobody but the man that's handled horses all his life can pick out one horse from another at night. Mighty few can do that even in day time, specially with a big bunch of horses that's strange and just been glanced at once. You can't see saddle marks at night, but you can get the outline of their heads and withers against the sky, and as the boys spotted the ones they'd wanted out of the bunches during the day they, natural like, took in the outline of their heads, necks and withers.

With the four bunches they'd gathered there was around sixty head of horses, milling around and making the old corral crack. Hugh was lost in locating any of the horses that'd been picked out during the day, the first eighteen years of his life had been spent in town, and that made the difference between him and the other two boys. He was put to handling the corral gate and to open it whenever Stub and Andy cut out a bunch of horses that wasn't wanted. They'd holler "all right," or "let 'em go" for the gate to be opened, and "hold it" if there was one horse amongst some bunch they'd cut out and wanted to keep.

Hugh was fine at the gate and no horse squeezed by whenever "hold it" was hollered. Stub and Andy, afoot and crouching in the corral picked out the horses by the shape of their heads against the starry sky. One bunch after another that wasn't wanted was let go till finally there was only eight head of horses left in the corral, not many horses out of sixty but they was good ones, and the ones they'd picked out that day.

It might be wondered why this work was done at night when, to a stranger the country looked so big and short of humans, but humans, specially riders have the bad habit of popping up at the time when you might think there's not one to within a hundred miles. No sane or healthy horse or cattle thief works in daytime, for the range, as scattered as the folks might be sometimes proves mighty populated when you get fond of somebody else's horses or cattle.

In daytime the running of bunches of horses will stir up dust that eagle-eyed riders can see and wonder about. They'd wonder who's rounding up horses at this or that time of the year, more so when they might be owners of the horses on that range. Then again, the corralling of horses in a corral that hadn't been used for many years, on a big flat, would create a heap of suspicion amongst them eagle-eyed riders, for, on a still day, that dust would soar up a mile high, like a signal and bellering to the whole territory of the goings-on inside of that corral.

The boys all changed their saddles from their tired horses to the fresh ones they'd picked out. Night is not a very good time to try out strange horses and there was quite a commotion stirred as that was done. Stub and Hugh was lucky enough to each get pretty well behaving horses with first throw of their ropes, and after they had their buck out them two boys knowed that they was mounted on horses that was good for a mighty long ride. Andy wasn't so lucky. His first loop settled on one of the fightingest horses he'd seen for a long time. That horse had to be throwed to be saddled, and when he was let up he done his best to tear the corral down while trying to get rid of Andy, he throwed himself a couple of times and the only time he stopped fighting was to take a breathing spell to do some more. It was finally seen that he wouldn't do because he was wearing himself out and as that night called on for a horse that could be depended on for a long ride when he throwed himself once more, Andy held him down, unsaddled and turned him loose.

The second one he caught was near as bad and it was figured best to turn him loose too, but the old saying that the third try is a charm proved to be true, and more of a charm than could be expected, for that time Andy's loop settled on a fine big horse, even in the dark his outline showed all endurance and speed, the feel of his wiry frame proved that. He never even humped up when Andy saddled and climbed on him, and there, Andy was surprised some more for the way that horse turned to the feel of the rein.

Only a few hours of the night was past when they let the horses out of the corral and started hazing 'em out of the country. They done some mighty fast riding during the hours that was left of that night, and when daybreak come they was near fifty miles away from the old corral. They hid themselves and the horses in a rocky canyon that day. A trickle of water wound down it, and with the good feed that was there the horses was glad not to move much. The boys fed up on rice and dried beef and went to sleep, all but Hugh who stood first shift on guard and had the luck to knock down a big sage hen with a rock while doing that. Didn't dare to shoot.

Andy took his turn on the middle shift of watching the backtrail and the horses and the while chewed on a hunk of sage hen. The sun was about center and up to high noon when two horses trailed down the side of the canyon and into it to water, and Andy's eyes popped with surprised and happy feeling at the sight of 'em, for them two was saddle

CHAPTER THREE

THEY MADE THREE LONG NIGHTS' RIDES and left over a hundred and fifty miles of mighty hard trail to follow before they felt safe to stop and rest their horses for a couple of days, then they rode on some more, slower and till they got to another country where there was plenty of horses to pick from. They come to such a country, and after looking thru a few bunches without much luck in spotting anything they wanted they rode square into one bunch of straight saddle horses all bearing the same brand. There was more than twenty head in the bunch and the boys knowed that they must of been part of a remuda of some big outfit and turned loose till round-up time.

Most of them was pretty fine horses and a dandy string could be picked out of that bunch, but the boys was a little leary of running off with any of them because the big outfits usually keep track of their saddle horses pretty close, they have their riders on the job all the time.

The boys talked it over for quite a spell before deciding, and when they did decide it was for taking a chance. Out of that bunch of saddle horses they could get what they wanted to make up the string that was needed for all three. They wouldn't have to stop any more to pick up any more and they could hit out in a high lope for the country they was bound for.

They found another corral out of the way, it must of belonged to the same outfit the horses did because the branding irons hanging on it was of the same mark the horses wore. That corral was in top shape, it was made up of four pens and there was a squeezer for rebranding or venting grown stuff. The separate pens made it mighty handy for the boys to cut out their horses, but all about that corral was so well kept up in shape and strong that the boys got to thinking that such an outfit as owned it was sure well organized and very much alive, and on that account they'd be apt to miss their horses mighty quick and be on their trail just as quick.

But they'd decided on taking that chance, and now that they'd started they sure wasn't going to let the sight of well kept corrals scare 'em out. So, by sunup the next morning there was fourteen head of good saddle horses missing from that big outfit's range and hid away sixty miles from where they'd been the evening before.

The boys now had their string to the size they wanted it. With their own three horses they had twenty-five head of picked horses, a few ornery ones but them was sound and with plenty of riding would come to time. The main thing now was to keep from being seen by any rider who might suspicion and give them away, or being caught up with by sheriffs or the outfit's riders. They'd have to ride hard for the next three or four nights, hide well during the day and cover their tracks all they could all the time.

They was now thru with the territory where their names was bad and hitting out for the country where they'd make their new names good, running wild horses.

On their first day of hiding after stealing their second bunch of horses the boys went to work to changing the brands on all the horses, not with a branding iron because that would show too new and take too long to heal and bring on suspicion. Andy had learned a heap from his dad in how to change an iron in a hurry and so as it'd look old and original and would pass if a feller only used his eyes, and didn't use his hand and go to parting the hair and looking for the scar and scaly ridge of the brand.

They was now thru with the territory where their names was bad.

With the tip of a broken knife blade he sort of plucked the hair out in line with his design in disfiguring the original brand. He didn't exactly pluck the hair, some of 'em came out by the roots of course but the idea was more to make a shaggy line of half length hair to match the looks of the original brand. With Andy's skill at that a feller could of stood three feet away from the hair brand and swear it was burned in at the same time as the original, all one iron.

Andy was most careful with the big outfit's horses, because all the big outfits' brands are well known for many hundred miles around, some are well known all thru the west from Mexico to Canada, and the reason for changing the brands was so that if any rider did pop up on 'em while they was hiding, as that sometimes happens, and got a look at the horses they wouldn't be suspicioning, with the brands being made over, that them horses didn't belong to anybody else but them men that was with 'em. Any rider seeing the big outfit's brand, unchanged, would of sure recognized it and more than suspicioned. The boys took care of that so no such a thing would happen.

In their first day of hiding from the big outfit the boys was not worried of anybody being on their trail and right close. They didn't think any of the riders would miss the horses so quick, and being they'd only took a little over half of the bunch they figured, like they hoped them riders would, that the missing bunch was just roaming on the range and was a little hard to find, as sometimes range horses are.

The boys worried more on their second hiding day because, as luck sometimes has it, some of the riders might of missed the horses right away, seen the fresh tracks in the corral where they'd cut out and fresh tracks leading away from there and acrost the country. They figured ways and means to cover their trail, and once in a while, while hazing the horses thru during the night, the boys would sight other bunches of horses. Most every one of them bunches was used to cover up their trail, two of the boys would go on with the saddle horses and the other one would fall in after the bunch that'd been sighted. That bunch would be brought in on the trail and behind the saddle horses and kept going for some miles that way, then they'd be turned off the trail of the stolen saddle horses and shoved on for some more miles and then let go. There would be only one rider doing that work.

According to some remarks that's been wrote or said a tracker could tell by the horses' hoof prints which one was being rode and which one wasn't, and how many riders there would be. The claim is the way they can tell is that a horse being rode makes a deeper print. If that was true the trackers wouldn't be fooled by the tracks of the different bunches of horses that was used to cover up the saddle horse tracks for they'd know there was only one rider with them extra horses that was picked up and then branched off, they'd also know there was three riders altogether and it could of been seen that even tho them riders tracks was zigzagging and once in a while scattering they always got together again, and that bunch with the riders tracks is the one they'd follow. None of the horses was shod, and being it ain't so that a ridden horse's tracks is any deeper or different than a loose one there was no way of telling which bunch of horses the riders was keeping with. The tracks of the loose horses that was picked up on the way, brought along for a few miles and then sent a scooting to one side and away from the saddle bunch for a few more miles would confuse any tracker and throw him off on the trail of the wrong bunch of horses a plenty so that the thieves would keep gaining lead along the way.

The boys brought on other tricks. Like for instance they kept their horses in file as much as they could so that the tracks would give the impression of loose roaming horses and not that of a driven bunch, for that same reason they'd sometimes let them stop and graze and scatter for a short spell, then they didn't keep 'em going one straight direction and it would of been hard for any tracker to guess that direction so he could make a fast ride like he could if he wasn't hindered by having to watch for tracks so much, and overtake the riders.

By the time daybreak come on their second night from the big outfit's range the boys was over a hundred miles away. They hid their horses up the side of a timbered mountain for that day, pretty high up and where a good sight could be got of the backtrail. They was more watchful of their backtrail that day than they was the day before, for now was a more likely time for the horses to be missed and riders setting out on the trail of 'em. They'd have to be watchful for a few days and till they got well out of the country, and if in that time they didn't bump up against anybody who might be suspicious and scatter their description and direction to the country they could then feel pretty sure of a safe getaway.

If a couple or three hundred miles is covered with stolen stock and the trail is not picked up and the winds and rains have a chance to wear it out a feller can then slow down and rest easier. On their second day's hiding the boys got to wishing strong for high winds to sort of smooth out their trail, and the devil, like in cahoots with 'em done better than that. It was on the afternoon of their third day's hiding when heavy clouds begin to gather over their backtrail, and that night a good steady rain caught up with 'em, the kind of a rain that'd level and wash out a horse track in an hour's time.

They rode on thru that rain and made good distance and all three drawed a long breath to rest. They rested for two days, their backtrail was smoothed out, the earth didn't show no sign of it, and now feeling pretty safe they didn't want to make no deep tracks in the earth that the rain had softened, for them tracks would of been so plain and there to show for a long time.

That rest was needed and mighty welcome by the men and horses, and it would of been enjoyed to the limit if the grub supply hadn't run low, very low. The only thing they wasn't short of was salt but they'd run out of dried beef and the rice had got down to just a few handfuls. They could of stopped at some of the ranches that they passed and stocked up, but, being wise, they'd kept to countries where ranches was mighty scattering, and when they did come to one they'd make a big circle around it, for a strange rider dropping in at a ranch and wanting grub would prove that that rider didn't want to be seen very much or he'd do his stopping and eating at ranches and not be packing grub with him and dodging the ranches. Such doings would most always draw suspicions, and no horsethief wants any of that on his trail for riders to pick up and follow him by.

But the devil being good to them again produced a chance for them to get some grub on their second evening of rest. Andy was sort of looking out over the dimmed backtrail when he spotted something white in the distance. He knowed at a glance of it that it was a sheep wagon, and figured that if he was lucky he could get in it while the herder was away tending to his sheep and supply up on the necessary without that herder seeing him. Andy caught one of the best horses, hit for the sheep wagon on a high lope, seen that the herder was over a ridge with his sheep and where he couldn't see his wagon and then proceeded to help himself with the grub that was needed. That's done often in the range country and most herders don't interfere even when they're in plain sight of their wagon and see the rider come in and out of it. The most of 'em know that all the rider is after is a little grub and that the herder would be welcome to the same if he struck a cow camp, —it's exchange of hospitality. But this perticular herder must of had something done to him that aggravated him, maybe a blanket or a rifle had been stole out of his wagon once, anyway, when his dogs barked and he stuck his head over the ridge and seen Andy coming out of the wagon he started blazing away at him with his rifle. Andy could tell by the whizzing of the bullets that they was from a high powered gun, and not wanting to be stopped with the grub he took his own rifle, rested his arm on a wagon wheel and done his best to hit as close as he could to that herder without hitting him. He must of done pretty good because the herder quit shooting and the dogs quit barking and went back with him over the ridge. There was two reasons for Andy doing that, one was to teach the herder not to shoot at him and another was to let him know it would be healthier for him not to try and follow. Andy had been hitting mighty close.

It didn't help things that that herder had seen Andy, for even tho he didn't get close enough to get a description of him he could say, if somebody asked him that some rider had raided his camp of some grub and that would leave some kind of a suspicious trail in case anybody asked. But Andy'd had to take that chance because there had to be some grub in camp as there was many a long ride ahead before the other end was reached.

Come time for the boys to hit out. If they'd known that the evening they started out again on their way towards their new country riders from the big outfit and two officers was as close to 'em as twenty miles they'd scampered a little faster than they did, as it was they just traveled natural and at mixed trot and walk, figuring to do about forty miles before the night was over.

*Riders from the big outfit and two officers
was as close to 'em as twenty miles.*

The officers and riders had no inkling as to where the boys was,
they'd been going on a blind and washed out trail and it was just plain
luck for 'em that they'd hit it so close. It was also just plain luck for the
boys, or the devil was on their side again, that they kept hid and didn't
move their horses while the ground was soft, for the officers and their
men was right in the country at the time and they'd sure seen the tracks.
Now, after not seeing a track, making a last circle and still not finding
any they come to figure that the boys hadn't come this way at all. They

then turned hoping to run acrost their tracks in some other country, and plum the opposite direction from the one the boys took.

Now all was clear sailing for the boys, and after they'd put another hundred and fifty miles of night riding between them and where they'd rested during the two days, and figuring they was now over four hundred miles from the big outfit's range they begin to ride in daytime. Of course they still kept to the most open country and was careful to dodge ranches by a big circle, also keep out of sight from any rider. Most every rider is suspicious, and specially in seeing such a good bunch of saddle horses and three reckless looking riders hazing 'em along.

They bumped into a couple of riders one day who squinted their suspicions as they sized up the saddle horses. Stub done the talking and eased them suspicions. He happened to know of a herd of cattle that'd been shifted some few hundred miles, acrost that country from one range to another a month or so before. The suspicious riders had also heard about that, and Stub went on to informing them, like as if he didn't care, that they'd trailed that herd thru and was now on their way back to the outfit with the saddle horses.

They met some more riders now and again but Stub or Hugh always had some story ready to throw off any suspicion they might have and make them forget that they'd seen a saddle bunch with three riders. Andy always kept quiet at them times for he knowed that he couldn't compete with neither of his two pardners when it come to that line of work, for they'd had plenty of practice at it at plenty of ticklish times.

They kept a making tracks that the winds and storms dimmed and now they was hitting pretty straight and at good speed towards their new territory. It was only while crossing some State line on their way that they'd travel at night for some two or three nights, and that was on account of not wanting to be seen by anybody who might scatter word of seeing them and so that no stock inspector would be on their trail, for even tho the plucked brands was good they wouldn't stand too close an inspection, and them inspectors have a way of knowing from the States around whenever any stock comes up missing. They'd be mighty apt to know about the big outfit's saddle stock and being they didn't want no conversation with no inspector and wanted to keep their saddle string all together they was mighty careful when it came to crossing a State line, sometimes even a county line, when they knowed about where it was.

The thousand miles or so to the new territory was covered without hardly any happening to worry the boys, and then, true to Stub's words and him taking the lead, they located one mighty big outfit that was mighty anxious to be rid of the many wild horses on their range and write a contract to that effect. They would give a bill of sale to the boys of all the horses that was caught on their range (usually the wild horses are claimed by the outfit's range they're on), the outfit's superintendent also agreed to let them keep whatever branded horses they caught with the wild ones. Such branded horses usually are renegades that join the wild bands. The boys would also be furnished with well-fenced pasture to hold the wild ones that was caught, but there was no agreement of any grub furnished (only beef they could get from the company's ranches) nor camping outfit or the necessary for the building of wild horse traps. Another thing was that the boys had to catch a certain amount of horses by a certain time or the horses they caught would be claimed by the company. That was so as to keep every inexperienced horse runner away, for such kind never catch any and only make the wild horse worse and harder to catch for the rider who knows how to catch 'em.

The boys thought the contract a little bit stiff and risky, but they figured it'd sure make 'em tend to work and if they caught up to the count that was wrote down on the contract they'd be high winners while doing honest work.

There was one flaw in that contract which was a temptation against that honest work and that was that whatever branded horses they caught amongst the wild ones would also be theirs. The boys knowed that there'd be very few branded ones amongst the wild ones, the superintendent had sure figured on that too but what was there to keep the boys from running in a few branded range horses amongst the wild ones once in a while, they'd look and act near the same in a bunch of wild ones and the boys could easy enough make up their count with the company's range horses in case they was short.

They wondered how come the superintendent of such a big outfit and knowing as much as he was supposed to to let such an opening in the contract. They figured that most any stockman would know better, but there wasn't a chirp about that from any of the boys and that flaw is what decided 'em to sign the contract.

They made camp alongside a brushy creek and inside a big pasture and turned their horses loose. They now felt safe in the heart of that big outfit's range, for to anybody suspicious they could say and prove that they was contracted to run wild horses on that range, and nobody would doubt that they was established and honest mustang runners. They wouldn't be bothered in that country.

The first thing they tended to was the brands on their horses, they used a hot iron this time and half scalded and half seared over the plucked brands that Andy had drawed. The new brands would take time to heal but the boys would soon take their horses up in the rough hills, amongst where the wild ones was, and what few riders they'd see wouldn't be inquisitive or even notice the fresh brands because they'd be company riders and would know of the mustang runners, the fresh brands could just as well been on wild horses that'd been caught up and broke and there'd be no wonder about 'em from them riders. When them brands healed they would stand the test of any inquisitive eye or hand, for the scald would bring on a few white hairs and the sear would bring on the scaly scar such as is with all good brands.

But before the boys took their horses up in the rough hills and started to work in catching the wild ones there was some things that was necessary to get to make camp with, for with all the wild horses they'd contracted to get they figured they'd be in that country for about six months.

While on the dodge and stealing horses they done most of their traveling at night. Riding kept 'em warm during the night and it was usually warm enough during the day so they could take off their coats and shaps while resting. Boots and underwear and shirts was not pulled off only when stopping alongside of plenty of water when there'd be a general cleanup, and then they'd be put back on again as soon as they dried, for a cowboy on the dodge has to be ready to go right quick any time, and he can't afford to enjoy the luxuries of time in the things he enjoys to do like other folks can.

It was decided that they would leave the horses in the pasture and all three ride into town to buy the necessary things to make a good camp with. Stub knowed of the town and he said it was plenty big enough for anything a feller wanted to do, it was about a hundred miles away. Andy was for staying where he was and keep an eye on the horses, but Hugh and Stub made him change his mind, remarking that the fence around the pasture was good and tight and that all the horses would be glad to stay on the good feed there was, and nobody would bother 'em.

The reason for Andy wanting to back out of going to town was that he'd never been in a town in his life, and even tho the thought of seeing a town sort of stirred his curiosity and interest he felt a little backward and leary of the experience. He'd heard a heap of stories about towns, how the people lived in such places and what went on in there, and that was so different than the life he'd lived that he felt it all would be mighty puzzling. All he knowed was range country, horses and cattle and ropes and branding irons, and the thought of town made him think of himself as a wolf in a pen of popping fire crackers.

Andy was like a snorty and spooky bronc being hazed into a corral as he got into the lanes and got his first close sight of the town. He wondered at all the tall chimneys, why they smoked so much, at the tall buildings, why they was so close together, and he felt as he got in the narrow noisy canyon of 'em that he was riding into a trap that he'd sure never get out of very easy. His horse shied at the different strange things and people, and Andy shied right with him. There was rattling wagons and slick buggies, a few automobiles and many bicycles, but what scared Andy and his horse the most was the many people on the sidewalks that went both ways and kept up a steady jabbering both of them ways as they went. Some of 'em would cross a street right in front of Andy's horse and so close that Andy wondered at the ignorance of 'em and wondered some more that his horse didn't paw the daylight out of 'em, for the horse he was riding was no more use to people than Andy was.

Hugh and Stub didn't pay much attention to the folks and goings-on around, they'd been in many towns in their ramblings, now they was headed for one place and it was some relief when Andy got sight of that place, for there was corrals with many horses in 'em and stables and sheds. It was a sales and livery stable.

They left their horses there. All three brushed up as best they could with a stiff stable brush, took off their spurs and cartridge belts and left 'em with the stable man, but they kept their guns and shoving 'em inside their shirts out of sight, let 'em rest at their waist.

The first thing they had in mind to do was to go to hardware and grocery stores and get what they needed for camp and grub and tools for trap building, but being that at that time of the year, springtime, the days was so long they didn't realize how late it was, and the stores they wanted to trade with was all closed.

Stub and Hugh both sort of throwed up their hands at that and Andy stood like a feller waiting for a verdict. The verdict come pretty fast. Andy was for staying at the stables and pick out a team and wagon to haul the things they was to buy, but Stub and Hugh had decided on some other things, doings that Andy couldn't get the drift of, and they'd also decided that Andy come right along with 'em. Andy did.

The stables was some ways from the main part of town, and sort of letting his pardners take the lead and him keeping in the shadow of 'em, the three started out. Andy didn't miss a thing or a hoof as he trailed along. He wondered why the buildings had doors and windows so tall and wide while the people around was no bigger than him. He wondered some more while going thru one part of the town he passed bunch after bunch of fellers standing or laying around and, as he'd hear some of their talk, he couldn't get the drift of what they was talking about. One and then another of them fellers came up to him and asked him for the money for a cup of coffee or a meal. Andy had never packed no money, had never had no use for any such, and now he was still without any money. Either Stub or Hugh would turn when the bums came around, hand 'em some change and the three would go on, with Andy trailing along and doing a heap of wondering as to such begging.

That part of town was passed and then they come to where Andy done some more wondering. They'd come to a better part of the town and Andy wondered why the stores was lighted up while dark was still an hour away, they wasn't lighted with lamps nor candles neither but with bulbs that throwed a better light. Andy studied 'em and the window displays till he come near losing track of his pardners a few times, and then, finally he got to figuring all of that as beyond him and went to putting his interest on the folks that passed him. It struck him a little queer that amongst all of them none stopped to speak. They all seemed to be hitting for some place in a hurry and none seemed to or cared to know one another. He finally figured the reason for that was that there was too many of 'em in one pile.

Another thing that struck him queer about the folks around was the way they dressed. They'd have stiff white bands around their necks that seemed to be choking 'em, and from there would hang some piece of colored cloth. He didn't mind the coats but he couldn't figure out why they buttoned vests on such a warm day as it was, and what puzzled him some more was from there down and the wrinkle that was so straight and even all the way up and down their pants. Andy looked at the wrinkles on his pants and they didn't at all run straight up and down and even the way theirs did, his run all ways wrinkled by rain and sun on the outside and by saddle leather and horse sweat on the inside.

Then there was the way they handled their legs and feet, their arms and hands and their faces and all of themselves. Andy figured they'd be poor ropers and riders, they seemed so loose or so stiff and with the most of 'em their legs seemed to be only two props they used to pack 'em around with. He knowed for sure that them props couldn't work on a bad horse and when he seen some fellers come along with big feet sticking along sideways and pants a flapping that reminded him of some snow shoed horse that'd got in the gumbo, only thing was that a snow shoed horse would keep his toes straight forward no matter how long they might be, and the flapping pants sort of spoiled Andy's reminding too.

As he trailed along close behind or alongside of his pardners, Andy was struck dumb and paralyzed by an apparition. Like the good horse thief he was he seen it, or her, first and half a block away over many heads of the males and females that'd went back and forth. He'd noticed some of the females and had only glanced at 'em short, being careful they wouldn't notice his glance. But when the apparition come along, Stub and Hugh lost a pardner right then, for Andy had just stepped to one side, squeezed himself where the lights wasn't so strong and waited for her to come by.

She came by, and if Andy ever wondered before he really learned to wonder as she did. How such a girl could be amongst these people was away beyond him. He didn't think it right to even look at her, but his eyes had the best of his brain that time and he looked, all while trying to compare her with something alive and the most graceful. He thought of deer and antelope, but as he watched her move along he got to deciding that deer and antelope would have as little grace as compared to her as a mud turtle.

He wondered how such neat slim ankles could pack a body, specially on such high slim heels, but that body didn't seem to be packed, it was like it was floating on air and carried with wings that couldn't be seen. But her face is what had first caught his attention, and there's no telling what a pretty tangling impression it made in his heart strings. If anybody had asked him what she looked like he'd of just had a helpless expression on his face and couldn't of said a word, but the light in his eyes would of told aplenty.

He'd plum forgot all about Stub and Hugh or where he was at. All he thought of now was to follow or maybe get ahead of the fairy so he could ease his heart with another long look at her. Just one more would do.

He'd just got out of the shadows started stringing along on the trail of the girl when both of his arms was took a hold of and he was stopped sudden, then Andy heard a voice say,

"We been looking all over for you."

Then another voice at seeing Andy's face. "Seen a ghost, or is there somebody on your trail?"

Andy couldn't answer, then the voices went on to say for him to come along, that they was going to get a few drinks and then something to eat. It was hard for Andy to come out of his trance, but the saloon was right close and when he walked in with his two pardners the strange goings on in there stirred up enough interest in him to bring him back to his regular senses. There was gambling tables, roulette, faro and along all that conglomeration of men and smoke and tables was a bar that strung along the whole length of the building. The three lined up to the bar.

"Here take this," says one of the boys, "It'll do you good."

Andy took what was put in front of him, and two more of the same, then the boys told him to stay close, that they was going to join in on a game or two. Andy sat down in one of the chairs against the wall and begin watching the proceedings all around him with a heap of interest. For a spell he'd near forgot the girl, but the few drinks he'd had begin to do their work, then there come visions of her, visions as fair as she'd appeared on the street, then come a time when them visions of her took queer twists and mixed up with gambling men and tables. The tables begin to spin and the men got to looking queer. There didn't seem to be half enough air for him either, and as his roving eyes sighted the door of the saloon he stood up and zigzagged his way that direction, the swinging doors slammed him as he went out and he managed to stand up against the wall of the building where he reached for air and fought the dizziness that'd come over him.

It wasn't the first time that Andy had drunk whisky, there'd always been plenty of that at home, and him and his dad and different outlaws had often took a few drinks. But with that day's long ride on an empty stomach the few drinks he'd just had sure had the advantage of him. The boys had said that they'd all eat after taking the drinks but they'd just wanted to play a few games first, and now Andy had no thought for anything but plenty of air, no sitting inside at no table of food, not for a while.

Andy managed to stand his ground against the building, kept a gasping for air, and come a time when he begin to notice people going both ways in front of him, people everywhere, and it seemed he'd seen more people in the short while he hit town than cattle and horses in all his life on the range.

As his gaze got steadier and he got to watching 'em he got to feeling conspicuous a standing there by the saloon door. Night had settled on the land by then but the town seemed brighter than if it was plain daylight, every story window looked like a sunrise and Andy begin to take interest enough to start walking along 'em and looking at whatever was spread inside.

That time he did look around.

He come to one window where diamonds and all kinds of jewelry was scattered and sparkling and stopped there. He was still mighty groggy and things sort of whirled at his sight, but Andy had never seen such sparkling things as there was in that window, and he was trying hard to study and think on some designs on a silver dish, how some of that work would do with decorating spurs or bits when he felt a sort of light shove. Andy moved away a foot or so and never looked around. A few seconds later he felt another light shove and that time, with a scowl on his face, he did look around.

But the sudden flutter that come to his heart at the sight of who'd done the shoving sure took that scowl off his face mighty sudden and left it blank. Andy had seen visions and things whirling from the last few drinks he'd had and even tho things still whirled some he thought sure he'd got rid of the visions, but it didn't seem that way for the one who'd done the shoving and was now standing right alongside of him was none other than the girl, the one he'd seen that afternoon and which he'd visioned in the saloon that evening.

But she wasn't looking at him. She seemed mighty interested in the jewelry in the window, and that was mighty good for Andy because that gave him a chance to get his breath, a lot of which he was short of right then, and also make sure that with the way things was whirling wether this girl alongside of him was just another vision of her or not.

To make sure he done a little light shoving himself. She seemed sure enough there, and when she looked up at him and smiled there come another flutter, plum up to his gizard, for as she looked up at him she smiled. Then she asked,

"Can you tell me where Mrs. Jones lives?"

Andy tried his best to smile back, but the best he could produce was a spooky grin. She had the prettiest voice, he thought, so pretty that he hardly took in a word she said. Things was sure whirling now.

The girl noticing his blank look repeated the question and then Andy come to his senses enough so as to get the drift and make an answer.

"No Mam," he says, "I don't know anybody by the name of Jones."

"She's my mother," says the girl, "and I wonder if you'd help me find her?"

Andy couldn't see how he'd be of any help to her. He wanted to tell her so and still he sure wanted to pace along with her. He was doing some debating on the subject, but he didn't get to debate long, for the girl took the lead and his arm, and Andy paced along by her side.

CHAPTER FOUR

TUB AND HUGH STAYED AT MORE GAMES than they'd intended to and sort of lost track of time along with thoughts of food. Stub, not caring so much about gambling, and breaking about even, was the first to finally quit and remembering his appetite. Thru the thick smoke he thought he seen Andy sitting at his same place against the wall. He spoke to Hugh, told him it was about time to quit too and get something to eat, but Hugh had been a heavy loser and wanted to play a few more hands so he told Stub to go ahead and order the steaks, that he'd be ready when they was.

There was a door from the saloon into the restaurant and Stub stepped in there to order. A talkative waitress sort of took it onto herself to entertain him after he'd placed his order and Stub lingered. He lingered till come sudden sounds of a commotion from the saloon and then the barking of six-shooters. When he opened the door into the saloon the first person he seen was Hugh standing by a table, gun in one hand and raking in all the money that was on that table with the other hand. One of the two men he'd been playing with stood against the wall, the other one was down and holding his hand to his shoulder. The rest of the people was just standing away and staring, even the bartenders.

But that didn't last for long. By the time Hugh had stuffed all his and the gamblers' money in his pocket, and before Stub could get by

Hugh standing by a table, gun in one hand and
raking in all the money with the other hand.

his side, there come a rush of two men with badges and, each pointing
a gun at Hugh, told him to drop his.

Hugh knowed he'd have no chance in fighting it out. There was too
many around that was now ready to help the officers. His back was to
them, and he layed his gun on the table. He was satisfied now anyway,
he'd cleaned up on the two men he'd found was crooked gamblers and
playing together to cheat him. He also thought right quick and before
he layed his gun down that no judge would go against him for treating
such men as he did, if the one he shot didn't die.

The officers had no liking for the gamblers either, they was only trouble
makers and they was glad to take 'em in along with Hugh. They even
allowed him to hand the money he'd raked in over to Stub, also his gun.

Hugh was took away and Stub was left behind to cuss the luck. With
the wild horse contract to live up to such a happening couldn't of come
at a worse time. Then he thought of Andy and wondered why he hadn't

been around at the rumpus. He looked for him amongst the men and then asking one of the bartenders he was told that he'd seen him go out quite a while before. He then walked the streets looking for him and forgot all about the fine steaks that'd been ordered. Thinking that he might of went back to the stables he went there looking for him, he even called up the jail house and a couple of hospitals but no sight of such a person as he described had been seen anywhere. The tenderloin district was also visited by him but that was a mighty big district, with many different kinds of houses and stalls, and many had their doors closed and the shades down.

On account of Andy not being town-wise, Stub didn't expect to find him in that district, but it was just another place he'd thought of as he kept on searching. Finally he went back to the saloon, took a stiff drink and then went in the restaurant and gulped down one of the steaks. He hardly tasted it for worrying about his two pardners, one in jail and the other one missing. But he had to have something to eat because his stomach sure said so and he felt that he'd be needing a lot of strength, put on a lot of action and do some fast thinking to get the outfit together again.

He walked the streets again after he got thru eating. He didn't see much use in doing that because he knowed that Andy had a heap better sense than to just wander around like a lost sheep. He knowed he'd been at the saloon and with him now if he could, that's what worried Stub and he walked the streets more to ease his restlessness than with any hope of finding Andy.

He'd go to the saloon hoping to find him come back there, then he'd rest a spell and walk the streets again. The bartenders changed shifts, and when three o'clock come Stub was sitting in a chair of the saloon, all tired out and with his chin resting on his chest. Finally he stood up, sort of shook himself and telling the bartenders where he could be found if any such feller as he described Andy come and asked for him, he hit out for a hotel, room and bed. He stretched out on top of that bed, too wore out to take his clothes or boots off. It was one thing for him to ride day and night and worry about getting away with stolen stuff, but worrying about his pardners the way he had, and walking the streets was all mighty different and wore not only on his body but his heart.

Stub had woke up and went back to sleep about ten times before daylight finally come. He got up, then washed, run his fingers thru his hair, sort of shook himself and went to the saloon. Nothing had been seen nor heard of Andy. His breakfast was a cigarette and a cup of coffee, and then he went to the stables again hoping to find Andy there. No such luck, and as Stub started to walk back up town he got to cussing that luck some, and getting a little desperate.

It was early when he went to the jail to see Hugh. His reason for going early was to see how many would be on guard at that place besides the jailer. He also wanted a good look around outside before there was too many people on the street. The outside looked mighty solid, thick stone walls, then there was heavy screens on the barred windows, and as Stub looked thru one of the windows he seen that there was a four foot space between the bars of the window and the heavy bars the cells was made of. There'd be three thicknesses of steel to cut thru and unless the fellers on guard was dead there'd be no chance of cutting thru the first thickness without being heard. Stub didn't know very much about jails but he realized it was past him to try and get Hugh out from the outside.

He went inside. There was no regular hours for visitors at that jail, and being so early only brought a second look from the jailer as he walked into the main office. There was three other offices adjoining, the doors of two of them was open. A man he figured was a deputy was in one, he felt pretty sure there was nobody in the closed office. He looked around for other offices or doors as the jailer unlocked the door leading to the cells but there was none. He noticed how the jailer kept his keys at his waist, alongside his six-gun, but his back had been to him while he unlocked the doors and the deputy hadn't even looked his way when he walked in. He figured that with Andy he could easy enough lock them up and get Hugh out.

There was another door of bars, the jailer told him to holler out to whoever he wanted to see and then he went and set down not far away. No chance to smuggle anything to Hugh while he was sticking around, besides, between the bars where he was standing and the cell bars was a space of six feet or so and a feller had to talk plain to be heard, there couldn't be no whisperings.

Stub looked down the hall between the cells. There was about a dozen prisoners, a few was pacing up and down slow and steady like caged tigers and one of them was Hugh. Stub hollered at him and that lanky boy stopped in his tracks, then recognizing Stub he got as close to him as the bars would let him.

"Hello Stub, old boy," he says, grinning his pleasure at seeing one of his pardners, "where's Andy?"

Stub didn't want to tell him about Andy being missing, but he couldn't think of no true excuse for him right then, only one and trying to make light of that as he could so Hugh wouldn't worry he laughed and said that he was in the room at the hotel and sleeping off a jag, adding on that Andy didn't know of Hugh's trouble as yet.

The two boys talked about nothing in perticular for a spell. That's the way it sounded to the jailer anyway, but while talking, Stub made signs the jailer couldn't see which went to tell Hugh that he'd already investigated and seen where if things got tough a break could be made easy enough, and hinting an answer to the plans, Hugh says,

"I guess I'll have to wait a few days till they learn if that tinhorn is going to live or not, then I'll be getting a hearing and know something of what to expect. There won't be no use of fretting till then."

Stub winked at him. "Me and Andy will be around in case you want anything. . . . How're you fixed for tobacco. Want a drink?"

He got as close to him as the bars would let him.

Hugh didn't have much tobacco, and he would like a drink. Stub asked the jailer to take the tobacco to Hugh and give him a drink out of the bottle he handed him. The jailer was good and done that, then Stub asked him to take a drink himself and he done that too.

That was Stub's way of feeling out the jailer in case he'd have to figure on a "break." But even tho him and Hugh winked at one another as the jailer took a drink out of the bottle neither of them was fooled. That old boy knowed when to drink and who with.

61

Saying he'd be back that afternoon with more tobacco he laughed and added on that he'd meet him at the same place then went out. But he wasn't laughing as he got on the street again, he was mighty serious and worried. If only Andy would show up.

He spent most of that day at the saloon, just sitting there, thinking and watching the door for Andy. He knowed that's where he'd come to soon as he could. Once he went to the stables and to see Hugh again on his way back. He talked to the sheriff some but there was no encouraging word from him, so he wandered back to the saloon. He felt sort of lost and mighty lonesome.

If he'd of knowed what news he'd be getting about Hugh on the next day he'd went to bed earlier and slept a heap better, even if there'd still be Andy to worry about. As it was he joined a small poker game, more to pass the time away and keep from thinking than to gamble, and he was sitting right where he could watch the door as he played.

It was late forenoon of the next day when he wandered down to see Hugh again. Then Stub got his surprise, Hugh was in front of the justice.

It'd been found that the gambler who'd been shot was safe from danger and would sure live. Then there was hurry proceedings for a hearing and the fixing of a bail. Stub looked blank and swallowed hard as he heard what the bail had been set to and he thought it was pretty steep, about *twice* as steep as the good amount of money he had, and he had all the money there was between the three.

He thought mighty hard for a spell for he'd hoped that he could get Hugh out on bail, that would of been a heap better than helping him break jail because with the jail breaking they'd all have to leave everything behind, ride light and fast and be on the dodge again, with only one horse to the man. Their picked string of horses would be lost to 'em, so would the contract on catching the wild horses.

The time for the trial was set for many months away, and with Hugh staying in jail all that time, there would be no hope of Stub and Andy making good on the contract because it sure called for three mighty good men to fill it. It couldn't be filled without Hugh, and being that the outcome of the trial didn't promise to be very cheerful, Stub and Hugh come to a silent agreement that, being no bail could be raised, there was other ways of fixing things so he wouldn't be spending no summer behind the bars, even if they would have to be on the dodge again.

It was as him and Hugh was talking things over that way, and about the contract, when Stub thought of the superintendent they'd made the contract with. He was the only man they knowed a little in the whole country, and being they'd be dealing with him they figured he might help on putting up the bail. Anyway it was sure worth trying, and that was no more than thought of and decided on when both of the boys sort of perked up. There was hope, and Stub sure didn't let no moss grow on his bootheels in following up on the ray of it.

If Andy was only with him now he'd of felt pretty happy. He hated to leave town without knowing what had become of him, but he couldn't do anything for him and he sure could for Hugh. He would leave word with the bartenders for Andy and ride on to see the superintendent.

But that day seemed to be a day of surprises for Stub. He'd hot-footed it to the saloon to get some stuff he'd left there when the bartender pointed to a feller sitting in a chair against the wall. The feller's head was down but Stub right away recognized the build of him, his clothes and his boots. It was Andy. But his build and clothes was about all that could be recognized about him, for as he happened to raise his head there was everything about it that didn't look like Andy's, it was all swollen and purple with bruises, he packed two black eyes and a cut lip, then there was a bandage on his head and both of his hands was bandaged too.

Stub stared a while hardly believing his eyes, then he begin to laugh, at the sight of him and the happy relief of seeing him.

"He come in just a while ago," says the bartender. "I gave him a good stiff bracer. He said he didn't want nothing to eat, but I think he's all right."

"Yes, if he hasn't got a few broken ribs or some such like. By the looks of him he must of tangled with a few too many, and he wasn't idle either while that was going on, not by the looks of them hands of his."

Then a sudden thought came to him, and walking over to Andy and just saying, "This is Stub, Andy," he reached inside of Andy's shirt and pulled out his six-shooter. It was loaded as usual, Stub smelled for powder smoke in the barrel. There was none, but to make sure he asked.

"When did you reload this gun?"

Andy had stood up at Stub's first words and being he could hardly grin his pleasure at being with him again he just lifted a bandaged paw to his pardner's shoulder and rested it there. It was hard for him to speak but when he did it was to say that his gun hadn't been used nor reloaded since he'd left the home ranch.

Stub believed him and that was another relief to him because he sure didn't want to see both his pardners cooped up on account of shooting scrapes, or on any other account. He didn't ask how he come to be missing the last two days and nights, where he'd been or what had happened for him to get all battered up the way he was, he only asked him if he was in shape to ride back to camp with him.

"Yes," Andy answered. There was something to that answer which hinted strong that he wasn't ready to go but that he would, and from that, Stub figured that Andy only wanted to stay to even scores. He would of liked to stayed too and helped him at that, but there was things a heap more important to do right now than fighting.

"Where's Hugh?" asks Andy as the two was sitting in the restaurant and trying to down a noon bait. Stub, not wanting to stir Andy up any worse right then, lied and said that Hugh was out of town hunting up a team and wagon to haul the stuff they'd bought. Andy felt pretty bad at the thought of how little help he'd been to his pardners the last two days and he done his best to cheer himself in knowing that he'd sure make up for that when time come to run the wild ones.

By afternoon of the next day the two boys had reached their camp, they'd rode over a hundred miles in a day and a half of daylight. During that ride, Andy had lost his stiffness, and he'd also learned what had sure enough become of Hugh. When Stub told him he brought his horse to a stop, he wanted to go back and get Hugh out somehow, but Stub finally got him to understand and explained how he was working to get him out in the quickest and fastest way, so they wouldn't have to scamper out of the country in a hurry and be on the dodge some more.

As Andy was told there was nothing for him to do but stay in camp and nurse his bruises and feelings. The watching over the horses would help heal that up. He savvied them.

Stub caught a fresh horse the same afternoon camp was reached and rode the thirty miles to the ranch where the superintendent held out before that feller had digested his supper. The two went to the cook house to talk, and while the chink brought Stub the grub, Stub went on to tell the superintendent his troubles and then to ask if he would help on half of the bail.

The steaming coffee seemed hardly warm as Stub took a couple of swallows of it while waiting for the superintendent's answer. It took a little while for it to come but when it did it was more than worth that while, for the superintendent agreed to do even better than go half on the bail. He said he'd go two thirds of it so the boys would have plenty of money to rig up their camp and outfit with. Then he went on to add, in a way that Stub would be sure to remember, that he might want the boys to do him some favors sometime too.

Stub sure didn't expect any such ready and generous help from the superintendent and there's no way of telling how grateful and happy he was. He wondered some how him and his two pardners could ever do any favors for him any time, but if any such a time come they'd be all three as one to jump in and do 'em. That's what he told the superintendent.

It was less than forty-eight hours afterwards when Stub and the superintendent got to town, fixed the bail and Hugh was turned loose till time for trial. The important presence of the superintendent sort of changed the tune in the court house and there was a wink and a hint from the sheriff that there might not be no trial and that the most likely to happen would be the gamblers getting kicked out of town and the case out of court. No square men of the law cares for crooked gamblers in their town, and with the superintendent of the big outfit, the biggest in the state, furnishing on the bail that boosted Hugh away high to them same men, also went a long ways towards the dropping of the trial.

Stub and Hugh was happy as two kids in a free candy store while they went to work of getting a team and wagon and loading that wagon with all the things they would need in grub and camp and tools for trap building. That took a whole day, and at daybreak the next day they was on their way back to their wild horse territory.

CHAPTER FIVE

ONE EVENING, WHEN ANDY SIGHTED the loaded wagon trailing into the big pasture and towards his camp he thought that was one of the prettiest sights he'd ever seen, specially when he seen there was two men with the outfit, both riding the wagon seat and a saddle horse led behind. That meant that Hugh had been set free.

There was a heap of rejoicing at camp that evening, and not with rice and jerky to fill the empty spaces. There was new skillets being initiated to the fire with thick slices of ham in one and eggs in the other, canned corn in a pan and coffee in a pot and other things they could of had in town but never had in camp. They hadn't seemed to have time to appreciate them things while in town but while in camp it was different, very different. Of course the meal of that evening couldn't be repeated for very long, the eggs wouldn't keep, neither would the light bread and butter, but they'd have their coffee and biscuits, beef and potatoes and that's what a cowboy never tires of.

They wouldn't be traveling "light" (on rice and jerky) no more now, they'd have their skillets and ovens, a solid camp they wouldn't have to jump out of in a hurry, a good tent, and each their own blankets and soogans all wrapped in a tarpaulin. That'd be a heap of a change from sleeping in coat, shaps, and boots with spurs always on 'em.

To a stranger coming into the boys' camp that evening it would seemed that they hadn't seen one another for months instead of days, they had

Both riding the wagon seat and a saddle horse led behind.

so much to say. Andy had already heard about what trouble Hugh had got into and knowed how he come out of it, but neither Stub nor Hugh had got to hear any of Andy's story, and being now that Andy's face had limbered up some he could tell it, and even smile a little while telling.

The way it come about for Andy to start on his story was from a remark that Hugh grinned at him.

"Daggone it, Andy," he says, "you look like you stuck your head in a sausage grinder, and look at them hands of yours, they're no better."

"Yes," says Andy, looking at his hands, "and I wonder what them other fellers look like by now too. I'll sure want to see them again."

"What other fellers?" asks Hugh.

Andy started on to tell his story and he brought on a crooked grin as he did. He told of seeing a girl on the street the first evening in town, he described her as he would a pretty filly, the prettiest of fillies and tried his best to picture her as an angel that way that'd just floated to earth for a spell. Both Stub and Hugh grinned and near guessed the rest right then.

"Anyway," as Andy went on. After he'd took the drinks he had he got to feeling like the world was whirling too much inside and he went outside to get some air, then, after he got to feeling steady enough he started to walk a bit and, stopping by a window to look at some jewelry, what snuggles up to him but that same angel filly. She'd said she was a stranger in town and asked him to help her find a place where some folks of hers lived, and he'd felt like he was on wings himself and off the earth by escorting and helping such a girl to find any place, or anything.

Andy didn't spare any laughs on himself as he told of his feelings during the happenings that went on.

Well, if there was a stranger to that town or any town, that was Andy, but he didn't dare say so to her for fear she would get somebody else to help her. She done right well finding the place. At first she wound around some, sort of aimless, and she'd talked about herself and them folks of hers. She was sure a fine girl, Andy thought, so must her folks be, "and they'd had a hard time of life." The folks the girl talked about amounted to four, her old mother, a little sister and two brothers. The brothers was a bit wild she'd said, they couldn't keep any work but they was good at heart. Andy couldn't understand that about the brothers but he let on that he sure did understand all about such things, even to the girl supporting the whole family from her small earnings at some job she said she had. Now she'd not only lost her job but there was a payment due on the mortgage on the house her folks lived in and they'd be ordered out unless that payment was made by the next day or so. If she couldn't get a hundred dollars before then she didn't know what her and her folks would do.

Andy seemed to understand all about such little things as mortgages. He liked to hear her voice so well and be near her that he hardly understood anything, only that she was in some deep trouble, and when she mentioned a hundred dollars as a way out of it he jumped at that in wanting to help her. Andy didn't know how much a hundred dollars meant and he didn't care, he'd never needed or handled any money. He knowed where he could get lots of money, there was some buried in the Badlands at home that he could find, Stub and Hugh had plenty of it, and he didn't hesitate at all when he said that he'd be glad to let the girl have a hundred dollars, or even five hundred dollars, or more.

Them words was no more than said when the girl stopped her aimless winding around and hit straight for the place Andy was to help her find. He paced alongside of her, too happy to think how queer that was, and his only worry there was that when they found the house which the girl figured was the right place he expected she would leave him at the door. She'd said that she couldn't accept help from strangers, and he was afraid he'd never see her again.

But Andy wasn't let go at the door. He was invited right inside and led to a parlor where the girl asked him to sit down for a spell while she went to other parts of the house to look for her folks.

Andy sat down on the sofa, about the only piece of furniture left in that parlor, and he thought as he looked around the big bare room that there'd sure ought to be a table with lamp or a candle on it, and a few knick-nacks such as there was at the Badlands ranch home. There was a light from the ceiling but no lamp and he felt that the room sure ought to be "stocked up" with something. Proof to him that the girl and her folks sure was needing help.

He thought of the girl mostly, and as he was trying to picture her folks here she come with two of 'em, her two wild but good at heart brothers, her mother was out trying to find work and had took the little sister along.

The brothers seemed to be very good at heart, gooder acting than anybody Andy had ever seen. They slapped him on the back, cracked jokes and brought on drinks, plenty of drinks. Andy wondered about that, he didn't care to drink, he wanted to look at the girl and talk to her. But after a while she'd left the parlor, saying she'd be back soon, and her brothers was so friendly he thought he'd be friendly too. The stuff they brought him to drink only looked like yellow water, anyway. They called it cocktails. It didn't taste strong, more like a drink to quench thirst and Andy was thirsty. He took one and then quite a few more of the drinks they offered him and the more he drank the more he got to liking them brothers.

Andy had got to where he thought them brothers was as good brothers as a feller could have, even if their ways and talk was strange, when one of them sort of stirred his horsethief instinct and set him to wondering. It was thru something that that brother asked. He'd said that his sister (Dot, he called her) had asked him to get a loan Andy had promised her, somewhere around three or four hundred dollars. That Dot had gone out to find her mother and told him to get the money for her. She would see him in the morning.

Three or four hundred dollars didn't sound like a hundred to Andy, and even tho he'd said he'd let her have five hundred, or more, he wanted to talk to her about that and not her brothers, which she'd said was a little wild. Andy knowed what wild meant in any way that word went. Andy had been a little groggy from drinks, but that brother asking for the money straightened him up pretty well.

"I can't give *you* any money," he says, "I was talking to your sister about that and she's the only one I would give it to."

The brothers looked at one another with understanding grins, and then proceeded to show more brotherly love to Andy by having him take one more drink, and many others. Andy got to forget about them asking him for money and he talked, saying he wished the girl hadn't left, how pretty she was and how such a girl as her could ever take a liking for such a feller as him. The brothers explained that to him very easy, that he was a handsome looking feller but that his frank and honest ways was what she liked him for the most. That pleased Andy, and as he talked and drank, his imagination got to working well. While he hoped for the girl to come back any time, he told of the big ranch his dad owned and by the time he got thru describing it that ranch had spread till it took up a whole county. But there something clicked in his mind and when he was asked as to where it was he moved the location of that ranch by a thousand miles or so. He also told of the many wild horses him and his pardners had caught and how many more him and them expected to catch, that was hope along with his imagination.

He told the brothers many more things, but always there was his "bringing up" that kept him from bragging about the horse stealing times, the badlands or any of the outlaw game he knowed so well. The brothers acted very interested in all he said, but a heap more interested when he finally begin to nod while he talked.

Come a time when Andy did quit talking. His head was down on his chest and he was breathing in deep sleep.

He was dreaming of running wild horses, the girl in the lead of the band and riding the prettiest horse he'd ever seen. He was catching up with her and the horse she was riding when he felt hands going all over him, into his pockets and even down his boot tops. That didn't fit so well with running wild horses, but it took quite a while for his senses to figure that out. Then one of his boots was being pulled off, and that helped some to make him come to, for nobody had ever pulled his boots off before. And when a hand touched his gun at his waist, under the front of his shirt, is when Andy shot up sudden to have a look around.

He stood up to face the two brothers. They hardly paid any attention to him, and figuring he was too drunk to realize they went to talking about "That fool girl, Dot, bringing just a plain bum for us to roll. What does she think we are anyway?"

One of the brothers started out of the room, remarking that he would see her about that right now, while Andy was shaking his head in trying to figure out what they meant, but even if he'd been plum sober he'd had a hard time understanding their lingo, for they sure wasn't talking the language he knowed.

The only thing he caught in their lingo was their tone of voice, about the girl and her being a fool. One of the brothers had already gone as Andy asked about that, and the other answered with words to the effect that she was a heap worse than a fool.

Andy couldn't recollect just what he did as he heard that answer only that he seen red and started to wipe the earth clean of such a feller, brother or no brother, for talking about his sister the way he had. He got a blow along one eyebrow and had only faint recollections of what the brother said. That was that she was no sister of his and only a bum like Andy was.

Andy landed on the floor with that recollection, then he forgot about that recollection and got another, that was about the one brother pouncing on him while he was down, and there's where that brother made his mistake. He could of whipped Andy easy enough in a stand-up fist fight, for Andy had never had any fist fights, but he'd wrassled many a big wiry calf and handled many stiff-necked broncs and he sure applied his skill that way till he got a holt and then he begin to do some pounding himself.

That one brother was ready to quit when the other one came back. Andy took one glance at him and figured right then that he'd only started to fight, for that other brother sure seemed on the warpath and coming Andy's way. It struck Andy queer afterwards, but right then he thought of the girl, that this big brother was no brother of hers at all, and neither was the other one, that they wasn't brothers at all, only a little wild, as the girl had said, but with *no* good at heart.

Andy sure enough got mad when he seen him. He rushed at the big feller and was knocked down once more, but he sprung up like a cat this time, and arms a swinging wild, made another rush. He was so mad right then and set on exterminating that big feller that his body was like solid steel, the blows hardly seemed to faze him, and when that big feller stuck his fist in Andy's middle is when he did connect with plenty of steel. It was a forty-five six-shooter, at his waist. And while that big feller was shaking his right from the connection, Andy's own right come to a smashing stop on the big feller's adam's apple and he dropped like a beef.

Mad as he was, Andy realized he'd better go while he had the chance and before more brothers came in. He could hardly see now anyway on account of the two fine black eyes he'd got. They was swelling fast, and with other blows he'd took, that day's hard riding with nothing under his belt since early that morning and plenty too much to drink that evening, the meeting of the girl, then the fight, that all was too much for any one man in any one day. Andy got as far as the door and he buckled under by it.

Andy's own right come to a smashing stop on the big feller's adam's apple.

He was still very much by it when morning come, not only morning but noon. He got to know it was noon by a feller who pulled on his shoulder and told him he'd sure found a hard place to sleep, and that, anyway, a human shouldn't be seen asleep at noon. Andy didn't get to talk to or see that feller, but there was one word that struck him at the right place and sure begin to wake him up, "Noon."

His head felt as big as a full grown pumpkin and ached about that size. With "noon" he thought of his pardners, he hadn't seen them since the evening before, and thru all that was confusing and aching in his head he thought of them, the work to be done and how he should be with 'em.

With that thought in mind he started to get up on his feet. It took him quite a while to do that, for it seemed like every one of his muscles had a thorn in 'em. Finally up on his feet he steadied himself, then he started down the steps, with no thought of what house he was leaving or how he'd come to be there. His only thought was to get back to the stables and find his pardners.

Andy's sight wasn't so good, both his eyes was near closed, and as he walked along on the sidewalk he wondered as to where the stables might be. But if his sight wasn't so good his hearing was, then he heard the sound of horse's hoofs on the street. He turned his head at the sound and strained his eyes to see. It was a horse all right and pulling a light wagon. Andy stepped into the street to meet it and asked the driver where the stables he described to him was. Andy didn't see the grin on the driver's face as that feller looked at him and told him he was going to within a few blocks of the stables, and for him to step up on the seat and ride. Andy was mighty glad of the chance, and as the driver made talk he drove out of his way a few extra blocks and took him right to the stables and hunted up the stable man for him.

"You need taking care of, boy," says that feller as he glimpsed Andy. He took him in his office, hunted up the vetenary and in a short while, Andy was patched up in good shape, then he was told to lay down on a cot and a big raw and bloody steak was spread over his eyes. Andy remarked at that, saying he wished he had another one just like it inside his stomach. He was powerful hungry.

He asked if his pardners had been around and he was told that one had a couple of times and again just a little while ago.

Andy layed with the steak on his eyes, licked the blood that run off of it, and wondered when Stub and Hugh would be down to the stables again. He didn't want to try and find the saloon the way he looked. He didn't know how to go about finding it anyway, for the streets had him all lost and he was as helpless in them as a town man would be in his home badlands. There was only one thing for him to do and that was for him to wait where he was till his pardners come again. But he'd have to get something to eat pretty soon or the steak that was on his eyes would have to do as it was.

As a couple of hours drug by and his stomach kept a hollering he got to thinking about some way of satisfying it. The stable man came in from some chores while he was thinking his hardest on that subject and he asked him where he could get something to eat. He was told that there was a little restaurant only half a block up the street, then Andy thought of something else which quieted his stomach for a spell. He had no money, and without hesitating any he told the stable man so.

He was handed a couple of dollars and he took the money with no more thought than if he'd just borrowed a smoke, or less, for even tho that money would get him food that was only more reason for him to snicker at the need of it and town. On the range he could make his own kill.

But his stomach didn't let him think much on that subject right then. He got out from under the steak that was on his eyes and started to where he could get one on a plate with potatoes.

He felt near like himself when he came back to the stables again and he went into one of the corrals where his and his pardners' horses was busy around a big manger of good hay. It seemed to him at the sight of the horses that he hadn't seen a horse for a month, and the reason for that is that the last twenty-four hours had been his longest time away from one since he was a three year old. The horses sure looked good to him.

The sun went down, Andy was setting on the edge of an empty manger, watching the horses eat, thinking and often glancing at the corral gate

He felt near like himself when he came back to the stables again.

for his pardners. He could see pretty well again now. Dark come but no sight of his pardners and he didn't think they'd be down to the stables any more that day.

As time wore on and he'd quit expecting 'em, something else started a pecking at the back of his mind, like wanting to be remembered. He did remember it all at one shot as he happened to think of the girl, the promise he'd made to help her. He stood up as tho he'd been stuck with a spanish dagger, for he should of tried to see her that morning and now it was evening. He wondered how he didn't think of her before and what she would think of him.

But how was he going to keep his promise? He needed at least a hundred dollars to go with that promise, and his pardners had the money. Then he thought of the stable man again and went to his office and asked him for that money as he would another smoke.

The stable man looked at Andy and laughed. He knowed his breed mighty well and helped many of his kind when they got reckless with their money, but as much as he knowed the breed he'd never seen one just like Andy before, so ignorant about money and his careless way of asking for it, like it was nothing.

He started to lighten him up on the value of the jingling or crackling stuff but that didn't seem to have no effect on him. He just said he needed the money right away and would pay him back soon as his pardners showed up. The stable man didn't doubt that but wanting to educate Andy a bit he told him he couldn't let him have the money, not unless he gave good security for it. Andy didn't know what security was, and after that was explained to him he didn't see no sense to it. But if that was necessary he would furnish his horse and saddle as security, which, the stable man knowed, was well worth three hundred dollars.

And that's what Andy asked for, three or four hundred dollars, but the stableman said he could only let him have a hundred dollars and no more. Well, that was the best Andy could do right then. That would at least meet the payment due on the mortgage. He didn't think of the girl's folks or how she lied about the two men being her brothers, he thought only of her and his wanting to see and help her.

With the money in his pocket, the next thing was how to find the house and the girl. Andy knowed he could never find the house by himself so he asked the stableman to help him. The stableman learning why he'd wanted the hundred dollars was willing to help him, he hooked up a driving team to a buckboard and the two started out.

Finding the house was near like finding one perticular bay horse amongst a thousand bay horses. Andy had no sense of direction in town, it sure wasn't like being in the hills where a feller can go by landmarks. He remembered crossing a railroad track, that the house was two-stories high and a hitching rack was in front of it.

They circled pretty well all over town, and was about to give up, when they met the feller who'd took Andy to the stables earlier that day. From him they got a close idea as to where the house was, for that feller had first seen Andy when only a couple of blocks from it.

The house was finally found, the hitching rack helped identify it, but it was all dark. Tying up the team, the stableman and Andy walked up the steps, Andy remembered the steps. The door was open and as they walked in and lit matches, Andy well remembered the parlor. They went into other rooms. There wasn't a bit of furniture in them, only glasses in the kitchen, and when Andy hollered a howdy the stableman had to grin. The house was vacant.

They was made sure of that as they walked out and met the same man who'd shook Andy to waking up that day. He said he was living next door and that the house had been vacant for months.

"Well," says Andy, wondering, "it sure wasn't vacant last night."

The stableman couldn't help but laugh at him and Andy drove back to the stables. "Anyway, you've saved a hundred dollars," he says, "and you're lucky you just got your hide nicked, because that girl and the two men was only crooks who figured you had money and tried to get it."

Andy finally had to grin at the stableman's true remark, but there was a lot of disappointment with his grinning, for it was hard for him to believe that the sweet and pretty girl who'd took him to the house was a crook too. That hurt him, he'd liked to seen her again to make sure, and her two would-be brothers, so as to tangle with 'em once more.

He slept on the cot in the stable man's office that night and the stomping feet of the horses in their stalls and their steady grinding on hay kept him from dreaming of the girl or what all had happened the night before.

His eyes was again pretty tight shut when he woke up the next morning. He splashed water on 'em and wiped his face with the front of his shirt, then feeling in his pockets he figured he had enough change left for a good breakfast, he'd given the stableman his hundred back. He passed a barber shop on his way to the restaurant and there he stopped a while as he seen a man stretched out on a barber chair getting a shave. He felt of the stiff bristles on his face and wondered if he should tend to them or his stomach, he didn't think he had enough money to tend to both, and being a little dubious about having somebody shave him, also knowing that a shave couldn't make him look much better, he decided to tend to his stomach.

He took on his breakfast, then went back to the stables, moseyed around there, looking at the many horses, talking to the stable man and helping him and the chore men, just sort of passing the time away while waiting for his pardners to show up. He figured sure that they would be at the stables that morning, but eleven o'clock come and no sign of them. Then Andy got restless and finally asked the stable man if he would help him again and find a certain saloon, that he'd like to go there. He described the saloon to him but there was many others like it, and being there was a driving team just come back and already hooked up on a light buggy he told Andy that he'd drive him around and help him look for it.

That's how come Andy was sitting in the saloon when Stub came back from seeing Hugh. Andy had been there about an hour, talked to the bartender, was told that Stub had been looking everywhere for him, and would most likely be back again any time. A drink had been offered to him, Andy'd took it and it'd been just enough to make him feel drowsy, so he went to set down on the same chair he'd set on two days before, his eyes closed and his chin rested on his chest. That's when Stub found him.

Stub and Hugh grinned and sometimes laughed out loud as Andy told his story. Sometimes his ignorance of town ways and use of money made 'em wonder. They scowled and closed their fists as he told of the fight, and as far as the girl was concerned they hardly thought about her. They knowed her kind and on account of not wanting to disappoint or hurt Andy any more than he already was they didn't tell him anything about 'em. They'd let him find that out for himself, but it was agreed right there and then that the next time they went to town there'd be no such trouble and scattering as there was the last time, and they would be coaching Andy a bit.

Andy's story sort of clinched the decision, for they could see that even tho he grinned as he told it he packed some hurt in his heart. But they knowed mighty well that as bunch after bunch of wild horses trailed around pinnacles to his sight that he'd forget that. Hugh didn't have to think about his trouble till late fall, and Stub had no troubles, only to keep his pardners together and with him. They was honest mustang runners now, with no snag in their way and with plenty of mustangs running wild as a good chance for them to prove themselves.

CHAPTER SIX

THE BOYS WAS ON A BIG CIRCLE, each going a different direction and getting the lay of the country, where most of the mustangs was and what pass or ridge they'd head for when stirred into a run. The stirring of 'em was easy, all a rider had to do was to show himself to within a mile of 'em and they'd do the running, they'd run on for many miles even if the rider didn't follow 'em and the dust the first bunch stirred would act like a signal for any other bunch that seen it and spook them into a run too. Dust after dust would be stirred in valleys and hills and mustangs would be running everywhere.

The boys wasn't running horses that day, they just stirred 'em and watched which way most of 'em went of their own accord. Letting 'em run natural that way gave the rider a good idea of what ridge or pass they would take most always in making their get away out of the country. The wild ones would have their run, in a day or so would circle back to the same country and could be pretty well depended on to run out on the same pass or ridge when stirred again.

The place where the most bunches of horses run out on was the place where a good trap site would be looked for, hid away just off the main trail down from the side of a steep ridge or amongst trees, never in a box canyon because wild horses don't take to box canyons when being chased. Their instinct warns 'em of the danger of being hemmed in such places, and instead they'll take to the ridges or open country where they can see well all around 'em.

The dust the first bunch stirred would act like a signal for any other bunch that seen it.

Another thing that had to be noticed was the amount of horses in the country, if there was enough of 'em to make it worth while building a trap. The horses counted on would be the ones that ranged in the country surrounding the trap site and not over twenty-five miles away from it. The ones further away than that wasn't counted in because it'd be too long a run to get them to the trap and too many things likely to happen on the way to make them turn, split or break back. That would only be spoiling the mustangs and wasting good saddle horse flesh.

In scouting around for the wild horses, where and which way they run, the boys figured that if the big outfit's range was as full of horses as it was in the scope of country they was taking in and caught only one third of 'em they'd easy enough make the count the contract called for.

It was near sundown of a long spring day when, one after another, the boys rode into their camp. Each had about the same story to tell, that there was quite a few horses but what was confusing and making things hard in picking out a site for a trap was that the bunches of horses when stirred into a run most all went different directions, only a few bunches would follow one another thru one certain place out of the country and them wasn't enough to give the boys a good inkling as to where would be the best place to build a trap.

They seen in that first day's ride that the horses had been run often by many riders, and the ones that was left had got mighty wise to mustang runners' tricks. Some wise mare in each bunch had took the lead to freedom, past riders and dodged back when sometimes a few yards more that freedom would of been cut by the wings of a trap. The bunch would follow the wise mare and the wise stallion would nip the stragglers and keep the bunch together.

As the boys summed up on their day's ride they come to figure they'd have to do better than just hard riding to trap one third of the mustangs they seen. They'd have to study the horse's actions, know every foot of the country, build good traps at *exactly* the right places and then use their heads all the time in trying to outsmart them wise ones. They wasn't too confident in being able to do that well, but as the coals of the fire was spread and the evening meal was started, there was a golden glow of the setting sun on the high soaring dust which hundreds of mustangs for forty miles around had stirred that day, like encouraging and promising that much of that dust would soon be also soaring above the traps they would build, where many trapped mustangs would stir it again.

They talked of mustangs during the meal and afterwards, went to sleep thinking of 'em and dreamed about 'em during the night. When morning come, daybreak and the sun, they'd lost all thought of how snaky and wise the mustangs they'd seen the day before had been. They would be still wiser.

That day's ride was in another part of the outfit's range. The boys scattered, stirred up about the same amount of mustangs as the day before, watched which way they run and seen that they was also as wise as them of the day before. Few bunches got together and the way they hit out at the sight of the riders didn't give no sure feeling they'd go that way again the next time.

The boys met and stayed at one of the company's ranches that night, talked to the riders there so as to get an inkling as to where most of the mustangs would be, the ones that was least spoiled, and asked for the locations of the best of the old traps other mustang runners had built. They didn't get much information from the cowboys because them fellers, even tho they'd rather ten to one run mustangs than handle cattle, had learned that there was nothing in running wild horses but the thrill of the run. There was steady wages handling cattle and they wasn't paying much attention to mustangs no more.

Their talk wasn't very encouraging but when next morning come the boys forgot about that too and scattered to some more new parts of the outfit's big range. They was out to get the lay of it and to find the best location to build their first trap, where there was the most horses and in a kind of country where they could get the edge on 'em. They wanted a rough country, the rougher the better and where there was few trails. Then after knowing that country well, seeing how the mustangs run in it and picking out a likely trap site they could easy enough, they thought, keep 'em on the trail they wanted 'em on by hanging spooky looking rags on the trails where they might branch off. Them rags would turn 'em to the right trail.

They was cheered up some by Stub running across an old stockade trap, by the way it was built. As Stub described it they all agreed that it was no wonder so many wild ones was still free. The trap was scary looking, could be seen too soon and gave the mustangs too much chance to break back, then it was weak and low in places and there was signs showing where many horses had broke out of it time after time.

"What was still worse," Stub went on, "whoever built the trap made their camp only a couple of miles from it. That right there was enough to keep the suspicious on the watch right around that country."

The boys rode day after day and near covered the outfit's range before they went back to their camp. In that time they'd found some more traps they figured could sure be improved on in location and building. They seen more than two thousand wild horses, all wary and wise, and located three places where they figured to build traps.

They would build good traps, and being the location is as important as the trap itself they was mighty perticular in picking out the locations. They done a lot of hard riding, when one of the boys would locate a promising location for a trap and where there was plenty of horses around, the three would get together on the next day and make a run in that country, a regular run of crowding and hazing to see how many horses would run by the spot that had been picked for a trap site, and how many more horses could be turned to run that direction.

There was many runs like that and many picked places was let go on account of not enough horses running the same way each time. Where mustangs run to of their own accord in getting out of the country is where the trap ought to be layed because them wild ones can seldom be turned, no easier than a bunch of antelope, and when they see a rider they run to where their instinct tells 'em regardless of where the rider might be. The rider could be on a very fast horse and close enough to them to slap the leader's head with his coiled rope in trying to turn that leader and the bunch but the wild ones will seldom turn, they'll most always scatter past him and run on the direction they want to as tho he wasn't there.

To save a lot of hard riding and disappointments it's mighty necessary to build the traps along the mustang's run, like agreeing with the birds in their flight from South to North when spring time hits the land.

Two of the trap sites the boys finally decided on was in the roughest part of the outfit's range, a high country where horses had to pretty well keep to a trail while traveling. That country reminded Andy some of his home badlands, only the hills was many times higher, there was good grass in parts of 'em, good springs too, and with the shade from the scattering scrub pine and cedars them rough hills was mighty fine horse range.

The third trap site was located at a point of a rough range of mountains where steep and hundred foot rims of rock made a sort of big winding chute down off of 'em to the big flat below. Many of the wild ones took to the point where the chute started and came down it in fine style to where the trap would be built. Once in that chute the horses couldn't very well get out of it. It was a downhill run and they sure traveled on their way down to the flat. A few openings would have to be closed with dead trees, and when the boys seen how they could hide their trap so well, away down at the bottom of the natural chute and by a tall rim they figured that location to be as good as any man could find. The horses would take to the chute because it was high and open, it wasn't pinching and spooky like a box canyon, for the chute was like a big stairway winding down the point of the mountain. On one side was a straight up rock wall of a hundred feet or so, then between that wall and another that made a drop of another hundred feet or so straight down was a near level strip where the mustangs made their winding run down to the big flat at the bottom.

Mustangs do their fastest running when turning some point out of sight of the pursuing riders, and as there was a tall rim jutting up at the start of the chute many bunches took to a hiding run around the point of it. It's hard to guess which way mustangs will go once they're out of the runners' sight, for then is when they sure use their heads to be

The chute was like a big stairway winding down the point of the mountain.

anywhere but where the runners would expect 'em to be. The wise ones often manage to do that, and by the time the runners locate 'em again them wise ones might of circled back or took to some country where there'd be no hope of turning 'em, and safe once more from the wings of the trap which they wouldn't know of. —Instinct.

But once around the top rim of the natural chute the boys didn't think they'd have to fear losing any of the horses, for they expected 'em to run right down that winding chute like for a sure get away. All open places would be closed along that chute and the boys would be right on their tail to crowd 'em into the trap they would have at the bottom. There'd be very little chance for the wild ones to turn back.

The boys wondered how come the other mustang runners to overlook such a trap site, and as they went to investigate they found signs where somebody had, but the signs was very dim, it looked like the trap had been built maybe a hundred years before, by Indians and with sage brush that'd been sort of weaved and piled up to make a high enough fence. But the entrance to the trap showed that the stairway hadn't been used, only the lower rim, the entrance had been used from the flat and as Stub studied the trap he seen it hadn't been built for wild horses but for antelope. That was the Indians' way of getting their meat supply while they still had only bows and arrows. There'd been thousands and thousands of antelope in the country, the Indians had lined up to make a wing leading to the trap and closed in at the wide entrance when the antelope was inside, and being that antelope is not a high jumping animal the six or seven foot sage brush fence held 'em easy enough. The fence had now sagged down till it was only about a foot high but showed well the shape of the trap. It was of the same shape the boys had figured on building theirs, only the entrance would be from the rims instead of the flat.

The boys decided on that location to build their first trap, at the bottom of the rock rimmed stairway. They was all mighty anxious to get to work at it and start running the wild ones in. Camp was moved to some rough hills acrost a little valley from the trap site and set up again by a little stream that broke thru the earth, run for half mile or so and then sunk back into the earth again. There was good strong grass for the horses, and now that there was no fence to hold 'em the boys put the hobbles on the ones that'd be most apt to drift, but there wasn't many needed hobbling because they was so far from their home range that they was satisfied to stay most any place so long as there was water and grass. Then to make them more satisfied, Andy took the team, drove to one of the company ranches and bought a wagon-boxful of grain. He would feed 'em some of that grain twice a day.

He surprised Hugh and Stub by also bringing a big quarter of beef, a sack of potatoes, and two men with their bedding. They was ranch hands.

"There was no more work at the ranch for these boys," says Andy. "They was leaving and I told 'em about helping us build our trap. Whatever you pay 'em you can take out of my share in the mustangs we catch, and me I'm just going to hold camp, take care of the horses, cut wood, start the meals then wash the pots and pans afterwards."

Stub and Hugh laughed and remarked that he sure must think he was some powerful worker to bring two men to take his place, then added on that whatever was put out for the men would be split three ways. They was glad Andy got the men because they didn't have no time to spare and their help would cut the time and work of building the trap to half. Stub and Hugh didn't care no more to get off their horses and go to work with shovel and ax than Andy did, so the help was mighty welcome, and to please Andy they told him they'd already decided on him holding camp and watching the horses anyway, that somebody had to do it.

The work on the trap was started. A mile or so from the site and where few wild horses ever went was a deep canyon that cut into the rough hills and both sides of the canyon was pretty well covered with fair sized junipers. It was steep and rocky climbing to get to them but once a tree was cut there sure was no need of dragging it down and it'd land to within short loading distance of the wagon. Stub and Hugh done the tree cutting while the two hired men was set to work digging the post holes along the line that'd been marked out.

Stub and Hugh was getting blisters and calluses on their hands while Andy's was getting soft and tender from too much dish water. The work went on, one tall cedar was stood up in a narrow trench alongside of one another, at every six or eight feet a bigger cedar was set deeper and then all the posts would be wound together close to the top with a strip of rawhide and sort of binding the corral like a hoop around a barrel.

On account of the good location there wasn't half the work to building that first trap as there would be with the others. The rock rimmed stairway made natural wings to the trap, then the lower rim went to make a good part of it. It only took a couple of weeks and then the trap was done, a solid trap of rock wall and cedars that stood eight feet at the lowest place like a tall shaggy picket fence. There was a big main corral with a wide entrance and then a smaller corral adjoining where the wild horses would be run into after they was caught. A heavy gate was on that one and would be closed and hold the horses inside till another bunch was run in.

The boys was pretty tired of "laboring" by the time they got the trap done, and thinking ahead to the next trap they'd have to build they kept the two men to go to work on it while they'd be running horses. Stub let them have the team and wagon. Their beds and part of the camp outfit and grub was piled in there and he went with them to show them the location for the second trap and map out how to build it.

It was a good idea to build that second trap right away because when the wild horses that wasn't caught got to leaving the country around the first trap the boys could go to the second one, which was forty miles away, and let the mustangs come back to the country where the first trap was, also maybe catch some of them that'd left the range surrounding

92

the first trap. They could work the same way around with the second trap, for when they run short of horses there they could switch back to the first trap, and back and forth that way to try and catch the horses that would return to whichever range the mustang runners was leaving rest.

The boys was in the saddle by daybreak for their first run. They'd long ago forgot the discouraging words the cowboys had spoke about trapping the mustangs of that country, and riding the best of their good horses they felt mighty confident that there'd be at least a couple of bunches of wild horses in the new trap by evening. They seen a few horses on the flat but by the short run they made it was easy guessed that they was branded horses belonging to the outfit. A couple of bunches of mustangs was at the foothills of the mountain. The boys was over a mile away, but the mustangs seen 'em and run up a rough ridge. That was encouraging, for that's where they wanted the mustangs, up on the mountain and running along the trails there, to the end of it and the winding chute.

With the starting of the first two bunches, Andy figured it best to hit on their trail, not to let them see him, but if they turned and hit for the point of the mountain and the rimrock chute he would ride to crowd 'em on down and into the trap before Hugh and Stub would run in with whatever more horses they could head that way. It was most likely that the two bunches would stop when reaching the top of the mountain, but as it is necessary to have at least one rider somewhere within a mile of the trap to be ready to help with the horses brought towards it, Andy rode on figuring to be on the watch there. Hugh and Stub was to go a few miles further, get up on the mountain and Hugh was to ride there while Stub went down the other side, rode the foothills and shoved what horses he seen up there to Hugh, then Hugh would haze 'em towards Andy. Stub was to ride up on the mountain again when close enough to the trap and help Hugh and Andy run in whatever horses was gathered.

But wild horses often spoil the best mustangers' best plans by running just the opposite direction or doing things they're not expected to. When Andy rode up on the mountain he seen the two bunches of mustangs about a mile ahead of him, they didn't see him in the broken and scrub timbered country and they was skirting around the point of a steep pinnacle at a walk, but in the direction of the trap. Andy hardly expected 'em to do that. He hid, and soon as they got around the pinnacle and out of sight he put his horse in a high lope. When he reached the pinnacle, stopped his horse and looked around a point of rock he seen the mustangs again, now going at a good lope. Their instinct had warned 'em that a rider was somewhere on their trail, and being they hadn't seen him as yet is why they wasn't traveling faster. They was still heading towards the chute and the trap, they'd went that way down off the mountain many times before, when there'd been no trap, and their good instinct wasn't warning 'em that there was one now at the bottom of the rims.

Andy kept hid by the pinnacle till the mustangs run out of sight around another jutting point, then he rode on some more, faster this time, and when he seen 'em again they was running faster too. He wished they would slow down and stop so as to give Stub and Hugh time to catch up with him with whatever horses they might bring so the whole work of trapping 'em would be done together. He wanted to be where his pardners expected him to be so as to help, but the mustangs kept running and straight for the top rim at the point of the mountain.

They was only within a mile of it now, and Andy's heart was pounding in his ears at the sight of 'em. And knowing that one mustang in a trap was better than three in the hills he rode past the spot where his pardners would expect him to be and run on after 'em. He seen that they wouldn't stop, and if they went on around the top rim and into the chute there was no way for 'em to go but into the trap, they'd of course turn back mighty fast at the sight of the trap, and if Andy wasn't right close to crowd 'em into it, them horses wouldn't only be impossible again but they'd be running loose to lead other horses away from that trap. They'd know its location and would sure never forget it.

Andy now rode to where he'd be at a good advantage to handle the horses in case they turned off the mountain before they got to the top rim of the chute. He kept out of their sight and his heart was beating fit to bust when as he'd get a glimpse of their ears and manes now and again he seen that they was heading straight for the rim. They went around it without them seeing him, and then Andy sure put his horse to covering space. He near took a chip off that top rim as he rode around it and fogged down on the wild ones. Then they seen him, spurted speed and tore the earth while they looked back at him and run between the winding rims. Their tails was just a-popping as they got to the bottom and the leaders spotted the trap, then they sort of checked for a second, but they was too late. There was a loud holler from the devil behind 'em, he was waving a long scary looking slicker which none dared turn back to face and, all mighty confused they run into the entrance of the trap.

Twenty one head of mustangs is what Andy counted of the two bunches he'd trapped. He felt mighty pleased and his heartbeats didn't slow down much at the thought that he'd been the one to initiate the trap. Such a nice bunch too, no little colts, but there had been little colts, for two of the mares was ganted up and had full bags. Mountain lions had got the colts, Andy figured.

The mustangs was running around the big corral of the trap, snorting, dodging at their own shadows and looking for a way out. Their only way out was the way they came in and they would rush the entrance once in a while, but each time the rider with his spooky slicker shot in plain sight sudden and scared 'em back, he'd hide again so the sight of him wouldn't make 'em more excited, and desperate. A wild horse will get mighty desperate when cornered and a rider stays in plain sight. He'll fret till he's near crazy then and is likely to run past or thru the rider to make his get away.

Andy knowed that and that's why he kept hid. The mustangs got to know he was there too, and the sudden scare he'd give 'em every time they tried the entrance finally made 'em quit trying it again. Then, with not seeing him they cooled down to huddling together at the far end of the trap, kicking and biting at twigs, one another or anything that touched 'em.

It would of been fine if Andy could of run the horses into the smaller corral and closed the gate on 'em, then he could of rode back up on the mountain and took his stand where his pardners would expect him to be when they come his way with their wild horses. But he didn't want to take the chance of trying to run the horses into the smaller corral while alone, the main entrance of the corral they was now in was too wide, they would be mighty likely to scatter if he went in there and beat him to that entrance before he could bat an eye. And if he did get 'em into the smaller corral the first try is seldom good and they would break out again before he could close the gate. No, there would have to be two riders to guard the entrance while another eased around to get the wild ones into the smaller corral, and then is when "Wild Horse" seems like a mighty tame name for the mustang.

Where Andy was hiding he could peek over a boulder and watch the horses inside the trap. A clump of low cedars hid him and his horse well on the other side and from any horses coming down the chute. He was some excited as he watched the trap and then turned to watch along the high rims. It seemed to him that he'd been there quite a while and that his pardners ought to be showing up any time now.

He'd smoked about ten cigarettes and was about to roll another one when there was a sudden clatter of hoofs, a dust and the sound of rolling rocks and, looking up, Andy seen a string of what first looked like about fifty mustangs a-tearing down along the rims, and Stub and Hugh right close behind 'em. The mustangs in the trap heard the noise the same time Andy did and started running around the corral, all stirred up again and looking for an opening. Andy had forgot about 'em in the spell of watching the other wild horses winding down along the rims, and only a sudden hunch made him turn his head at the right time. But he was in a predicament where he couldn't move right then, for if he did the coming horses would see him, sense a trap, and turn back in spite of hell, riders and damnation. Then again, if he let his trapped horses go they couldn't be turned back into the trap, they'd jump a high rim first or dodge past the riders and take the other horses along with 'em, for the other horses would be quick to see by their actions that all wasn't right at the bottom of the rims.

Things was too fast for thought. Something just seemed to sort of take a holt of Andy, held him where he was for a split second and till the horses coming down the mountain was out of sight around a bend. In another split second they'd be in sight again but that seemed to be time to spare for Andy. He shot up sudden to within ten feet of the trapped horses, swished his slicker and they near broke their necks in turning back, then Andy was in his hiding place when the other horses come into sight again, scattered gravel over him and run thru the entrance of the trap.

Squinting thru the flying gravel and dust, Andy got a rough count of the horses as they went a few feet past him, and he was surprised to see Stub and Hugh so quick, for he'd only counted ten or twelve head of horses, just a small bunch compared to what he'd seen at the top rims.

There was a mixture of disappointment and glad surprise on Stub and Hugh's face as they come to the entrance of the trap. The glad surprise come as they seen the horses already in the trap. Then Andy came out of his hiding place, grinning.

"Where did you lose the rest of the horses? I thought there was about fifty head when I first seen the bunch."

There was the disappointment. "We had about thirty head," says Stub. "The bunch split just around the bend over here. This little bunch here was in the lead and kept on a-coming, but some long-maned fuzztail took the lead of the second bunch and made a hole right thru the fence of dead trees we'd made to close an opening between the rims. Of course the rest followed and tore down all the fence."

A mustanger don't think much of having a few bunches scatter away from him while away from the trap and making his circle to run 'em towards it, the closer he gets 'em to the trap the more he minds losing a bunch. Losing a bunch within half a mile after he'd run 'em for fifteen or more sure aggravates him, but having them break away while in the wings of a trap and within only a few hundred yards of the entrance is apt to make him see red and bite a hunk out of a granite boulder.

But such is often the mustanger's luck, more of a gamble than cards on a table. Stub and Hugh had lost most their horses when they figured they sure had 'em. They'd lost another bunch before that on account of Andy not being where he was supposed to be but that was only eight head and Andy had well made up for them by bringing in the twenty-one head.

They now counted thirty-two head of wild horses in the trap, very wild and excited horses, and the sight of them made the boys forget that day's disappointments, for they seen that they done mighty well for the first day's run, better than they'd expected. Stub worked to get the horses in the smaller corral while Andy and Hugh rode the entrance, and the horses was finally corralled, the heavy gate well closed on 'em, and the boys rode back to their camp very encouraged. They cleaned up a warmed-over beef and potato stew, started cooking another one for the next day, another day that promised good, and as they crawled into their soogans and went to sleep they rode on some more in their dreams and hundreds of mustangs was caught before daybreak stirred 'em again.

The boys rode back to their camp very encouraged.

CHAPTER SEVEN

THERE WAS "LABOR" TO BE DONE at the trap the next day. The opening where the big bunch had broke thru the day before had to be mended and the fence of dead trees made wild horse proof. When that was done they only had time to make one little circle, but they caught one little bunch that made that day's ride very worth while.

On the next day the boys worked in the smaller corral and amongst the trapped wild ones. There was a commotion and a jarring of earth as each one of 'em was roped, throwed and tied down and let up again with a short rope tied from a front ankle to the tail. The front foot was tied back so it could just touch the ground and hindered a horse so that he couldn't go no faster than a skippety-hop lope.

It was sometimes mighty ticklish to work amongst them wild ones, so close and penned in with 'em. The stallions' eyes showed red fire thru the long foretops, their ears was at a murderous slant and the boys was careful not to turn their backs to them as they worked. For that reason they caught and throwed the stallions first and as strong sticks was used to pry their jaws open to see how old they was, there was a couple of them sticks snapped in two as tho they was toothpicks. But as one after another of them stallions was roped and throwed and then let up with the short rope on the front foot that gave 'em something else to think about besides murder, they went to wondering why they couldn't put one front foot ahead and then to fighting the rope that held it.

100

*Each one of 'em was roped, throwed and tied down and let up again
with a short rope tied from a front ankle to the tail.*

They'd quit fighting and stood sullen before the last horse was throwed
and foot tied up. Then the corral gate was opened and they come to
life again, so fast that they near throwed themselves. The bunch jammed
thru the corral gate and scattered all directions into the big corral, fighting
the foot rope, some of 'em falling, and all hitting for the main entrance
as fast as they could. But the boys was there and turned 'em back to
let 'em have their fight out and till they cooled down some.

When they did, and started to bunch up, two of the boys took the
lead out of the trap and one stayed at one side while the bunch skippety-
hopped out of the entrance. There didn't need to be no rider behind
'em, only at the front and sides to hold 'em back and keep 'em together.

That was quite a job because the horses was excited and mad and
sure had lost none of their wildness. Every horse wanted to hit out by
himself and the boys had to slap many heads many times with their coiled

ropes before each one could be turned and the bunch kept together. That's what's called "herd-breaking," teaching the horses to turn when a rider come near, to stop when he stopped in front of 'em and to keep together all the time.

The herd-breaking lesson was hard on the mustangs, caused by their own wildness and fighting what all was strange, they'd throw themselves as they'd kick at a rider who come near to turn 'em, run short of wind in their trying to get away and every hide was wet with sweat. But the mustang learns fast, and the bunch was only a few miles from the trap when they'd quieted down to traveling in one bunch, turning or stopping as the riders wished 'em to and without them riders having to use their coiled ropes.

By the time the fifteen miles from the traps to the pasture was covered they was well herd-broke, and mighty tired. There was a good fence around that pasture, good grass inside of it and there, by a good running creek, the riders left 'em be.

They wouldn't forget the herd-breaking lesson for many months, not unless they got out of the pasture and run free again for a spell, then a rider would sure have to ride again to get near 'em.

The foot rope wasn't took off of 'em as they was left in the pasture. They would have to pack it for a few days to sort of keep 'em quiet, so they would get used to things and not make a fast run into the fence before they got acquainted with the danger of it. Then, when another bunch of wild ones would be brought into the pasture the bunch brought in before would get a tryout as to how well they remembered their herd-breaking lesson. The ones that remembered it and behaved well would be roped and the foot rope took off, the ones that didn't would be left to pack the foot rope till a next time or till they did remember and behaved.

Of the good and bad there is to mustang running the boys figured the worst part of the game was the tying up of wild horses' feet at the trap and trailing 'em to another enclosed place. The wild horses sort of

The foot rope wasn't took off of 'em.

reminded the boys of good fighting men, in the right and fighting for their rights, till handcuffs and leg-irons makes 'em see the uselessness of fighting. The dejected looks and actions of the mustangs on their last miles to the pasture was like that of prisoners being hazed from one prison to another, only no man had ever enjoyed the freedom they did.

Running them, trying to outfigure 'em, tricking 'em to running towards the trap and then seeing 'em run into the entrance was the good and thrilling part of the game. The mustang enjoys that as much as the runner, all but the getting into the trap, and when he outfigures the runner and makes a good getaway he seems to laugh proud all over, the same as the runner does when he gets the wise one into the trap. After that the fun is over, it's a lost freedom for the mustang and "work" for the runner.

"It looks to me like we're going to be sending many good ponies to grief," says Hugh as the boys brought in a second bunch to the pasture. "They'll be jammed in cars, scared to death, shipped to where nobody knows anything about wild horses, and put to hard labor for no harm they ever done only to be on earth like us."

Stub and Andy looked at him sort of queer and agreed. They'd thought the same.

But such thought sort of wore out on 'em as long days after long days of hard riding and figuring brought 'em few and small catches, and now it was the mustangs that was getting the thrill and proud laughs at most every run in outsmarting the runners. The boys would also get some thrills during the day but there was no proud laughs after the long days' runs, only disappointed grins, for the trap corral was often empty.

There was only ten head in the third bunch they took to the pasture. That little bunch had to be took out just the same as if there'd been a corralful on account if they was left in the trap too long without water they would get the lockjaw and die. Them ten head was the result of two days' hard running, just one bunch out of the many that was still in that country, and trying to hold an eel with soapy hands would of been easier to do than to get them bunches near the trap. If crowded to a turn they would dodge past, around, and even under or over a rider if necessary, and every direction but towards the trap. They was stubborn and wise. Tricks was tried where the rider would sort of act to agree with 'em and manœuvre for 'em to turn towards the trap like as if that direction was the only way of escape, but the wild ones wouldn't agree. The boys often tried to even crowd 'em away from the trap, expecting by their stubbornness, that they would crowd back and scatter past towards the trap, but the wise ones only agreed there and didn't crowd back.

It was thru them disappointing runs that the boys begin to think of branded range horses. There was quite a few bunches of them in that country, fine horses, and it was getting mighty tempting to run a bunch of them in the pasture and mix them with the wild ones there. The contract read that branded horses caught with the wild ones would be theirs and count as wild ones, and who could know that whatever branded

horses they might run in hadn't been caught with the wild ones? . . .
So far they'd caught only six branded horses, old renegade geldings that
had joined the wild ones and made wise leaders, wiser than the wild
ones because they wasn't afraid of man. Them six would be a small number
as compared to what might be expected to be found amongst the wild
ones, for them branded horses run on the same range as the wild ones
did and they was bound to mix. The boys had been surprised that they
hadn't mixed more than they did and surprised some more that good
range horses had been allowed to run on wild horse range.

Anyway, as they dug in the subject oftener and oftener they figured
that the way things was there ought to be at least one-fourth of the branded
good horses amongst the wild ones caught.

But they'd decided to be honest mustangers. It was mighty hard
to be that while they seen good bunches of range horses every day that
they could as well mix with their wild ones. A bunch or two would
sure help make up the count the contract called for. But they agreed
against that, for a while anyway. They'd do their best to straight
mustanging. Maybe they'd do better at the second trap, if they didn't
then they *might* make up the count with company horses before a
shipment was done.

Many branded bunches was glanced at as the boys went on their
rides after the wise mustangs. They would be so easy to get, while the
mustangs was like reaching for clouds, for clouds of their dust is about
all they was getting.

They kept on riding and resisting temptation, taking a little bunch
to the pasture once in a while, and gathering and holding the ones they
caught for a spell so as to keep 'em herd-broke. Then one day, when it
seemed they could get no more horses near the trap they caught two nice
bunches. It was sure a good surprise to 'em, but as they went on trying
to get more, with no luck, they figured that the two bunches they caught
had come from some other range and wasn't wise to this one.

Then, as the wild ones begin to disappear in the country around the trap the boys figured it wore out, for a time, and they decided to move to the second trap they was having built. They seen many horses as they neared it and they recognized some bunches that had ranged in the country around the first trap.

They was pleased with the sight of the second trap. It wasn't in as good a location as the first, but it was well built and hid, and so that when a wild horse seen the trap he would already be in the wings of it and couldn't very well turn back in the steep drop down to it. Another advantage was that after a horse seen the trap it looked like there was a wide opening thru it, the kind a mustang would take, but there was no opening. What made it look that way was a small point of a ridge that run into the center of the trap and hid the high juniper picket fence on the other side.

There was a few more days' work to be done on the trap. That gave Andy plenty of time to set up a good camp and make a trip to one of the company stores and supply up on grub and grain. The horses needed a rest, too, more so the spoiled ones because they'd been used for the hardest and longest runs so as to make 'em come to time and behaving. They was now behaving and didn't waste much more efforts in meanness.

The second trap, with the many horses around it, stirred up new hopes with the boys. But they was undecided some whether to have the hired help start with the third one or not. Then, thinking things over, they come to figure that if they was to carry out the contract they'd sure need the third trap, and need to save time by having the two men build it. So Stub went with the two men to the third trap site and mapped out the plans for that one.

The first day's run to the second trap wasn't so good. They'd had to change their style of running on account of the lay of the trap and the surrounding country, and it took a couple of runs to get an idea how the horses went. They got as good an idea as they did at the first trap but they wasn't catching as many horses as they did there. The horses acted like a cross between kangaroos and goats in that rougher country. They was on top of a sharp pinnacle one minute and along the side of a steep canyon the next. Now you could see 'em and now you couldn't, and where you could see 'em was most always in some daggone place where no rider could get around to turn 'em. Not unless he was riding an eagle.

It was middle summer, half of the time to fill the contract was past and only a little over a third of the horses that contract called for had been caught. Now the second trap was fast petering out and the horses was beginning to leave the country around it. Them that was staying was as hard to turn as the breezes that blowed and the boys would snort grins of disappointment at one another as day after day the most they caught of mustangs was the sight of their fantails waving a good bye at 'em as they made their getaway.

With the discouraging work, the boys begin to get restless and Stub and Hugh got to talking of other times, when they was running good bunches of range horses out of one country and shipping 'em to another, and cattle too. Of course there was no thrill in running them, only the big thrill of getting away with 'em and not get caught doing it. That life seemed to sort of look good to 'em again, maybe because of their disappointments and not living it right then. Anyway, that got to be a pretty popular subject of evenings and mustangs was hardly talked about only to map out another plan for their next day's run.

Andy was sort of neutral in their talk. Running mustangs or running off with somebody's horses or cattle or anything was just the same to him. He'd do what his pardners would do and take and share with good or bad and any chances they took. He wasn't so serious or worried about things as his pardners was, all he wanted was plenty of horses around him, plenty of hills and open country, and mustang running suited him as well as anything could.

Now you could see 'em and now you couldn't, and where you could
see 'em was most always in some daggone place where no rider could
get around to turn 'em. Not unless he was riding an eagle.

The boys got to camp early one evening, after another day of plenty of runs and no catches. They was more disappointed than ever and seen where something out of the ordinary had to be done. They talked things over well as they rode and that's how they finally come to decide to run about twenty head or so of range horses to the pasture and mix them in with the wild ones. The superintendent might ride in on 'em most any time now, they thought, and they'd better get the range horses right away so he would count them in as caught with the wild ones. Then they would get his okay on all horses and ship them out.

But the superintendent rode in on 'em that very evening and spoiled their plans by one day. They was talking about him when he rode in, and the sight of him at just that time sort of made 'em feel like everything was in cahoots against 'em. They tried not to show any disappointment as they seen him, and done their best to act mighty pleased as they handed him plate and cup and told him to help himself to what there was around the fire.

As the superintendent et and little talks went on he sort of sensed that the boys wasn't in any too high spirits. He figured that they was disappointed with their mustang running. That's what he expected and wanted, and he grinned to himself.

"Well, boys," he says, looking at 'em over his tin cup, "I rode by the pasture yesterday and I see where you've caught about enough horses to make a shipment. How many have you caught so far? The horses was running in bunches and I couldn't get a count on 'em."

He was surprised when Stub told him how many horses was in the pasture. The boys had done mighty well, he thought, about twice as well as any mustang runners ever had in that country. That pleased him, they was good horsemen, the kind he wanted and it pleased him some more that as good as they was and as well as they done they still was short of about one third of the count the contract called for. Of course there was still a few months to go to fill it but the superintendent knowed his range and the wild horses on it, and he knowed that the boys wouldn't do so well as they had from now on. They'd been running in the best part of the mustang country and there wouldn't be much more than hard riding and disappointments in the other parts.

In a round about way he told 'em that. Such talk made the boys look at the fire pretty hard and not with cheerful thoughts, and that's what the superintendent was working for. Then, when he thought he had the boys worried enough he remarked that he'd be riding over to the pasture on the next day. They would come with him and get a count on the horses, he would give his okay and they would start the horses to the shipping point.

The boys slept on that that night. If they'd only had one more day they'd had some range horses to swell the count, but it was too late now. They would sure run in range horses before the next shipment. They would sure have to if the other mustang countries proved worst, as the superintendent said, than the ones they'd already trapped in.

They rounded up the horses in the pasture the next day. That turned out to be a pretty ticklish job because the boys hadn't been to the pasture with new bunches for a spell and the mustangs was getting to forget their herd-broke manners. They went to running and scattering as the riders tried to bunch and hold 'em and it was high noon, after a lot of manœuvring, that was done.

The herd was being held still so they'd cool off and quiet down when the superintendent rode to a stop near Stub and went to sizing up the horses.

"Looks like," he says, acting dubious, "you boys will have to ride some between now and fall so as to make good with the contract."

"Yeh, we'll have to ride all right."

Stub was thinking of a heap more than riding when he said that and when the superintendent spoke again he seen that that feller was thinking of other things too.

"You remember, Stub," he says, "when I said I might need you boys to do me a favor sometime in return for the favor I done you by furnishing most of Hugh's bail." Stub well remembered. "Well," he went on, "the time is here now when you can start returning that favor and in a way that will be for the good of you boys as well as me, because what I have in mind for you boys to do for me would be the only way that you could make good on your contract."

Stub's ears perked up at that. He didn't say anything as he looked at the superintendent, but that look of his said aplenty that he was anxious to hear more.

"Before I tell you of my plans," said the superintendent, sort of mysterious, "so we'll keep them plans to ourselves and understand one another well I'd like to let you know that I know where you boys got most of them good saddle horses you have. . . ."

Stub squinted at him, trying not to show his surprise.

"Yes," he says, "I read the original brands on them horses while you boys was in town last spring."

The superintendent went on to tell him that the outfit the horses had been stolen from was of the same company as the one the boys was now contracted to run mustangs for. That was how come the superintendent to know about the boys and the stolen horses. He'd been advised to warn the authorities and his riders to watch out for 'em.

"But they don't think you came this way, and now that the brands are disfigured and about healed up you're safe here. We're the only ones who know, and nobody else will."

The superintendent rolled a cigarette and grinned at Stub. "Now that I have something on you boys," he says, getting no remarks from Stub, "I'm going to give you a chance to have something on me and it'll pay us all well to keep quiet about it. . . .

"For one purpose I've let the company's range horses accumulate to more than the range should carry. That purpose was so that I would get a good share of 'em by shipping them out with wild horses, as renegades, and without the company knowing any different. That's why I left that part open in the contract. I expected you boys would help me sort of round out my flat purse that way, by mixing half and half wild range horses with each shipment. My inspection will stand with the inspector at the railroad and you won't have no trouble there, nor nowhere else."

Stub still hadn't said anything, he'd been listening and thinking, and the whole proposition went well with his ears and thoughts. He was some surprised at the superintendent stealing from the company that hired him and that didn't strike him as the right thing to do. That feller was trusted, the stealing was easy and that wasn't on the square like stealing from outfits that suspicioned you and was ready to be on your trail if only as little as one scrub horse was missing.

But Stub didn't put too much thought on that subject, he figured it was none of his daggone business anyway, and that he'd be doing well to take care of his own along with his pardners'. There seemed to be a good way out now with the superintendent's proposition and he was ready to agree on it without even first talking to his pardners. He was sure they would agree too.

"It all sounds good to me," he says. Then he asks, "What's going to be our share on the horses?"

"Well, you of course understand that I'll be fixing things so you boys won't be taking any chances. Another thing you'll be getting full count of all the horses you ship, and that'll go to fill your contract. All I ask for that is the money that you get for two-thirds of the range horses. Whatever you get from the wild horses and one-third of the range horses is all yours. Don't that strike you fair enough?"

That did strike Stub fair enough, and when he talked the whole thing over with Hugh and Andy later they thought it was fair enough too, and good.

CHAPTER SEVEN

The superintendent wrote out a slip where a count of a certain amount of horses had been inspected by him and rode back to his headquarters ranch. The boys would have to gather quite a few bunches of range horses now to make up the count. They knowed that any horses over that count would have to be throwed back and the number would have to be exact so as not to stir suspicion from the inspector at the railroad.

They went to gathering range horses the next day. That was easy, and to make things more worth while they didn't take every horse they found amongst 'em. They run bunch after bunch into the trap, cut out the ones that wouldn't bring a good price and kept only the best. They figured the superintendent would agree with that well because, as he'd said, his purse needed rounding out, and shipping only good horses made things more interesting in every way.

It took four days to get the horses to the railroad. The mustangs being mixed with the gentler range horses didn't give the boys no trouble. There was no trouble with the inspection either, and to save time more than to save money, they turned the horses over to a commission man and hit for a hotel to catch up on a lot of sleep. They'd been in the saddle pretty steady for four days while driving the horses and four nights while holding 'em to graze.

A tenderloin steak to each and a good night's sleep made 'em feel brand new again. But they didn't waste no time on spirits nor cards nor women on this trip to town, that all could wait, for now summer was slipping by and there was a heap of work to be done before the snows come, when the contract come to an end.

Andy thought of the girl Dot and grinned to himself, Stub and Hugh thought of cards and fun in general, but as the three rode out of town for wild horse country again the jingling of their spurs sort of scattered them thoughts to the winds and the thoughts of gathering another big shipment of mixed mustangs and range horses took place in their minds. Things looked good.

CHAPTER EIGHT

T HE SECOND TRAP BEING PETERED OUT the boys moved to the first one again, thinking they could catch a few bunches that'd went back to that range. They did catch a few bunches, and figuring on how they could add on the same amount of range horses, that numbered up pretty well. When the first trap petered out again they moved camp to the new and third trap which was now finished. They let the hired men go then, for they figured that with the three traps and working from one to another they would about make up the count they needed in mustangs. If they didn't they knowed of other ways of getting mustangs without a trap.

The third trap was as well built as the other two and different again. It was hid over the edge of a steep ridge and where the drop off was natural for a mustang to take if something spooked him to turn at the right time. That had been took care of, a few sticks had been set in the ground on the main trail on top of the ridge and where the wild ones wouldn't see them till they come to the turning off place down to the trap, and spooky looking rags stirred by the breeze was hanging on the sticks and the sudden sight of them was expected to turn the horses as was wanted. There was many of them spooky looking rags hanging at the right places, where the mustangs wouldn't see them if they went for the trap, but where they'd sure bump against 'em if they took any trail away from it.

The trap itself was well located, and with the lay of it and the many horses in the country around the boys felt pretty hopeful of catching many horses there. They went to work at catching the wild ones with

114

There was many of them spooky rags hanging at the right places.

the same spirit as they always had, and with hardly any thought that with every wild one caught they could add on a range horse that might be worth twice as much as the wild one.

The boys figured hard to outsmart the wild ones, rode according and done well with the third trap, as well as they had with the other two, but they seen that as well as they done there would of been no chance to make up the count that was called for without chipping in the range horses. After a few weeks the third trap begin to peter out, some wise old tangle-maned mares had led their bunches right past the spooky looking rags when only a few hundred yards from the entrance and made clean get-aways. Them bunches couldn't be brought to within miles of the trap again and would lead other bunches away from it, and when one day the boys seen a wild one rubbing against a stick that held a spooky looking rag they figured that as a mighty strong hint that the trap was petered out. What mustangs was left in the country was wise to it.

They went back to running at the second and then the first trap, with not much luck, and when they tried the third trap again, with no luck at all, they figured it best to try some other way of getting the wild ones. They would run 'em to a "Parada."

A parada is a herd of stock horses, and to be of any use to the mustanger they have to be herd-broke or range horses, stand in a herd when wanted to and wild enough so they can be stirred into a sudden run without a rider having to do much scaring. It takes around a hundred head of such kind of horses to make up a good mustanger's parada.

With the superintendent's permission, the boys made up a good sized parada from the range horses, well herd-broke and plenty wild enough to be ready to run. The studs was took out on account that with them there'd be too much fighting and the bunch would be hard to hold together, for each one would be trying to haze his bunch out.

The parada, stationed in plain sight on some big flat, is used as a decoy for the wild horses, but the wild ones won't take to the decoy when fresh and just stirred. They might run into the parada but they'll go right on thru like as if it wasn't there and keep on running. It ain't till a wild bunch has been run a long ways, is sweated up, pretty well winded and tired, that it will slow down to run with the parada. Then the company of so many of their kind seems good and like sheltering from the runners that kept so close to their heels.

Stub held the parada on the first day's run to it while Andy and Hugh went on the trail of a few bunches of mustangs and followed 'em on a high lope on a thirty mile circle around the mountain. The wild ones was running their natural circle, there wouldn't be no need of having to turn 'em and the boys figured they would run close by the parada on the way back. They kept to within half a mile of the mustangs, close enough so the wild ones would run at a speed that would wear on 'em by the time the thirty mile run was made, and not close enough so that they would want to split or scatter.

Andy and Hugh had picked on their orneriest and toughest horses for that day. They was rangy, grain fed and strong and they covered the ground with a long lope that seemed of no effort and agreeing mighty well with their spirits.

It was along early afternoon when Stub seen a tall dust over a ridge, and later bobbing objects coming around the point of it. The wild ones was coming. Stub was glad at the sight because herding is tiresome and monotonous, there'd be action soon now and he prepared for it. He bunched the parada a little closer, not too close, and sort of stirred 'em to be ready so that when the wild ones come amongst 'em they would start to run too. Mustangs would go right thru a still bunch of horses when being chased but if the bunch starts to run when they hit it they will mix and run with 'em, and stay.

There's many things to know with running mustangs to a Parada and the boys knowed most of them things. Stub stirred the herd once more and shifted 'em to where he figured the wild ones would run. When that was done and the wild ones was within a mile, he rode to one side of the Parada a ways and got off his horse, keeping the horse between him and the coming mustangs. For the sight of a mounted rider would of turned 'em away.

But Stub wasn't standing flat-footed to the ground as he got off his horse, he kept one foot in the stirrup, and as three bunches of sweated-up mustangs hit the parada he was in the saddle to jump 'em into a run with the mustangs. They did that well, for they'd been wanting to run, and the scared mustangs coming in amongst 'em, and no rider to hold 'em, they went to splitting the breeze at as good a speed as the mustangs had. The mustangs mixed with 'em, Stub rode low on the side of his horse trying not to show himself to the wild ones, and looking back he seen his two pardners riding at full speed to help him. Their horses was tired but they was good for quite a run yet and now there was three riders to try and keep the herd together.

All went well for a spell. Then as the gentler horses of the parada begin to get their fill of running and went to slowing down is when the wild ones begin to looking around, noticing things and getting together again. They was getting their wind along with glimpses of riders near 'em, too near, and now the big parada was running too slow for 'em.

One bunch of wild ones broke out in the lead and near bumped against Stub, but as he straightened up in the saddle they spooked back, glad to hide themselves amongst the many horses. Another bunch broke out and was scared back the same as the first. But the boys knowed they'd try again and again and might make good their getaway. Many of the parada horses was now wanting to lag behind and Andy and Hugh had a hard time keeping them laggy ones to taking any lead around the wild ones and keeping them wild ones in the center so they wouldn't be so apt to spook and break away. The boys had to be careful in stirring up them gentler ones, too, for any commotion or noise would make the mustangs quit the parada in a hurry.

One bunch finally did get too nervous, and shot out of the parada as tho out of a cannon. Stub, riding a fresher horse than his pardners', took after the bunch, gave 'em a fast ten mile run and by then they was easy enough turned back into the parada again. But while Stub was doing that another bunch broke out at top speed, and being if one rider went after them would leave only one rider with the parada and the third bunch, they had to decide to let that bunch go. One bunch lost.

With some ticklish manœuvring the boys finally got to one of their traps. There was careful work in running the horses towards and in it and many of the parada horses had to be made to take the lead before that was done.

Once in the trap the wild ones was separated out and closed in the small corral, then the parada was drove out of the trap to a rough canyon where there was good feed and water and left loose. They wouldn't scatter much before the next day come, for it had been a long day and they was tired and hungry. So was the boys and their horses, going since daybreak and now it was sundown, with still ten miles to go to their camp. Hard work, along with steady disappointments that mustang runners have to stand.

But two bunches for the first day was encouraging. There was four good bunches brought into the parada the next day and all went well for a while, till they got near the trap, then they lost three bunches all at once. The fault there wasn't the boys', it was that there was too many horses and not enough riders to hold 'em. The parada had to be the size they had it, only there ought to be at least five or six riders when running horses that way.

The boys realized that, but their traps had wore out on 'em and now they was running mustangs in the only way they could so as to make up the count to fill the contract. They needed quite a few mustangs yet, but with the range horses they could throw in they figured they would make out easy enough, if they worked hard enough.

They worked plenty hard enough. In a week's time they'd caught six bunches of wild ones, about sixty head altogether. About then the parada was getting logy, they wasn't caring to run when the wild ones come amongst 'em and a couple of bunches was lost on that account. Another parada of fresh range horses had to be gathered and the tired ones let go.

The second parada was mighty willing to run, too willing. Stub had to ride like a wolf to hold and keep 'em together, and when three bunches of mustangs lit in the middle of it that parada was right in cahoots with the wild ones and went to running too, and so well that the parada, wild ones and all got out of control of the boys, scattered and got away.

The boys had to laugh. Another parada was gathered on another part of the range and the work went on, mustangs kept a-being caught, shoved into one trap or another then hazed to the pasture with one foot tied up. Of course they wasn't catching any big numbers of wild ones, just enough to keep 'em in good hopes to living up to the contract, and one advantage they had, now that they was running to a parada, was that there was no time lost to building traps, no certain place to have to run to. A good parada could be gathered anywhere on the company's range in a day's time, stationed anywhere, moved any time to meet the wild ones, and they caught some wild ones with the parada that they hadn't been able to catch in a trap.

It was now getting along early fall, the boys had been hard at running mustangs since early that spring and there'd been no happenings much, outside of the superintendent's visit and the shipping of the horses, to make any day much different than the other in all that went with the game of mustang running. Once in a while a rider would drop in at camp, stay for a meal or over night, talk of other ranges and ride on. Sometimes it'd be a prospector and his burros who'd tell the boys they was fools to waste their time running them "dad-burned fuzztails" when there was gold under their very hoofs just a-hankering to be found. The round-up wagons of the outfit would camp close some time and the boys would go visiting there, leading a pack horse and riding back with a quarter of beef tied on him.

None of the visits or visitors was much break from the regular happenings on the range, and the boys wasn't wanting nor looking for any breaks nor strange happenings. The running of mustangs still had 'em mighty interested and was seldom monotonous, and when they reached camp at night they was satisfied to do no more than just eat and then stretch.

But there finally come one day that brought on a happening that was a little strange and not fitting with mustang running. Stub was holding a parada on the outskirts of the company's range that day and Andy and Hugh was off that range to get some of the mustangs that had run out of it. Hugh was riding alone on a good ornery horse and chasseying a bunch of wild ones the direction of the parada when his horse stuck both feet in a badger hole and turned over a few times. Hugh done his best to hang on to a bridle rein but his grip slipped to the knot at the end of it and then it was snapped away from him. He was afoot, and his horse and saddle was gone, to the wild bunch.

It's very seldom that a rider ever gets to see his horse or saddle again in such a case. The horse will naturally follow the wild ones, and that's what Hugh's horse had done as soon as he quit rolling and got on his feet.

Hugh cussed as he watched his horse run, then he begin picking some crushed granite out of his face while looking around for some sight of Andy or any rider or ranch, somebody who might catch his horse, or some place where he could get one, so he wouldn't have to walk. It was many a mile to where Stub was holding the parada and many more miles to camp. He just stood still, like as if it was just as well to do that as to try and walk all that distance.

But with no sight of Andy or any other rider or ranch in the whole big country around him he begin to figure that he would have to do something, and walking was the only thing he could do. He started the direction of the parada. The boys wouldn't start it towards the trap nor go back to camp without him he knowed, and they'd sure look for him when he didn't show up.

He was walking along, spurs a-ringing, and watching for the sight of a rider when he seen something standing half a mile or so to his right. He stopped and squinted, it was no stump of a tree because there was no trees in that flat open country he was in, not for miles around and that was in the mountains surrounding. Then whatever it was that was standing begin to move, like a human, but it seemed too small for a human and Hugh's eyes blinked and he got as curious as an antelope. Anything like a human afoot was sure a curiosity in that country, to man and animals, specially such a small human as Hugh thought he was seeing. He could account for small humans in towns but not in the middle of big deserts.

Hugh hardly believed his eyes as he walked towards the upright object and that object walked towards him. Sage brush hid it from sight at times, and Hugh had to stop, eyes a-popping in wonder when he seen for sure that that object was a little human, a little tow-headed feller who now was jabbering and running towards him.

Hugh stood his ground and stared. When the little feller come near enough he touched him to make sure, then he grinned his surprise at the smiling freckled face of a boy, looked to be about ten years old. He didn't seem lost nor scared nor thirsty nor hungry and that sure made Hugh wonder some more.

The little feller was the first to break the wondering spell.

"Gee whillikin, mister," he says, "you sure took some fall. I seen the dust from your horses quite a while before you took that fall and I was watching. You're sure afoot now, ain't you?"

122

"Yes," says Hugh, still wondering at the boy, "but where in samhill do you come from, son?"

The boy pointed towards where Hugh had first seen him. "Over there," he says.

Hugh looked hard but couldn't see a sign of anything "over there." The country seemed too level to hide anything like any kind of a house, and then seeing how Hugh was puzzled the boy says,

"You can't see our house from here. You come with me and I'll show you. It's pretty near dinner time now anyhow."

They'd walked quite a ways when the boy pointed ahead. "You can see the stove pipe now. Our house is right under it."

Hugh seen the stove pipe all right but it seemed to be sticking right out of the ground and he couldn't see no house under it. But as he walked on he seen a drop in the ground by where the stove pipe was, a little flat that couldn't be seen from where his horse had fell, a little fenced-in flat and so green and cool looking that it seemed like a lost gem in that big ocean of bleak and sizzling country around it. Hugh got a whiff of the little green alfalfa field, it was like a drink out of a cool shady spring. He seen a cow and a horse in the shade of a little rock, dirt roofed shed, a neat little stack of hay by it and then a garden surrounded by berry bushes and small trees. There was a bunch of chickens too that cackled and hit for cover at the sight of him.

He didn't get to see the house till he walked down into the little flat, then only a little of the front part of it, the other part had been dug into the bank of earth and the roof had been covered with that same earth, making the house as part of the bank. It was a dugout. But not like most dugouts, it was neat and well built, made out of stone and pinion timbers and looked comfortable and cool.

At the sound of the cackling chickens a woman came to the door of the dugout. She was a young woman, not big nor small and, Hugh thought, not over thirty. At the sight of her he showed as much surprise

It was a dugout. But not like most dugouts.

as she did. She fumbled with her apron a bit while she remarked that it'd been weeks since she seen any stranger or neighbor, that he must excuse her and such like. But Hugh didn't see where she needed to be excused for anything, and then as the boy went on to tell her how come Hugh to be with him that gave them both a chance to get over their surprises and to feeling more at ease.

When the boy was thru talking she looked at Hugh and says, "I'm sorry you had such an accident but it's lucky you're not hurt. I'm Missus McKay," then she layed her hand on the little boy's shoulder, "and this is my little Joey."

"Sure glad to make your acquaintance," says Hugh, "and little Joey's too. If it hadn't been for him I'd never knowed there was such a pretty little place as this hid away out here."

Hugh was invited in the house and to stay for dinner which would soon be ready. He would of liked to stay but he was a little fidgety and he said he ought to get back to his pardners as soon as he could before they went to too much trouble looking for him. He asked how far was the closest ranch, where he could borrow a horse. He was told it was fifteen miles or more, but that there was no need for him to go there to get a horse, she would be glad to loan him hers. Of course he was old and slow and better for harness than saddle but that would sure beat walking, and as she didn't need the horse for a few days he could take his time returning him.

Hugh thought it was mighty fine of the lady to offer her only horse to a plum stranger like him. He seen where she'd be pleased if he borrowed her horse and so he was glad to accept, and before he left he was glad to please her and the boy some more by staying with 'em for dinner. She didn't seem lonesome but visitors was mighty scarce at her place, scarce enough that any of 'em was sure welcome.

As Hugh jogged along on the old work horse, sitting in a saddle that was just as old, he wondered how and why that woman lived on her little place, in the heart of the wild horse country, far away from neighbors and town and alone with her boy. He'd got the drift from her talk that her husband had been dead for some years. She didn't hint as to how she managed for what was necessary to live on besides what she raised. She could be pretty sure of raising what she cultivated in the little patch of ground because there was a good sized and steady running spring by her house which she could always irrigate from, but there was clothes and other necessary things to buy and she was too far from market to sell anything she raised on her land. That was a country where everything marketable had to be raised on the hoof, either cattle or horses.

Hugh remembered now that her and her boy's clothes was pretty well patched up and mended and faded. He hadn't thought much of that before because they'd been so clean so as to throw off the sight of the patches. He hadn't thought much of what had been spread on the table either on account of being so busy listening to her and Joey, but he remembered now that the food had tasted mighty good and appetizing. There was plenty of vegetables, butter and milk and bread, and more vegetables with some eggs mixed in. Hugh had et many a meal without sugar and drank his coffee black, but that woman and boy sure must like some sweetening, and as he thought of it now he didn't remember seeing any sugar on the table. Them berry bushes in the garden sure must of bore plenty of fruit but there was no preserves, nothing sweet only some kind of syrup. Then he thought of something he did miss on the table and which, to him, was the most important thing, that was beef. There'd been no meat of any kind.

Folks sure can't live long that way, Hugh thought. Then what about when the cow run dry, there'd be no butter nor milk. Or when the chickens quit laying as they do sometimes, there'd be no eggs. And the vegetables, there wasn't many of them that'd keep all winter.

Hugh looked down at the old horse he was riding. The old horse

126

done the work on the little place and hauled in the wood and maybe pulled a rickety buggy to town once or twice a year, but a few more years and that old horse wouldn't be no more.

Hugh thought of many things about the woman, the boy and the little place as he rode, such thoughts was so different than the ones he'd been used to, not so cheerful but they was kind of homey and quiet and throwed him back many years past, when he was Joey's age.

His thoughts didn't get back to horses, the parada and his pardners till his vacant sight took in a moving object on a far away ridge and to realizing that that object was a rider. Then he seen that the rider was leading an extra horse, saddled. It wasn't hard for Hugh to guess who was the rider and what was the extra horse, and he stirred the old horse he was riding to a little faster gait. The other rider rode faster too, and soon, Hugh recognized Stub, leading his horse.

"Well," says Hugh, grinning, "I never thought I'd see that horse and saddle again, not so soon anyway."

Stub grinned back at the sight of Hugh on the collar-marked old work horse then he went on to tell of the catching of his horse. That horse had followed a wild bunch that happened along just right for Andy to pick up with another wild bunch he was hazing towards the parada. The wild horses run in the parada in fine shape but at the sight of Hugh's horse they thought of many things that might of happened and they held the horses just long enough so Andy could sneak up and rope him, then all the horses was let go.

"Too bad too," says Stub. "We had two nice bunches and I think me and Andy could of got them in the trap by ourselves. They stuck good with the parada."

"Why in samhill didn't you run 'em in?"

"Well, it would of been late after we had and made it hard for us to find you in the dark."

Hugh grinned. "Why find me? I knowed where I was."

"Sure," Stub grins back, "but we didn't know that you did know, and besides we couldn't think of you walking."

"And I'm not walking."

"Not far from it," says Stub looking at the old horse. "How did you get him, run him down afoot?"

Hugh changed to his own horse and being he was now much closer to camp than the widow's place he rode on with Stub. It was getting late afternoon anyway, and he would take the old horse back to the widow the next day. A ways further on, Andy caught up with 'em, he'd been looking for Hugh too and sighted the two riders from up in the foothills.

Without anything being said, the next day was decided on as a day of rest, that is, a day of rest from running mustangs, but there would be many things done around camp. A few tender-footed horses would be shod, clothes would be washed, whiskers clipped or shaved off, beans and beef and dried fruits cooked up and camp straightened out in general. The boys would seldom take such a day off for that work, and what decided 'em was that when Stub and Andy woke up at daybreak they seen a big fat calf tied to the quakers close to camp. Hugh had been out riding to get that calf while they slept and tied it to cool off before killing it. He was in his bed and asleep again and at the sight of him his two pardners turned over and done the same.

The sun was shining into camp when they woke up again, but it was a fall sun and it hadn't as yet scared away the frost that'd come during the night. Hugh had got up, made some coffee, had killed the calf and was skinning it when his pardners stirred out of their soogans.

It wasn't in the contract that the boys could kill their own beef, they was supposed to get their meat by quarters from the company ranches or round-up wagons, but Hugh, like his pardners, had done many things that wasn't in contracts and against what was law, and the killing of a company beef didn't bother him no more than if he'd just killed a jack rabbit.

That calf made mighty fine meat too, not at all like the bluish and stringy dairy stock meat that's sold on the block and called "veal" in the butcher shops. Like all range calves, this one hadn't been robbed of it's milk, and even tho it was about three months old it hadn't touched much grass as yet. Stub and Andy helped Hugh dress and hang it up in the shade, two hundred pounds of red, juicy and tender meat, then Hugh chopped the carcass in two, along the backbone, wrapped one half in heavy canvas and layed it in the shade on the frosty ground.

The saddle horses filed into camp as the boys was eating their breakfast. They was used to getting their grain much earlier. One of the boys usually came to get 'em but being that none had showed up that morning they'd filed in like to see what't went wrong and so they wouldn't miss out on their grain. There's nothing like a feed of grain twice a day to keep horses close to camp.

The old work horse that Hugh had borrowed was amongst the saddle horses. It'd been a long time since he'd had the company of any of his kind and he sure seemed to enjoy that, also the feed of grain that Hugh gave him. While he was eating it, Hugh wrapped the half a beef that was hanging and packed it on his back. He'd of like to put in a small sack of sugar with the pack too, but he didn't think that would go well, too much like charity. With beef it was different, that's accepted like in trade amongst range folks, the next one that kills is supposed to return that meat and if that person don't there's no wrong thought of, specially when that person can't make the return.

Hugh had told his pardners of the widow, her little boy and the place, and they would of also liked to chipped in with some of the grub supply but they agreed with Hugh that only beef would do right then.

"We sure don't want to queer you," says Stub, winking at Andy while Hugh was saddling a right good horse, "but it don't seem fair. Here we're holding down camp while you go galivanting around visiting a pretty widow."

"By golly," says Hugh, grinning at his pardners, "she is a right pretty widow."

He got on his horse, and leading the well packed old work horse he started whistling, for his pardners' benefit, as he rode thru the grove of aspens and out of sight of camp.

It was a little after noon when Hugh rode in to the widow's place. She'd just got thru washing dishes, and as she seen him at the door she put the dried dishes right back on the table and stuck another stick of wood in the stove. It was no use of Hugh saying that the noon meal was a meal he was well used to go without, for he soon found himself sitting at the table while hot dishes was put in front of him. It was the same food as he'd had the day before only cooked different, and now there was meat, not of the beef he'd brought, but rabbit which, as he was told, Joey had got with a rock the evening before, just plain jack rabbit, not a young one either, and like all cowboys, Hugh figured that folks must be mighty hungry for meat when they'll eat "jacks." He was glad he'd brought the beef, and the widow couldn't hide all her surprise and pleasure as he unwrapped the hundred pounds of it and put it away in the cool cellar and cut it up in hunks so it'd be easy to handle.

To sort of make talk he told her to hang the meat out at night so it'd chill and put it in the cellar in day time so it would stay cold. It would keep a long time that way, and if there was more than she could use before it spoiled she could salt some down. Joey said they only had a little can of salt left. But that was all right, Hugh had said, he'd have to kill another beef after a while anyway and he could always bring some more along.

In the days that followed, the boys got to running pretty well in the big country surrounding the widow's little place. There was more mustangs there than anywhere on the company's range, and the country itself accounted for that. It was mighty dry during the summer months and nothing much but a few antelope would feed on it, consequences was that there was more untouched feed there than in most places. Then a couple of heavy rains come, filled up the natural tanks in the dobie flats, moistened the earth and made the grass more tender. The wise mustangs around knowed what the rains would do in that country and many bunches left their overgrazed ranges to go there, followed by many bunches of range horses.

The boys had no trouble making up a parada there and they got many wild ones in the parada but the closest corrals they could run 'em into was trap number one, thirty miles away. They stationed the parada as close to the trap as they could and gave the mustangs a long run to it, but there was still quite a ways to go to the trap and they'd lose quite a few of the wild ones in that distance.

But, even at that, they was doing pretty well and they was getting more mustangs from that country than they could of from any other at that time. Stub and Andy was satisfied and Hugh was pleased. The camp had been moved, and when Hugh killed another fat calf he now had only ten miles to ride to give the widow another half. He'd brought a sack of salt along too.

Little Joey had got to riding the old work horse quite a bit since the boys begin running horses so close to his home. He was like any town kid might be if a circus spread the tents in a vacant lot next to the house. He'd be out watching the wild ones run and often put the old horse into a stiff-jointed run too, till that old horse begin the show wear and bones. Hugh noticed the old horse as he rode in with his second hunk of beef. Then as he went on to talk a bit and say that him and his pardners would be taking some more wild ones to the pasture on the next day he seen an expression on Joey's face that he understood well. That boy would of sure liked to went along.

Hugh took another glance at the old work horse as he started back for camp, and it was only a few evenings later when he rode to the widow's place again. He wasn't bringing no beef, this time, it was a good and gentle little saddle horse, it was for Joey.

The little horse had been caught amongst a bunch of wild ones a couple of months before, and seeing he was gentle and well broke they'd kept him with their saddle horses. They'd altered the brand on him, and it wasn't at all likely that anybody in the country would know or claim him. He was a little tall for Joey but that pleased the boy all the more and at first he could hardly believe Hugh when he said that the horse was his. Now he could ride far and fast and the old work horse could sure rest.

Joey did ride far, a heap further than his mother knowed or agreed for him to, thought Hugh, as he seen him trying to be of some help in holding the parada with Stub one day. The boy got a great thrill at seeing the wild horses run into the parada and all into a fast run towards the trap. He'd forgot he had a home right then and rode along till Hugh told him to hit back for home.

But a few days later, Joey was again keeping Stub company in holding the parada. He didn't have to be told to go home when the wild ones come in that time, he'd understood Hugh's grin and stayed back, but he'd watched till the fast running parada and wild ones disappeared before he'd turned his pony's head towards home.

If Joey's mother minded her boy being away from her for near a whole day long once in a while, Joey sure didn't show no sign of it, and he kept a-being with Stub every few days and wherever the parada was moved.

Little Joey was a lot of strange and enjoyable company to Stub, and he was a lot of information too, information that Stub would sometimes pass on to his pardners by the evening fires. From that information, Hugh got an inkling that even tho Joey's mother fretted while her boy rode so far and stayed away so long from her, she was bearing it so to let him have the fun he'd so long been deprived of, action and the company of others.

But a few days later, Joey was again keeping Stub company in holding the parada.

Hugh had got that inkling of her thoughts from the things Joey had said about her to Stub while the two was holding the parada, things that was as far back as Joey could remember, and some things which his mother wouldn't of liked to heard him tell. But whatever Joey told was all the same to him, the boys didn't ask him any questions but it was so seldom that he had the chance to talk to anybody besides his mother that he took advantage of it and turned loose on everything he knowed that would make talk.

From him the boys easy learned how he and his mother come to be in the desert country. His dad and mother had been city folks and earned their living behind counters, they seen very little sunshine, the climate was damp and the air was close and smoky, and Joey's dad begin to ail, his lungs was dwindling away and a doctor prescribed dry air and plenty of sun, the desert.

The folks was pretty well lost in the desert country, no town job would do, and then they met an old feller who had a little place where it was thought they could make a living. He had. They couldn't afford to buy much of a place, nor the cattle the old feller had, but figured they could make out by farming on it, raising chickens and such like, and parting with most of their little savings they bought the little place. Joey was four years old then.

Not knowing anything about farming they had it pretty tough at first, but with the help and advice of the scattered neighbors they finally got onto the hang of it and to making a living from the place. There was very few things they needed to buy. The desert was good to 'em, their first big scare of it evaporated and was replaced by a great liking. They worked in the sun, planted things and turned water on 'em from the big spring. They tore down the old timbered dugout and rebuilt it out of stone and improved the place in general. They was happy, never lonesome, and Joey's dad seemed to be getting well right along, then, when he seemed to be all cured of what ailed him, he took sick one day, his wife rushed him to the closest hospital, a hundred miles away and it was only a few days later when he died there.

Joey was eight years old when his dad died. His mother was sick with grief and she decided to try and sell the little place. She'd spent what money there was left and tried to get work in the desert town, but she couldn't get no work and couldn't find anybody who'd buy her place, so there was nothing she could do but hook the horse to the buckboard and go back to the place.

In time, with Joey's company and help, she was near happy again in the desert, happier, she thought, than she could of been anywhere else. Joey was strong and full of life as a bear cub, and the health shining thru his smiling freckled face made her love the desert for him. She couldn't think no more of cooping him up in any town, and even tho they had only what was most necessary to live on, they didn't have to break their backs getting it, and there was hopes for something better, for in a few years more, Joey would be taking a holt and making the little place pay more than a living. She'd teached him reading, writing and arithmetic well and that was all. His geography was in the big country around him and there's where life's real schooling also was from, he was growing fitting that country.

CHAPTER NINE

TIME FOR THE CONTRACT WAS NEAR UP. Only a few more days and then the superintendent would be along to get a last count on the wild ones caught. The boys had done well, and if the superintendent again added a range horse for every wild one caught that would swell the count to many more than the contract called for.

They kept on running and catching wild ones up till the day when the contract was to close, and as the superintendent didn't show up on that day they kept hard at it till he would show up and caught more horses. But it was also nearing time now for something else besides the closing of the wild horse contract, time for the trial and for Hugh to account for his wild actions the spring before. The date set for the trial was only two weeks off.

The superintendent showed up about a week before that time. He was pleased in seeing how many wild ones the boys had caught, and was more than agreeable to permit them to add on a company range horse to every wild one. The boys was a little worried in doing that, thinking that the foremen and riders of the outfit might notice the disappearing of so many range horses and get suspicious. But the superintendent had took care of that. He'd had carload after carload of range horses shipped from many parts of the outfit's range and the shipping of them was marked down as should be on the company's books. He'd been wise to also have different riders gather and ship the horses, so that none would get a straight count on all the horses shipped nor wonder about any bunches

They kept on running and catching wild ones.

on any other parts of the range disappearing, and with the thousands of horses on that range it would of been impossible for anybody but the superintendent himself to know how many horses there was or where how many was shipped. The foremen and riders only kept track of them on their own part of the range, each part gave their reports on cattle and horses and only the superintendent knowed the outfit's full count.

So, feeling safe, the superintendent wasn't backward in telling the boys to go ahead and run in range horses to the count of the wild ones and he wrote 'em another inspection slip to that number.

The boys done some fast riding, and in a couple of days time had the exact amount of horses the slip called for. They was now thru on the big outfit's range, for, as the superintendent told 'em, it wouldn't be a good idea to draw another contract for the winter months, not unless they wanted to cater to only wild horses. He didn't want to ship any more range horses with the wild ones, maybe he would later again. Then there was Hugh. It was likely that he would have to serve some time for raising the rumpus he had, even if not for smoking up the gamblers, and being that things was all unsettled that way and that they was done with the big outfit for the winter they sort of prepared for that.

They made arrangements with the superintendent to leave their saddle horses in a good pasture, then, in wondering as to where they leave their camp outfit and wagon till they'd decide what to do and would need it again it was natural for Hugh to think of the widow's place. The boys killed another fat calf. The weather was cold now, snow was on the ground and the meat would keep for a long time. They brought the meat to the widow, and as a good excuse that they wouldn't have no more use for it they also presented her with what grub they had left, a good supply of flour, bacon, sugar, dried fruits and many things she'd run short of or didn't have. Of course they'd need that grub sometime again soon but they could buy it, and all they wanted to keep, they said, was their camp outfit but she could use any part or all of it if she wanted to.

The widow didn't have much to say as to accepting what all the boys turned over to her, she just fidgeted around and could only point out where to lay the things they brought out, and there was a general rejoicing as she cooked a meal that evening, of the kind she hadn't cooked for a long time. It was Stub and Andy's first acquaintance with the widow and as they partook of the evening meal with her and Joey they could well understand how Hugh seen to it that she didn't run short of beef. There was a combination of all that was fine about her, and with seeing her happy as she was that evening the boys wished they could do more to keep her that way. Joey didn't roost early that night, neither did the boys. The crackling of the juniper in the stove made things cozy and cheerful inside, and the general talk that went on run the same way thru the whole evening long.

The boys had to shake the snow off their tarpaulin covered beds the next morning, they hadn't bothered to set up a tent. A cold wind was blowing, but after they washed by the spring and went in the house there was warmth there, the smell of frying bacon and the greetings of "good morning."

With each a light pack of grub to last for the next four days, and a good breakfast inside their belt, the boys saddled their horses, bid good bye to the widow and Joey, who both had queer looks on their faces, and rode away to the pasture to gather the mustangs and range horses and start 'em for the shipping point. They didn't have much trouble in gathering and holding them and, as before, no trouble with the stock inspector when four days later they turned the horses over to the commission men and loaded 'em into the cars.

The boys didn't get to town nor take care of the shipping of their horses any too soon, for after that was done, Hugh only had till the next day to answer to the charges the law had against him, and now it was too late for him to even see a lawyer that evening. He'd have to hunt one up first thing in the morning, and talk fast so as to have him understand his case and be able to fight for him.

But there was no need for him to worry about that, for as the boys was lined up at the bar of the same saloon where the rumpus had took place, and talking on the subject, the superintendent of the big outfit lined up alongside of 'em, greeted 'em with a long grin, remarked that the drinks was on him and, after swallowing his, winked at Hugh and said that everything was "all fixed."

The superintendent had got in town the day before, seen the company's attorney and put him to work on Hugh's case. That attorney

The boys had to shake the snow off their tarpaulin covered beds the next morning.

had worked well, and with the important presence of the superinten-dent sort of appearing for Hugh, it looked now like Hugh wouldn't even have to stand trial.

And Hugh didn't have to stand trial. A trial would of been expen-sive, specially with the company's lawyer, and right then the county wasn't wanting much expense, not on a case where it concerned only a tinhorn gambler, against a rider who seemed to be well backed by a big outfit the officers wanted to stand well with, and being the gambler was mighty satisfied not to appear in court, the case was dropped and everybody was happy.

There was several rounds of rejoicing at the saloon. The boys had decided to take a great liking for the superintendent, for even tho he was a little underhanded with the outfit that was a small thing as com-pared to the good work he done for that same outfit. He'd also showed there was a lot of white man about him in helping the boys out of their trouble, for if it hadn't been for him there might of been a jail break in getting Hugh out or, if not, Hugh might of had to serve some time, which wouldn't of done nobody no good.

The bail money was divided back, then a big check from the first shipment of horses was cashed, the superintendent took his share with a happy grin, and now, as soon as the commission man sent the check for the second shipment and the superintendent received his share of that they'd all be square, excepting, the boys thought, to be on the look out to do the superintendent some more "favors," maybe by spring, with running more mustangs, or anything he might have in mind. He didn't have anything in mind for the boys right then, but he winked again as he left 'em, as much as to say that he might have any time.

"Be good boys," he says, as he went, "and if you can't be good be careful."

Well now, for the first time in a long time, the boys had nothing to do, nothing to worry about and not a plan thought out. They sort of let down in the big chairs of the hotel lobby and looked at one another in a way that asked plainer than words "What next?" They eased a little deeper in their chairs, it was nice and warm in the lobby, and looking out the big window into the street where folks was bundled up and walking fast against the cold, a dry snow whirling amongst the buildings and everything looking gray, it seemed mighty comfortable to just sit and look out at that and not think much.

Stub and Hugh figured they could easy enough stand a week or so of such a life, and Andy didn't figure at all. When his pardners looked he looked, when they drank he drank and when they et or done anything else he done the same.

After a day of plain loafing the boys finally stirred out of their chairs, like something ought to be done. Maybe a little play or fun of some kind wouldn't go bad. There was now many cowboys in town. It was at that time of year, after the season was over and beef herds was shipped, when them riders stayed in for a spell, celebrated after long months on the range, and sort of took over the town.

When Stub and Hugh and Andy left their hotel and walked into their favorite saloon they found that it had been bought for the night. A wise cow foreman had bought it for the use of his riders, to keep them together all he could, and he figured that the buying of the use of that saloon for one night would be a heap cheaper than paying bail for many and have a scattered crew to worry about getting together again. He had very much use for his crew yet, for there was another big beef herd to meet, get to the railroad and load into the cars.

The foreman was also wise enough to furnish some entertainment. He'd dug up a combination of singing and dancing females and an orchestra, which all went to keep the boys in good spirits and from hankering to hit out and see what the town was made of. Riders from other outfits walked in, and the hospitable feeling was the same there as when on the range. Consequences was that the foreman was sure of a good crew when the fun would be over, whether that crew was made up of his own riders or others.

The three mustangers mixed in and sort of visited. It had been a long time since they had been in such a big gathering of cowboys, or seen such entertainment, and they enjoyed the company and all to the limit.

Nobody was thinking of anything but the present. Stub was thinking of the present very much, he was dancing with one of the entertainers, when happening to glance around he seen a hawk-eyed face staring at him. Stub recognized that face, and so quick that with the first glimpse of it his hand went to his gun. That face must of reminded him of some long past happening, and whatever that was sure didn't seem to please his memory.

He was glad that so many other dancers was around, hiding the move he made to his gun. As it was now he hoped that he hadn't given himself away by his surprised expression, and he kept on dancing and trying to act not at all spooky.

Stub danced on, glancing as much as he dared at the face that so upset him. He was brave enough to dance to within a few feet and make a sure glance at that face, then when the dance was over, he finds Andy and whispers for him and Hugh to come to the hotel room when they can, but not to hurry.

"Daggone your hide," says Hugh, as him and Andy came into the hotel room a while later, "here we was all set for a high old time, like we ain't had for a coon's age, and you quit us as if a scorpion had fell down your neck. You still look like you'd just seen a ghost."

But Stub was acting more peeved than scared as he paced the floor. "I wish that what I seen was only a ghost." He stopped and faced his pardners. "I seen a man tonight who knows about a fourteen year sentence that I haven't served. He was on the jury that convicted me, and he knows that I got away from the officers without serving any of that sentence. Now, I suppose that if you gazabos would run acrost such a feller who was so well informed about some of your past you'd just walk up to him, shake him by the hand and offer to buy the drinks . . ."

Such news set Hugh and Andy to being mighty thoughtful. After a spell, Hugh says, "I remember you telling me about them doings, Stub. It's sure tough that it's got to be remembered now after so long a time."

"Yes, about ten years, and this feller sure remembers. Of course he might not tell the sheriff, but I didn't like the way he sized me up, like as if I was something he could turn over for a big bounty. And, boys, he's not going to get that bounty, I'm hitting out now and get a head start on the sheriff before he sets him on my trail."

Hugh jumped up at that. "Wait a minute there Stub. You talk like you're going to ride on alone, and there ain't going to be no such a thing. If you ride we ride. But before we all go to making tracks, me and Andy are going to investigate that feller. You're safe in this room for a spell, he don't know your new name and can't give more than a description of you, and being there's so many cowboys in town now it'd be hard to describe you as any different than the others. Sit quiet here and don't be wearing a trail on this carpet while we're gone."

Stub gave his pardners a good description of the man they was to investigate and the two hit back for the saloon. Everything was going on in there as when they left, and in a short while they'd spotted the man they was after. That was easy to do, as the man was going around and making it plain that he was sure searching for somebody. Finally he stood still, Hugh walked up to him, and sticking out a hand like in glad surprise, he says,

"Why, hello there, Simpson, where in samhill do you hail from?"

The man looked at Hugh, and then grinned. "My name is not Simpson, stranger."

Hugh acted very surprised. "You're not Simpson? . . . Well I'll be a son of a sea cook. You sure must be his twin brother then."

The man, like wanting to convince Hugh, says, "My name is Morris, and I'm from the Antelope Basin Country."

The boys knowed of that country being a few hundred miles away, and Andy, who had his part to play, speaks up. "Let's have a drink, Hugh, I'm thirsty as a mud-hen on a tin roof," and at them words it was only natural that Hugh invited the stranger, Morris, to join 'em.

Morris joined 'em, and as he took one few drinks after another he kept his back to the bar and went on searching the faces of the cowboys. From the talk that went on, Hugh and Andy learned that Morris was a stranger in the country, that he'd come to buy some mixed stock for his outfit in the Antelope Basin. Also, as he took a few more drinks, that he was now using some spare time to watching for a certain feller. He said he'd seen him less than an hour ago but he had somehow slipped away, and laughing, remarked that the bounty he would collect by turning that feller over to officers would pay the freight on all the cattle he figured on buying.

"That man is bad to arrest," Morris says, "so I went to the trouble of getting a couple of officers ready, but he's slipped away. If I only knowed the name he's packing now maybe the officers would know of him and his arrest would be easier, but all I have is his description and there's a hundred in town who look about the same. . . . Well," he went on, "I'll be around for a week or so before I have to go back and I might run acrost him again in that time."

Hugh and Andy felt relieved as they went back to the hotel, and before they got thru talking to Stub he begin to feel relieved too.

"That feller, Morris, expects to find you around while buying stock," Hugh says to Stub, "and I know he won't tell the officers or anybody any more than he can help because he wants to point you out and be present to collect the reward. He lives too far away for you to worry about and as he's leaving town in about a week all we have to do is go back to our outfit and stay quiet for that time."

Stub begin pacing the floor again. "Yep, that's all right," he says, "but we been working our daggone heads off all summer and now we can't take a breathing spell nor have a little fun, and we got to hit out before we're ready on account of some galoot with too long a memory."

Stub was for riding back to camp alone, leaving Hugh and Andy to have their town play, bringing up as a good reason that they could keep an eye on this Morris feller at the same time. But Hugh and Andy only laughed, saying that town play would sure wait till when the three could enjoy it together. "Besides," says Hugh, "I'll have to get the team and come back here to get a new supply of grub and I can easy find out if Morris is still sticking around or not."

"Why get a supply of grub?" says Andy. "You must be figuring on us sticking in this country for the winter."

"Well, we haven't decided as yet just what we're going to do, and while we're deciding we sure got to eat, and we sure don't want to eat the grub we left with the widow. Anyhow I don't know of any country where we can be safer than on the Big Outfit's range right now, do you?"

Andy grinned and agreed, and Stub was also agreeing.

It was a couple of hours after midnight when the boys went to the stables, saddled up their horses and rode out of town. The town was alive with cowboys, and many places that was usually closed at that time of the night was wide open and well lit up, catering to cowboy trade. It was a cow town.

Little Joey was watering two horses one evening. There was a thin hard snow on the ground, a cold wind blowing, and a gray sky, like all in cahoots to make the evening dreary. Little Joey didn't feel no dreariness. He rubbed cold hands against cold ears and, natural-like, glanced at the country around him while his horses drank. He was looking in one direction when his saddle horse of a sudden raised his head and looked in another. Natural-like again, Joey turned to look where his horse was looking, to a low ridge, and there was the plain sight of three riders.

If the evening was dreary, if the wind was cold, little Joey more than warmed up to all of that at the sight of the three riders, and recognizing them he lets out a whooping holler that was well heard inside the dugout and near made his mother drop a skillet as she heard it and rushed to the door, wondering, then smiling her happy surprise as she looked the direction Joey pointed—. There was a cheerfulness in the little dugout cabin that evening that no king's gathering in castle could of competed with.

The next morning was still gray and dreary, but there was two smokes, one from the dugout and one from a tent, and voices that sort of warmed up the atmosphere. A team and wagon was just starting for town, Hugh was driving and no other than little Joey was alongside of him. His mother, standing in front of the dugout, watched him and wagon out of sight while Stub and Andy got busy with the few chores, tending to their horses, and then setting up camp in a better location a short ways out of sight of the dugout. It had been set up in a hurry the night before and shelter hadn't been much thought of.

If Stub was worried about anybody being on his trail he didn't show it as he worked with Andy to make the camp comfortable, for he worked like to make it permanent and not a camp he figured on leaving right soon.

But after the camp was well set and the skies cleared there come a day of restlessness for Stub. Andy was craving action too. The few chores to be done for the widow was no work and no action. Another day come and the two rode away to where the saddle horses was pastured, seen they was all there and doing well. They corralled 'em, changed to fresh horses and rode back in time to do the chores.

The next day was spent in wondering what to do. It seemed like they couldn't just take a rest. They washed their clothes, picked things up only to lay them back in the same place, and it was as if a whole day had gone before noon come. They looked in the cellar to see if there was plenty of meat, and there was plenty, so that spoiled their hunting for a little action in getting another beef. In the afternoon they rode out anyway. A cowboy seldom rides just to be riding but two did that afternoon, and the only excuse they could think of was to see how many mustangs was in the country and which way they would run. They seen many bunches but didn't notice which way they run. Instead, they noticed the good feed in the country, how strong the mustangs would winter, and then Stub and Andy stopped their horses. Stub had went to looking at the hills around, wondering, and Andy looked at Stub, wondering why he was studying the hills and the whole country around so close.

Hugh and little Joey got to town on the evening of the third day, in time to store away a good feed before the show at the Opera House started. Little Joey had never been to a show before, and even tho what he seen was past him to understand he took on the songs and dances with as much interest as a wolf pup would in watching a bear fight. The rustling noise he made with his bag of hard candy didn't go well with the folks around, but it was the best candy he remembered tasting and being so busy grinding on it and watching the show, there was no other folks around to him but Hugh, and the queer dressed ones on the stage.

Early the next morning, him and Hugh got busy getting a grub supply in the wagon. When the main things was loaded, Hugh took Joey to a clothing store and outfitted him from head to foot with a couple of changes to Joey's taste, so much to his taste that he agreed to help Hugh in picking out some ginghams and other cloths he thought his mother might like. Joey wasn't much help there but Hugh couldn't of done without him. They done more rambling thru town, Hugh got to see that feller Morris, there was another show at the Opera House, more candy for Joey, a good sleep, sun up, and then the loaded wagon with two drivers on the seat, two rested horses hitting the collar, started on their way back for home.

About that time there was a rider in the rough hills surrounding the big flats from that home. That rider had all the earmarks of a cowboy but he acted more like a prospector, for every once in a while he'd get off his horse, dig amongst some rye patch hollow and before riding on would study the sloping ledges of the hills around him. Another day went by with that cowboy still acting prospector and digging holes down in every rye patch he could find in range after range of hills, all the while studying them and the good feed covering the country on both sides. When another day come he didn't dig no more, instead he just looked down the holes he'd already dug. He'd smile while looking down one hole and with only a glance at another he'd ride on.

It was getting along sun down when that rider, after covering sixty miles of the rough hills, headed his tired horse for the widow's place. A short half a mile from there he stopped his horse once more to smile, at another cowboy who'd gone prospecting. That cowboy had a wild range cow tied down, and squeezed enough milk out of her to fill half a five pound lard bucket. That second cowboy had gone prospecting for milk.

"Little Joey ought to get back before dark," he says. "Him and Hugh has been gone for a week now, and I got to get in a supply of milk for him.— You know, Stub, that Mrs. McKay's cow has gone dry."

"Yes, I know," says Stub. "Any cow would quit giving milk with you handling 'er, Andy."

Andy was no good at milking cows. To do all he could to help the widow he'd took it on to himself to milk her cow, with the result that she quit giving milk. She'd been about ready to quit anyway and, with Andy's strange treatment, she did.

That worked fine with Andy's craving for action, and while Stub was prospecting in the hills he prospected in the flats and for whatever range

That cowboy had a wild range cow tied down.

cow that had any milk. He didn't care what outfit a cow belonged to or if she showed much of a bag. He'd rope one, tie her down, squeeze as much milk as he could out of her and then let her go and he'd catch another, till his bucket was near filled. He'd brought in a filled bucket two or three times a day, preparing, as he said, for when Joey would come home. Each bucketful meant the roping of a cow or two and that kept his rope arm limber and his craving for action eased down. The widow used the milk for cooking, and even tho she wondered some at his ways of getting it, she trusted to him as she did with Hugh and Stub that all was right, with consequences that when time come for Joey to show up she had twice as much milk, butter and cheese stored away than ever before.

With one more half a bucket of milk, Andy rode in towards home and camp. Stub was riding alongside of him. The sun had gone down and the two was just in time to see a team pulling in a loaded wagon.

The widow was first to meet the wagon as it creaked in under the heavy load. With night coming on she hardly recognized who the boy was alongside of Hugh, for Joey was sporting his new clothes. Finally getting ahold of him she half strangled him while he tried to tell her what all he'd seen and done and et while in town. She had only glimpses of the heavy load of grub that was being carried off the wagon and put away, and with them glimpses it all looked as enough supplies for an army.

Like as if it had held off till Hugh and Joey returned a storm broke loose with the next day. The mustangers stayed inside their tent and was plum contented, for once to just do nothing but keep the flap of the tent closed and the little tin stove to throwing a little heat. The storm was wicked enough to make things plenty cheerful there, and while a strong wind made the tent sag and flap the boys went on to rest and talk, with no fear that their words would be heard from neither the widow nor Joey.

Hugh told of seeing Morris while in town. Morris hadn't mentioned any more about looking for Stub, and not wanting to stir suspicions by asking Morris any questions, Hugh went to the stock yards and found out from the inspector that that feller had a trainload of cattle in them yards and would load and start out on the next day. . . . Stub sort of leaned back and took a long breath of relief at the good news.

The storm bowled on and gave the boys a secure and satisfied feeling as they went on talking, and then come the time to lay plans as to what to do during the winter.

They wasn't wanting to be laying idle. They had plenty of money, more than they could use for a long time, unless they went to gambling and to spending it for a high old time. But with their last experiences every time they went in town they sort of lost their hankering to play there, and being they was so well supplied with money, grub, good horses and a good camp they didn't see no reason, outside of for a little fun, to gather and run off with any bunch of cattle or horses. The boys was very satisfied with things the way they was, but there'd have to be some action.

Stub was the first to speak on the subject.

"Well, boys," he says, "here we are, all on velvet and leading lazy men's lives. What do you expect we ought to do?"

"Danged if I know," Hugh says. "Can't improve on anything that I can see, unless we start a saloon or go to killing sheep."

Stub grinned and looked at Andy.

"Well," says Andy, "I ain't seen much country or anything yet and I'd just like to see what it looks like beyond these hills we been in all summer. But I'll want to do whatever you boys decide on. Point the herd and I won't be no drag."

Stub thought for a spell and, eyeing his pardners, he says,

"I don't know how this will strike you, but I've prospected on something which I think will beat any ramblings on and where we'll sure have to use our heads and do plenty of careful riding, along with it all being mighty interesting, I think."

Hugh and Andy perked up some as they looked at Stub.

"You boys know this country around here," he went on. "You've run horses all over it and noticed the good feed everywhere, and most likely thought on what a fine big bunch of cattle could be run on it, if only there was water. As it is it's good only for winter range when snows and rains come to fill the dobie flats with the necessary water and then it's used mostly by wild horses. No stockmen have layed any rights to the country because they haven't found enough water to make it worth while taking any such right. These stockmen haven't as yet learned to develop water as I've seen it done in other countries. I've prospected for seepages the last few days. I've dug in most every place in the hills where there was a blade of rye grass or any other indications of water and out of every three holes I've dug, I've found moisture in at least one, and in some of the holes I've found real water. That all was enough to prove to me that with a little developing of the good seepages we can dig up enough water to take care of at least a thousand head of cattle. There's plenty of range around to take care of many times that many cattle, all depends how much water we can develop.

Hugh and Andy had by now got Stub's idea, and it went well, all but the digging out the seepages. Stub could easy see that part sure didn't agree with them and he hurried on to say,

"Us fellers wouldn't know how to get the most water out of the seepages and small springs so they'd run enough to water any stock much. I've thought that all out and I figure that only real good prospectors, fellers that knows how to follow any kind of a vein thru the earth, could do that work well. There's many good old prospectors in town now that'd be aching to get at such work so as to make a grub-stake and it wouldn't cost us much to get a few of them, fit 'em out with camp and grub and scatter 'em in the hills. In a couple of months' time we'd have all the good seepages to running water and then we could clamp our water rights on 'em. Later on, when we get our country well stocked up, and we want to make our range bigger we'd be able to buy a carload of second-hand pipe, and pipe the water from the best springs out to where the better feed is. . . ."

"Yes," Hugh interrupts, "that water would be fine for the mustangs too, and we'd be overrun with 'em."

"Sure. But we wouldn't be stocking up so fast that the mustangs would bother us. We'd be building traps for them wild ones and them same wild ones would be paying for the developing and piping of the water, with maybe enough money from them to buy more cattle too."

Hugh had to agree that Stub was right, and he seen many sidelines in the whole proposition where it would all be mighty interesting. Andy naturally thought of the same sidelines as Hugh did, and even tho he'd liked to rambled on, he seen where he could stir up enough action in the building up of the cow outfit to make things at least peaceable for him. Stub went on.

"We got plenty of money. We can outfit half a dozen prospectors and set 'em to work, and we can afford to buy a nice size herd of cattle for a starter. We already have a good camp, plenty of grub for the winter and each a good string of saddle horses. We're adjoining the Big Outfit's range, surrounded by all good sized outfits and with using the "long rope" sort of careful we can sure see that our herd increases well and steady. . . . Daggone it, I sure think this would beat roaming and dodging around like mangy cayotes. I've sort of got my bellyful of that.

"And just think," Stub went on, grinning at Hugh, "just think of what all we can do for the widow and little Joey. They might want to go into pardnership with us, we'd make a real cowboy out of little Joey, and the widow could keep books for us and such like."

CHAPTER TEN

S TUB'S HOME-MAKING INSTINCT HAD WON OUT. His idea of home wasn't of house and wife, it was of range land and cattle bearing his brand. A good house and wife could be for later, but now a tent or log cabin would do, and with his pardners to work with him in the building up of the outfit he couldn't think of anything else to wish for. Hugh was close second with him on that, and being that Andy had already said that they could count on him not being a drag with whatever his pardners done, was neck and neck with Hugh.

It was after breakfast of the widow's usual good cooking the next day that the boys sort of stuck around the table. The storm was still running wild but that wasn't the reason for the boys to stay when they was done with the meal. The widow noticed their actions, which reminded her some of school boys about ready to recite something, and she sort of prepared for whatever was to come, something strange and important, she thought, but she couldn't guess what. Stub up and spoke.

"The three of us have decided to start a cow outfit on this range, Mrs. McKay, and being you're located in about the center of it we thought you'd like to join us in pardnership. We . . ."

Stub stopped at the widow's surprised look.

"Why, what could I do? . . . and I have no money to invest."

"Well," says Stub, "you have this place and the only good location on this range for headquarters. You have a good running spring and many of our cattle could water here when the water is not being used

*His idea of home wasn't of house and wife, it was
of range land and cattle bearing his brand.*

to irrigate the patch of land. We'd take this place and give you a fourth
interest in our pardnership. Then if you'd care to you could take care
of the books for us and sort of keep track as to how we stand."

The widow couldn't quite hide her pleasure as she realized the full
meaning of Stub's words. Little Joey didn't at all try to hide his pleasure,
and his eyes was shining with excitement as he looked at his mother,
then at the boys. It was hard for him to sit still and not holler his joy.

He took another look at his mother, wondering why she didn't decide right away and accept the proposition, and he seen that she was doing a heap of considering.

Finally she says, "But this place, and what help I could be is so small to offer in return for a pardnership in such as a cow outfit . . ." Then she brightened up some at a thought. "But I could cook, wash and mend clothes if that would help."

The boys grinned. "We hadn't figured on you doing that," says Stub, "and just with your doing the cooking while we start will make us feel like we're cheating you with giving you only a fourth interest in pardnership."

No agreement papers was made as the widow finally decided to accept the pardnership, but the agreement that went on with words and hand-shake all around was more secure than any which a notary every clamped a seal on.

"We overlooked one pardner," says Hugh, as the boys started for the door. He grinned and pointed at Joey.

"We'll make him a silent pardner," says Stub.

But Joey couldn't be silent right then. He let out a holler of joy, and scampered outside with the boys.

If Hugh and Andy was at first for rambling and against settling down to one range, the agreement that was just made with the widow sort of clipped their wings for any thought but what the agreement called for, the starting of a cow outfit, and with her as a pardner they would make good where without her they'd be apt to ramble on if all didn't go well, and take Stub along.

Before the weather cleared, Stub rode over to see the superintendent of the big outfit and had a long day's visit with him. The superintendent was mighty pleased to hear that the boys would be neighboring, for that worked well with some plans he might have, later on, and he was glad to advise Stub as to the range they was figuring on taking control of.

He brought out maps surveyors had made of that country and in looking it over it was found out that there was two springs inside of that range which was marked as claimed, and there was no signs of any other springs in that whole country.

"It might be," says the superintendent, as him and Stub studied the map and claims, "that that feller might sell his rights to them springs. If not that will put a kink in your control of that range. But first let me look into this, it might be that the claims on them springs are just took for granted and not filed. I'll find out thru my office in town.

"Anyway," he went, "I think you're safe to go ahead with your plans, and if that feller has a right to the springs and you can't buy him out we'll find some way of making him forget about 'em. For, if I place this feller right, he's a pretty slick hombre and maybe we can dig up something against him that he'd like to have us keep quiet about in trade for the spring rights."

Stub was pleased with his confab with the superintendent. He got all the information he wanted and of the kind he couldn't of got from the recorder's office. He was also advised as to where a good herd of cattle could be bought, a drought and mortgage would make that herd easy to get.

Being the boys craved action there was no delaying with the starting of the outfit. Hiding behind a good growth of whiskers, Stub drove to town with the wagon. The superintendent had been there ahead of him, and had left word at his office that the two springs that had been marked as claimed on the map could not be held because no rights had been filed on 'em. There was advice that he should file on the rights of 'em right away, and feel safe to go ahead with his plans.

Stub did as he was advised and then went to looking for prospectors to work on the seepages and small springs he'd found. He had no trouble getting the prospectors, and being he had so many to pick from he took them who still had their bedding and camping outfits, that saved a considerable expense. The men, with their outfits and grub piled into the wagon and all started for the Four-Square Cattle Company's range. That was the name the boys and the widow had thought of and agreed on for the new outfit, and Stub had a brand registered which read

Hugh and Andy wasn't laying around while Stub went to town. They'd saddled up and hit out the same morning he did and in the direction of where the cattle was that the superintendent said could be bought so cheap. That gave Andy a chance to see plenty more country, for it took a week of hard riding to get to where the cattle was. There the country was sure enough hard hit with drought, there'd been none of the storms the boys had experienced. The cattle was sore footed and lean and the boys figured sure on an easy deal. But the cattleman they went to see didn't seem to be anxious to sell, not even with the mortgage and the drought bringing gray hairs to his head. He would sell, he says, but he set a price on his herd that the boys thought was pretty steep. They prospected around for a few days, looking for a cheaper priced herd, but it seemed like all the cowmen was bound to go down with their herds rather than take one cent off the set price. That wasn't good business, but it was cowmen's sentiments, to stand by their herds as long as they could, regardless of times and droughts.

The boys finally decided to deal for the herd they'd first set out to get, for they figured that if they was to get any cattle now was the time to get 'em. They knowed they couldn't do no better in price nowhere, and if they waited till spring, taking chances of the drought breaking by that time, they would have to pay at least the same price, and much more if moisture come. If moisture come and water filled the dobie tanks where the feed was good the cowmen would take on hopes and hang on to their cattle for all the longer.

Hugh and the cowman rode to a town to fix up the papers while Andy and a couple of the cowboys went to gathering the cattle. The full count was gathered and when Hugh came back from town the herd was ready to start. It was a pretty good sized herd, a little too big for two men to handle, and seeing they'd have to be on the trail a long time on account of the cattle being sore footed, Hugh dickered for the use of some extra saddle horses, bedding and grub on pack horses and two of the riders, one to bring the saddle and pack horses and the other to help with the herd.

It took Hugh and Andy only a week to get to where they'd bought the cattle but it took 'em a month to drive the cattle to the Four-Square range. It was a good thing too that Hugh had dickered for grub and canvas shelter from the cowman, for they was only a few days on the trail when a heavy storm hit 'em. The cattle sapped up the moisture like sponges, the soft muddy earth felt good on their feet and the boys let 'em graze as they took in shelter during the worst of the storm.

"Looks to me like the drought is broke up," Hugh says to Andy, as the two rode thru the storm one evening, "and we got these cattle just in time too, because after this storm they'd be worth a few dollars more per head."

The storm over, the herd was trailed along at a grazing pace, and even tho it took a month to get the cattle on what was to be their new range there was a considerable gained by that. The cattle had took on weight and strength, and on the good feed of their new range they'd winter thru in good shape.

Only one thing had worried Hugh and Andy along the trail, and that was if the seepages Stub was working on would pan out as he expected. If not the cattle would have to be sold before the country dried up, by early spring. But Stub was wise as to them seepages and what could be expected from them or he wouldn't of been for getting the cattle so soon, and as he came to meet the herd on the last day's drive, packing a pleased grin, they seen that they'd been worrying for no reason.

"Of course," he says, as he went to tell of the chances on the water, "we got to expect that some of our watering places will go dry during summer months or droughts. Some of the best springs will go down too, but even at that we'll have all the water we'll need most any time, and for twice this amount of cattle at the worst times."

The herd was drove on to the widow's little place, which was now the headquarters of the Four-Square outfit, and left to water at the little stream which run out of the little field. Joey had got on his horse at the sight of the herd and loped to meet it, and now his mother was outside, watching the herd with a queer feeling. She couldn't make herself believe that one fourth of so many cattle was really hers. She'd seen cattle come to water by her little field before but she'd hardly glanced at 'em. Now she was all eyes and interested. The bellering of the cattle, the voices of the riders and the sight of them, all of a sudden transformed her quiet little hollow into a regular well running cow outfit's headquarters, like the kind she'd passed on her way to town the spring before, and she hadn't ever dreamed that she would ever be a pardner of such holdings. There was work, action and peace now that all meant a safe home and future for her little Joey, and when he came running to her a while later, all happy and excited, she hugged him four times in one. Three of them hugs was for the three mustangers.

The widow counted cattle by the thousands as she went to bed that night, but that sure didn't bring on no sleep like counting sheep might. For with counting the cattle she was full of happy thoughts. She could see her little Joey riding amongst 'em, and her three pardners coaching him in the cattle game. She pictured him growing, capable, a lean and wiry cowboy riding amongst bigger and bigger herds, and then she'd doze for a spell, wake up again and start all over in picturing her happy thoughts.

She was the first one up and long before daybreak the next morning. The boys would be up at daybreak, and with the extra two riders, she had quite a crew to cook breakfast for. But she hummed as she warmed skillets, made biscuits and sliced bacon. There was plenty to eat now and she felt mighty cheerful as she cut in the big side of bacon. She'd never had no bacon nor many other things while she was alone with Joey, now a cellar was filled with grub and there was plenty of cattle on the range, all which gave her a great feeling of security and contentment.

Little Joey jumped out of his bed as his mother closed the oven door on the pan of biscuit dough. He'd been counting cattle during the night too, but not like his mother had. He'd counted 'em while picturing himself roping and branding, and that'd been a plenty to keep him awake some few minutes at a time.

All dressed and washed, he was sent out to tell the riders that breakfast was ready. It was daybreak, the riders was up, and when Joey called 'em they was ready for their coffee.

The inside of the dugout had the atmosphere of a regular cow camp that morning, and was tamed down only by the presence of the widow, clean table cloth, stone dishes, and curtains on the windows. That sure didn't spoil the good meal, but after it was over there was the hankering for a cigarette, and the riders filed out to roll them.

A bright sun peeked over an eastern ridge to warm the hides of the saddle horses in the little pen by the little shed. They'd been fed good hay from the widow's fast disappearing little stack and was strong for another day's ride. The two extra riders caught their horses, turned out the others that'd been borrowed, and falling behind 'em headed back for their home range.

The three mustangers caught their horses, and Joey caught his. There was a lot of work to do that day, and the widow, now outside and looking as far as she could and seeing no cattle nowhere was glad to see the boys ride away, for she feared that all the cattle had left the country and many

And falling behind 'em headed back for their home range.

would never be found. But her fears was only from not knowing the ways of range cattle and she wondered why the boys didn't seem to worry and rode away so slowly. If she'd been along she'd rode much faster. Some day she would be along, soon as she got around to making a riding skirt from the cloth Hugh had bought her that time him and Joey was in town.

As the boys had figured, the cattle had scattered only to feed and was all accounted for to within ten miles of "Headquarters." Bunches was gathered from the scattered herd, each of the boys took a bunch and drove 'em short distances to the most open watering places and where the best feed was. The fresh opened watering places had brought many wild horses to the country, but at the sight of the riders they suspicioned that that country would no more be their winter range. Many bunches spooked up and left, but they wouldn't be leaving for good right yet and in a few days they'd be circling back again.

The boys didn't worry much about the mustangs, but there was cattle that didn't belong on what now was the Four-Square range, and them is what they started to drive away, like letting every neighboring stockman know that they'd claimed this range. That was a doing that every stockman would understand and respect, for all of them would do the same.

Little Joey had a great time that day, he rode along with Andy, helped shove a bunch of cattle to a spring where a prospector was still working. There was a fair sized dirt tank of water already filled and running over from the little spring, and the prospector claimed that he'd get the spring to running twice as good before he was done with it. He'd tunneled deep into the side of a hill and showed Andy where all along the tunnel was little spoutings that went to make the little flow of water, about the size of a finger.

"With a good sized tank to catch and hold the water," the prospector had said, "and with the cattle coming in natural and a bunch at a time instead of a herd, this spring will water two or three hundred head of them, even in a dry year."

The bunch of cattle Andy and Joey had brought over was held to water till all had their fill and then left to graze as they wished. There was plenty of good feed around everywhere and the cattle would come back to the same watering place when thirsty again. There'd be no fear of them straying off the range as long as the water held out.

High noon come and little Joey got hungry. He near felt ashamed of that and tried hard not to pay attention to his stomach's hollers, for he already knowed that a cowboy only thinks of eating and resting after the work is done. Now there was some cattle belonging to neighboring stockmen that had to be shoved off the Four-Square range and it was quite a ways to the outskirts of it. By the time that was done and they was in sight of headquarters and home again it was near sundown. Somehow Joey had lost some of his appetite by then, but he was getting tired and as he unsaddled his horse he was ready to quit playing cowboy for that day.

He came into the dugout where his mother was busy starting the evening meal, and worried as she'd been about the cattle disappearing that morning she hardly gave Joey a chance to get near the stove to warm up when she begin to ask questions, and as tired as Joey was he done his best to answer them as a full grown cowboy should.

"Yes, Mom," he says, "they was scattered a considerable, but we found every one of 'em. They most all was in Badjer Flat."

"Badjer Flat," his mother asked, wondering, "where is that?"

"That's the flat down the country about five miles. Hugh named it that this morning on account of all the badjer holes there."

The next day and few days following went by with pretty well the same work. Cattle was drove in small bunches to different watering places, a rough count was made of the cattle already scattered so as to keep tab on how they was ranging or if any strayed away, but that didn't seem necessary, for the cattle had took to the new range like as if they'd been calved there. It was the first time in their lives when they didn't have to travel miles of rocky trail to scarce water, and back to scarce feed, and they wasn't hankering to do anything but stay where they was. Stray cattle was shoved off the range most every day, mustangs spooked away only to make a big circle and come back, and the riding from then on was about the same as with any old and well run outfit. It only took one or two riders to keep tab on the cattle now, and little Joey was riding by the side of one or the other most every day. Tired every night but anxious to go again every morning.

The watering places had all been named by then, mostly by the prospectors that developed 'em and according to some mineral in the water or by some rock formation or by some happening. One prospector named one after a big rusty cartwheel spur he'd found while digging, he'd called it Mexico Springs on account of the spur being Mexican. Other springs went by the names of Antelope, Sulphur, Jericho, Needle Rock, Wild Horse and such like. Only the best watering places was named, the kind that could be depended on the year around, and Joey had got to well know the names and locations of each, along with what cattle ranged near them.

As Stub had figured, most of the prospectors was done with their work in a couple of months' time. Depending on the water vein, some prospectors had dug out two and three springs in that time, and some only one or two. Very few that Stub had put 'em to work on had proved not worth digging.

With one prospector and then another done with digging, Stub put 'em right to work in the higher mountains and to cutting dry standing timber for use in building corrals, also any straight logs that could be found which would do for house logs. When more prospectors came to him he put 'em to work to digging holes for the corral posts. There was to be a big square corral, with smaller ones adjoining, and a good round corral for handling and breaking horses. A couple of the prospectors was put to hauling posts, and in a short time the corrals begin to take shape.

Hugh and Andy, with Joey, done the riding while Stub superintended the corral building. Another beef or two was killed. There was quite a crew now and a lot of meat was needed, so the beeves killed wasn't calves no more but big three years olds, and not out of the Four-Square cattle but from any other outfit whose cattle the boys happened to run acrost. The widow, thinking the boys was killing Four-Square cattle, felt inclined to be saving on the meat, she wasn't used to plenty, and the butchering of a big steer struck her as a big loss out of the herd. The boys thought it was a mighty good thing she only thought they was killing Four-Square steers. If she'd knowed they was butchering neighbor cowmen's cattle she might of felt guilty in cutting even a steak off the fine quarters of meat, and that would of been a heap worse feeling for her than cutting on her own beef. But the boys felt very different about that.

The prospectors wasted no time in wondering whose beef they was eating. The meat was good and that's all that mattered to 'em, they wasn't at all saving with it but they wasn't wasting it either, and as the widow would see one prospector and then another walk out of the cellar, packing a big hunk of meat, she wondered if them prospectors was men or wolves. They was only healthy and hard working men, and as the meat was dropped into pots and skillets at their camp and was cooked to taste over the sage brush fire it had a better flavor than when cooked on a stove, and the appetites of the men eating it out of doors was better too.

Juniper and Pinon posts was being cut by the hundreds and hauled in, and as most of the timber in that country was short and scrubby the corrals was built with all timbers standing upright and close to one another like with a picket fence. There'd been no timber long enough so the corrals could be built panel way. One patch of straight white pine had been found but that patch was a long ways off and wouldn't be cut down only when time come to build the log house the boys had planned on.

Like with all cowboys, the building of home and ranch always starts with the corrals. Corrals are first, on account that they're needed to run in and hold the stock that's necessary for work, also other stock that might stray away during the night. With wide open country all around, a good corral is more important than a house.

The corrals was about finished and a couple of men was now building gates when Stub and Hugh started pacing off squares in a pretty location not far from the dugout. The widow wondered at that but she asked no questions, only from Joey who told her that the boys was going to build a good stable there. She thought that was a sort of queer place for a stable and a heap more fitting for a home. Fact is, she'd long ago planned on building a house on that exact spot, if the time ever come when she could.

She was hurt, and felt a little peeved at the boys picking on that perticular spot as a location for a stable. She come near interfering a few times, but thinking on how good they'd been to her she figured it was sure worth sacrificing that spot rather than object.

A shallow trench was dug and flat stones was fitted in for a foundation, then the peeled pine logs begin to appear, and at the sight of them being grooved on the well layed foundation the widow thought on what a shame it was to use so much time on good foundation and such clean and straight logs only for a stable. What a fine house them logs would make, and as she seen the solid walls go up she got to staying in the dugout and trying hard to keep her mind on her work. She didn't want to see that building go up, knowing it would only be a stable.

The sounds of the ax cutting grooves on log after log wasn't good for her to hear. Then one evening, like wanting to picture a house there instead of the stable she looked the direction of the building. Her first thought as she looked at the half completed walls was that it would sure be a queer looking stable. She seen there was quite a few partitions, the doors was too narrow for a stable too, and looking where other openings had been left in the walls she knowed that there would be windows, but why so many of 'em? She'd never seen a stable with more than one or two windows.

Curious and wondering she walked towards the building and the closer she got to it the faster her heart begin to thump, for she seen that that building wouldn't be no stable, not the way it was partitioned up. There was four rooms, one or two open spaces for windows to each and when she seen places in the foundation that had been built for floor timbers to lay on she knowed for sure that that building would be a house, a roomy one too.

She knowed for sure that that building
would be a house, a roomy one too.

169

For a spell she felt like screaming with happiness as she realized that, but it came to her as she went from room to room that the boys had been wanting to surprise her and she kept quiet, even dodging past the window openings for fear they might see her. She didn't want to spoil their fun at surprising her, and she would act on as tho the building was only a stable and of no interest to her.

But she couldn't very well keep from joking a little about it as the work went on. She remarked to the boys that it was a queer looking stable they was building, so many rooms and windows, and when Hugh drove the team to town and came back with a load of floor and roof lumber she remarked at that, saying that she'd never seen a stable with a wood floor only in the East.

The boys would look at one another at her remarks, and even tho they suspicioned that she was wise to their game they kept up the play that the building would be a sure enough stable and nothing else. It was all right to have partitions they said, each room was a box stall. They didn't like a dark stable either and that accounted for the windows. As for the wooden floor they claimed that was better for the horses' feet than a dirt floor, and that they could show as much style in building a stable as Eastern folks could.

"But," says the widow once, remarking about the floor, "aren't you afraid the horses might get slivers in their tootsies?"

Then one day, after the windows and doors was put in, the logs chinked and dobied, the widow stopped all joking by taking holt of a bucket of paint and started to paint the floor. The boys grinned at one another at that, and tried to think of a way to tell her that that house had been built for her without hearing any remarks that she knowed it all the time.

But they didn't have to worry about that, as Stub took a long breath and went to tell her she come near crying right then with appreciation, and there was no joking back of that.

CHAPTER ELEVEN

I T WAS GETTING ALONG TOWARDS SPRING. The little hay stack by the shed had long ago disappeared, and the saddle and work horses had to be turned out on the range. As the feed was good they didn't stray far during the night, and being they was fed grain night and morning that was another good reason for them to stick close. Little Joey had been given the work of corralling them twice a day and giving them their grain. His horse was the only one that was kept up at headquarters, and now that the little patch of alfalfa was bared of snow and turned green that pony grazed there, with the milk cow.

There wouldn't be no hay to cut when summer come, for the little patch of alfalfa would be pastured. No hay was needed in that country anyway, for the winters was mild, snows seldom stayed on the ground over a few days at a time and stock could feed on the range the year around. Saddle and work horses would be brought in early every morning, fed their grain and when the day's work was done they'd be given another feed of grain and turned loose on the range again, with freedom to graze thru the night and no fence to hold 'em.

There wasn't much for the work horses to do now. The hauling of corral posts and house logs was all done, good sized tanks had been scooped out with scraper to hold the water at each spring, also at other places where rain waters could be caught, and when the prospectors was done, hauled back to town and paid off and another load of grub was brought out that was the end of work for the team for some time. They

That pony grazed there, with the milk cow.

was separated from the saddle horses, and with the widow's old work horse was turned loose on the range for the summer, or till time come when they'd be needed again.

It looked like now they wouldn't be needed no more only to get a load of grub from town and wood from the mountains once in a long while. The headquarters, house, corrals and all, was as much improved as was possible. New furniture, and fixings had been hauled out, and put in the new house, even a new stove, the spring had been piped and there was running water to sink and bath. All the hard labor was done.

The widow had took possession of the new house, and her only trouble now was to keep believing that she wasn't dreaming. She had a cheerful bedroom all to herself and one for Joey, then there was a big living room with a fireplace at one end, a good kitchen and bath room, and all with being fixed up to suit her taste she couldn't even try to think of what else she could wish for, only sometimes that her husband was alive to share it with her and Joey, but she kept so busy with her new home, cooking for the boys and all that there was a big scarcity of cloudy days for her.

As contented as the widow was in her house, the boys was as contented in taking over the dugout she'd lived in for so long. It made a dandy bunk house, plenty big enough for six bunks and as the boys was out on the range all day most every day the dugout felt mighty homey when night come. It was a good place to rest, and now they had a place to hang their cloths and put their things away in, their home quarters. The tent was let down, rolled up and stored with the rest of the camping outfit.

Things was now organized and running as smooth with the Four-Square as it would be with any old and well established cow outfit, and the big expense of starting the outfit was over. It was good that it was over, too, because the boys had run out of money. The last money they had had been spent for a saddle for the widow, a good stock saddle that Joey could use when his mother didn't.

Joey had the use of it for a whole month and had it pretty well broke in when the widow come out of the house wearing a riding outfit one day, one she'd made herself, and surprised him by appropriating her saddle and his horse. She looked mighty neat in her outfit, and now she wanted to take a little riding practice while the boys was away on the range. It had been years since she rode horseback and she didn't want them to see her riding the first few times, not until she got onto the hang of it again.

It had been years since she rode horseback.

It took only a few rides for her to get onto the hang of it again, and then the boys riding back earlier than usual one day caught her at it.— When they went to the big pasture a few days later to change horses they caught one good gentle horse for her to use. They brought a fresh one for Joey to sort of make up for his loss of the new saddle, for he now often had to go back to using the old one.

With the boys saddling up her horse for her most every morning as a strong hint that she should use him, the widow went to riding pretty regular. They told her she ought to see her range and cattle more often, and the work that had been done at the springs, that she shouldn't be putting so much of her time to cooking and such like, advised her as to what to cook so she'd be more free, and come a time, when as she went to riding oftener, that the boys pitched in and helped her with the dishes after a meal. With all of that there was a homey friendship taking holt, the widow quit fidgeting in her aim to please them when they came in the house, she got to feel at ease while discussing things and to smile and laugh with them. By the fireplace of the big living room is where the boys had got to gather of evenings, with the widow and Little Joey. When the evenings got warmer they'd gather on the porch, and with every such gathering there was the feeling of one happy family.

Many new born calves begin to appear on the range. The boys had been branding the biggest ones as they came onto 'em, but they was accumulating fast, and soon now there'd have to be a roundup and general branding.

When that time come, the widow was right on hand to help gather and hold the cattle. A pack outfit of bedding, grub and cooking utensils was made up and camp was set by a big spring thirty miles away from the headquarters. They rounded up the cattle in that country, the widow, Little Joey and one of the boys held each herd while the other two roped and branded. The three mustangers took turns about at that work. There was no rushing nor hard riding and the round-up trip was more like a vacation and change from the headquarters.

They was on their third day of rounding-up and branding and had moved camp to another big spring when two strange riders driving a strange bunch of cattle came to the spring. They turned their cattle loose there and rode up to camp where the three mustangers was helping the widow with the evening meal.

The boys had a hunch of who the two riders might be soon as they seen them turn their cattle loose at the spring, and they was prepared for them.

"Howdy," says Stub, as they rode to within hearing distance. "You're just in time, get off your horses and come and eat with us."

"No, thanks," answers one of the riders. "We got our camp just a few miles from here and we're going right back." Then he went on to ask, "Is it you folks' cattle that's been ranging at these springs? We been noticing 'em all winter."

"Yes," says Stub, "they're our cattle."

"Well, don't you think it's about time you ought to shove 'em to your own range and watering at your own water? They sure been here long enough."

Stub grinned. "Maybe I should of hung up a notice so you fellers would know, but these are our springs. You're on our range and the cattle you just brought in are the ones that need shoving off."

"Since when?" says the rider. "This spring and the other one by Cayote Holes belong to the Crane Cattle Company, and have belonged to the company for forty years that everybody knows of."

"Yes, I know the springs have been claimed, but with no rights on 'em. Nobody went into the trouble to find that out, and we wouldn't either only we needed the springs and we've filed our rights on 'em, like we did with all the water we developed on this range."

The rider was surprised and puzzled, but there was nothing he could do only to make sure from Crane himself or the foreman. He sort of changed his tune then, and asked if it would be all right to leave the cattle they'd brought over, for a few days, till he found out.

"Sure," says Stub, "we want to be neighborly."

There was a few more days of camping at one watering place and then another, rounding up and branding, and before starting back for the headquarters the boys killed a good big calf from the Crane herd and packed the meat home.

All the cattle furthest away from headquarters had been rounded up, a good count made of 'em and the calves all branded. A few bunches had strayed a little but they'd been brought back and none was missing. Now the rest of the rounding up and branding was with the cattle closer to headquarters and the corrals was used from then on. Little Joey got more chance to play there, for he didn't have to help holding herd as he did while the branding was done on the range. Hugh told him to try his hand at roping calves and Little Joey did, but roping from a horse was new to him, his rope twisted, tangled up with the bridle reins and his aim was not good when he throwed a loop. A couple of times his loop settled on the horns of grown stock instead of the calf he'd aimed it at and there'd been some little excitement to get the ropes off. The grown stuff was pretty wild and with the rope tied hard and fast to the saddle, Little Joey and his horse got jerked around some till the boys come to rope the critter, stretch 'er out to lay and took the ropes off.

But Little Joey did manage to rope a few calves and bring them to the fire. He caught 'em by the neck, of course, and the boys acted as tho they wouldn't handle calves that was roped by the neck on account that that made 'em hard to wrassle and throw. They said they wanted the calves brought in roped by the two hind legs, and that roped by only one hind leg wouldn't do.

The boys had a lot of fun with Joey, it was good fun and with plenty of practice and learning for him. He tried hard to catch calves by the two hind legs, but either his loop didn't get there, or layed dead or tangled up amongst too many legs. Anyway, he didn't catch but one calf by the two hind legs and he no more than got to feeling pleased and proud of that catch when he seen that the calf had already been branded. He let his rope slack and the calf kicked out of it while the boys tried hard not to laugh.

All the branding over with for that spring, the boys went to tallying up on the calf crop and was pleased that it was an eighty percent one. Later on they would make it a hundred and twenty percent, but they had to go at that gradually and so none of the neighboring outfits would get suspicious. They wasn't in no hurry about using the "long rope" with reaching out of their range and putting their own brands on somebody else's stock, for they'd come to figure that it would be safer to hit away out of their country when wanting to increase their herds or stirring up needed cash. They didn't want to take many chances of doing much in their own country, for here's where they started a home and outfit, here's where they wanted to keep their names in the clear, and not only for their own good and safety but also for the widow's and Little Joey's sake.

So they figured that if they was to go on any rampage on a big scale they'd do like they used to, change their names and their horses' brands and hit out for far away country where they wasn't known, gather in a few carloads of good cattle or horses, drive and ship 'em out and get the cash for them, then ride back home with the money and play honest some more, all excepting when killing a beef from a neighbor's herd and branding a few now and again that they'd hid away from them neighbors.

The boys didn't hanker so much to go on any horse or cattle stealing trip but something would have to be done pretty soon, for there wasn't one red cent on the Four-Square outfit and being they wouldn't have any cattle to ship in the coming fall, not till the next year, some money would sure have to be stirred up from somewhere before then. There'd be grub, grain, clothes and other necessary things to buy.

With the branding over with, the cattle all accounted for and ranging where they belonged there wasn't much work for the boys to do now. One rider could keep good tab on a thousand head of cattle the year around in that country, all excepting for maybe one month in the spring of the year when rounding up and branding, and one month in the fall when rounding up and branding again and shipping the beef. There was no hay to cut and no fences to fix, only plain riding to see that the cattle didn't stray when rains made more watering places, and that no big calves went unbranded.

Facing a whole summer with very little to do, and thinking up ways to stir up some money without going on a stealing trip unless they had to, the boys thought of the superintendent of the big outfit. Maybe he'd draw up another contract to run wild horses and add on range horses to them again. That would be about the quickest and safest way of making money. They could run with a parada and not bother with building traps, then they could also start in on clearing their range of the many mustangs that had accumulated on it since there now was so many watering places.

The boys had gone to their bunk house, the dugout, to talk of their plans one evening. They was stretched out on their bunks, talking free and with no fear of the widow nor Joey hearing when there come a sound of spur rowels ringing and in the next few seconds a tall hatchet-faced feller come to sight at the opened door. The boys sit up in their bunks, greeted the stranger, invited him in and asked if he'd wanted some supper, but the stranger only glared and scowled at all the hospitality and friendly welcome.

"I'm Mr. Crane," he says, as he stepped inside, "Crane of the Crane Cattle Company and I've come to see you 'claim jumpers' about taking over my two springs."

The boys now well realized what was up. They didn't exactly blame Crane for being peeved at losing the two springs, but they sure didn't agree with his tone of voice and his way of bringing up the subject. Hugh was the first to speak.

"You're accusing us right in taking over the springs," he says, "but mighty wrong as to us being claim jumpers."

"You can't hold the springs," says Crane, as tho he hadn't heard Hugh. "Why they're on my father's original range and was turned over to me in his will."

"Maybe so, maybe so," Hugh says, "but neither your father nor you filed any claim nor done any improvements on 'em. We have. And anyhow," he went on, "you sure can't condemn us for taking the springs, you'd

179

done the same if you was opening a new range, and maybe this will only do you good and look into what claims you have on your other holdings."

Crane's face sort of twisted and the boys expected a real howl from him. They wasn't disappointed there, and amongst the howls was threats of court fights and suing, also remarks that he'd range cattle at the springs as usual and he dared the boys to shove them off. He went on blabbering that he had plenty of influence in the country, that he was president of a bank and so on, and then, as the boys only acted sleepy at his raving, he cooled down, more and more, and finally wound up with a quiet tone and to asking the boys how much they would want for the springs. Hugh took the lead once more.

"With all your range, bank and holdings," he says, "I don't see why you have to worry about two little springs. You say we can't hold 'em anyway, so why try and buy 'em from us?"

Stub winked at Hugh, and chipped in. "You don't have to move your cattle either, we'll take care of 'em.— Now you better turn your horse in the pasture and turn in yourself. It's after dark."

Andy lighted a lamp, and the light showed that Mr. Crane was about to bust loose some more. But he somehow held himself and acted like he hardly dared speak for fear he would say too much. Finally he said a few words of warning, that the boys had better consider selling him the springs or there would sure be trouble. Them was his parting words as he turned and went out the door. A short while later there was sounds of horse's hoofs hitting a lope on hard earth, and as the sound dimmed and all was silent again the boys looked at one another and grinned a little.

"That old boy acted a little peeved," says Andy, "and sounded like he sure might start trouble."

"He can start all the trouble he wants," says Stub, "we'll put the finishing touches on it and head it back his way."

As short as the nights are at that time of the year it had hardly passed and there was only a faint light in the eastern skies when the widow woke up at low sounds coming from the kitchen. She got up wondering, dressed in a hurry, and coming into the kitchen she caught the boys at eating the breakfast they'd cooked. They'd tried to be quiet so as not to wake her, they said, but that day was going to be a long one for them and they wanted to get an early start.

They saddled their horses and rode towards the springs Crane had claimed, figuring on being there long before any of his riders would. For they suspected that Crane wouldn't be slow in starting trouble, and they wanted to beat him to it. In the surrounding country of the springs they gathered all they could see of his cattle, cut out some of the good steers, and shoved all the others back on Crane's range and mixed 'em in with his herds. Then they rode back on a high lope, fell in behind the steers, and shoved 'em on the fastest twenty miles they'd ever seen, inside the Four-Square range and in an entanglement of hills where they'd be hard to find.

The boys didn't like to do that kind of work in day time, but they figured that such doings would be well worth taking a chance for right then, for, if Crane sent any riders with more cattle or to see if his cattle had been moved back to his range, them riders would soon see that the cattle had been moved back. And mixed in with the herds the way they was, would take it for granted that the steers had been moved back too. It would of been mighty hard to tell that they hadn't without a round-up and careful count.

The boys was happy that they hadn't sighted any riders that day. They'd answered Crane's challenge in his saying that they didn't dare move the cattle from the springs and out of their country. They'd not only called his bluff but with moving his cattle out that went a long ways to make it appear that they'd moved *all* his cattle out, and throw off suspicion that they'd held back and hid the steers.

With all that might prove interesting with new plans, the boys sort of forgot about mustang running for the time. Something had fell right into their lap that pleased their outlaw spirits and they seen where they could have a lot of play along with the satisfaction of furnishing plenty of trouble to the maker of it. If Crane'd had any idea of what kind of fellers it was he threatened to start trouble with he'd stayed home and been glad to keep quiet.

But he didn't know. . . . He sent a few of his riders with more cattle to the springs, remarking that he would crowd and starve them smart alecs out of their country. The boys seen the cattle from a distance and grinned. They'd already took a good bunch of good steers from the first herds they'd shoved to the springs and drove 'em many miles from where the Crane riders would ever look for 'em. They could take on many more, as many as the Crane riders brought in.

Crane's war declaring called for only one kind of action, and the boys was again to their old tricks. They hadn't wanted to do any cattle stealing in their own country, but with Crane's actions there was the temptation of beating him at his own game, winning at it and in a way that looked so safe that they had decided to play it.

With all the Crane cattle being shoved on the Four-Square range the boys begin to do plenty of night riding. Little bunches of good steers was cut out of the herds now and again, the herds drove back and the steers hid away. When a good enough bunch of steers was gathered they was trailed thru a thirty mile strip of the Four-Square range, shoved over a summit and left in a country where it'd be natural for them to drift down into. They'd be a good fifty miles from the Crane range by the time they'd stop drifting.

Crane and his riders never suspected that the boys was doing such work, the steers was cut out in too little bunches at a time to be missed, and as the herds was being drove back the Crane outfit figured that the boys was only very patient and wanted to keep peace by not making a squawk. They had a right to drive the cattle back and could of settled and won the whole argument in court if they'd wanted to, and as it was the Crane riders and foreman only thought that their boss was a daggone hard headed fool, and that he'd ought to stick with his bank and let them handle the outfit, for the cattle being drove back and forth only made more work. They begin to get sore footed and sure wasn't making no flesh.

The boys worked as fast as they dared to get as many steers as possible, before any riders noticed 'em in that out of the way country and got to notifying the Crane riders about 'em. But if that was done there would be no proof that the steers hadn't drifted there of their own accord, even if it did look that they was in a handy place for anybody to get away with. The worst part then would be of the steers being drove back to their range, and the boys being suspicioned.

The boys had sure thought of that, and come the time when figuring they had a good enough number the three rode to that country, separated the steers from the other cattle that was there and started 'em on the move as dark come, on the move to a far away railroad and market. The steers was in good shape but by the time they'd be trailed to the shipping point and shipped to market they would lose considerable weight and sell only as "feeders." But they was big steers and would bring a good price in their class.

The three drove the steers on thru the night and made plans. They would take them acrost the line into another state and to a shipping point where Stub knowed of a buyer who would pay spot cash at railroad for such cattle and take his chances on the shipping. He wouldn't be taking the chances the boys had, for he had a bill of sale and he couldn't be connected with the stealing. The worst that could happen to him would be to have the cattle took away from him.

There was thirty miles of country covered with the steers on the first night, a long distance for cattle. The boys hid the cattle for the day as the sun came up and took on a few hours' sleep. When they woke up and looked over the back trail they figured they'd have an easy time delivering the bunch. They had a good lay of the country they was to go thru, had a good idea of where every Crane rider would be at right then, and with their knowledge of the cattle stealing game they could steal without being suspicioned where less experienced riders would of got caught up with and strung high to a tree before they'd got a good start.

Rested up, and while chewing on dry grub, the boys then decided that two of 'em would go on with the cattle and one would go back to take care of things on the Four-Square range. Andy, always wanting to see new country, said he'd like to go on with the cattle. Stub looked at Hugh, and as Hugh seemed very neutral he grinned and said that he'd go on with Andy. That left Hugh clear sailing back to the Four-Square.

"And I'm thinking that you're apt to get into more trouble there than we are," says Stub. Then he went on, "Of course I don't mean at the Headquarters."

It was near noon when Hugh started back for the Four-Square. He hummed on tune after tune as he rode, feeling that his pardners would be humming too, also maybe the widow and Little Joey. All was hunkydory. He was still humming along when evening come, and getting near the country where the stolen steers had been ranging, when his humming of a sudden stopped and his heart missed a thump or two as he seen four riders coming out of a cut in the hills. He seen them first but he was in plain sight and where he couldn't duck to hide without them seeing him. He decided quick that the best thing for him to do was to ride on straight ahead and as tho the sight of them didn't worry him none at all, and when they turned to come his way he had plenty of time to do some thinking before they got to within talking distance.

As they got closer he recognized one of the riders. He was one of the two who'd brought the herd of cattle to the spring during branding time. Hugh figured that the other three with him was also Crane's riders, and he was prepared for the questions he knowed would be asked, while he wondered how come for them to be here, at just such a time. He sort of cussed the luck.

The rider he remembered said howdy, told him they was hunting some steers they'd heard had been seen in this country and asked him if he had seen 'em. Hugh looked natural, not at all interested and didn't hesitate as he said he hadn't seen the cattle.

"Been hunting for some of ours too." Hugh says, "and thought they might of drifted this way. I rode this whole country the last three days and found some few of ours but not one hoof of yours. I don't see how Crane cattle would drift this way anyhow."

"We couldn't figure how either," says a Crane rider, "but some feller rode in and told us about seeing quite a few head of ours here. It's likely that we misunderstood him as to the country because we haven't found any. It's likely they might of drifted back."

The rider didn't seem to doubt or suspicion Hugh as he agreed, but amongst the cattle tracks in and out of the country they talked and wondered about one string of 'em that lined out. It was seen by the horse tracks zig-zagging on top of 'em that the cattle had been drove. Hugh said that he'd seen the cattle and the riders who'd made them tracks the day before from a distance, and he thought that some outfit around was bringing home cattle that had strayed away.

As it was getting late, Hugh invited the riders to come and spend the night at the Four-Square. That invitation was to put them off the trail and so he could keep his eye on 'em. But they wouldn't take up the invitation. Instead, and as Hugh feared, they was for following the trail of the cattle that'd been driven and catching up with 'em.

Hugh seen there was no use trying to talk 'em out of that, too much talk would only stir suspicion, and he was sure worried as they started at a fast gait on the trail of his pardners and the steers. But he didn't act worried, and he rode on as tho he was headed for home, but soon as he got on the other side of a little rise he got off his horse, peeked back over the rise and watched the riders. His horse went to grazing.

"Yes, you better be feeding up, old boy," Hugh says to him, "because we'll have to do some tall rambling tonight. Doggone the luck anyhow, them fellers had to come investigating at this time."

But that couldn't be helped now, and he felt glad for one thing, that he could warn his pardners and have 'em leave the cattle in time. Another good thing was that he had the advantage over the Crane riders, they would have to travel by daylight so they could trail the cattle, where Hugh didn't have to. He knowed what country the cattle would be drove thru and he could ride on at night, and figuring that the cattle would be drove another thirty miles that night that would make him have to ride sixty miles from where he was to catch up with 'em by the next morning.

The Crane riders disappeared in the distance, and it was getting dark as Hugh got on his horse and started to ride. He'd rode for about an hour, and it was good and dark when he seen a little fire which he felt sure the Crane riders had made to camp by for the night. The sight of the fire pleased him, for he seen they'd only rode about ten miles that evening and the cattle and the boys would have a good fifty mile lead on 'em when daylight come.

Hugh passed within half a mile of the fire and rode on thru the night, over rough hills and acrost wide valleys, and even tho it was hard for him to make sure of his whereabouts sometimes, he didn't go out of his way none. He came to the place where he left his pardners that day and rode on the direction they had told him they would take. Against the starry sky was the dark outline of a mountain which had been pointed out, and he headed for a jagged peak which they said they'd drive close past.

The nights was short but by daybreak, Hugh had near rode all of the sixty miles, and his horse was tired. With daylight he now begin to cut for the tracks of his pardners and cattle. He'd long ago went past the jagged peak. He was now in a wide valley, and heading for a low range of hills, he run acrost 'em. His pardners would be hiding the cattle in them hills by now, he thought, and he was careful to sing or whistle as he rode along, for he figured that one of 'em would be watching the backtrail from some high point and he didn't want to take the chances of being mistaken for a sheriff or any such like.

He was getting well up into the hills and figuring he would come onto the hidden cattle most any time when he heard a voice, and looking up to a clump of boulders and twisted pinons he seen Andy's face grinning down at him. But Andy's grin soon disappeared as he wondered of what might of went wrong to make Hugh come back. Hugh told him of the trouble in mighty few words and then the two went to Stub who was sleeping in a hollow in a ledge.

"We've got fifty miles the lead of 'em," Hugh said as he went on to tell about the Crane riders. "I think our best bet is to leave the cattle right now, ride back to that range of hills over yonder and watch the backtrail for 'em, and if they come this far and find the cattle we'll be too far away to ever be connected with the stealing of 'em, and we'll have too much lead for them to catch up with us."

That was the only safe thing to do. The boys got on their horses, rode back to the next range of hills, hid themselves and horses by a high rimrock. The horses was left to graze and rest while the boys climbed to the top of the rim to take turns at sleeping and watching over the back trail. From where they was they could see about fifteen miles of the back trail, the riders following it would pass to within less than half a mile from where the boys was hid and they would be in plain sight of the boys all the way till they found the cattle.

It will sure be tough luck, the boys thought, to have to go back empty handed after scheming, and working so hard to get away with the cattle, and having such a good start with 'em too. But that's a happening that would have to be accepted along with the game they was playing.

Looking up to a clump of boulders and twisted pinons
he seen Andy's face grinning down at him.

Stub had to grin a little as he remarked, "And wouldn't it pleased Crane if his riders had caught up with the cattle?"

Watching from the high rim the boys now knew just about when to expect the Crane riders and where to look for 'em, and after they'd well rested up and middle afternoon come they wasn't at all surprised to see a dust in the distance, and moving specs under it.

Being the cattle tracks was plain to see and easy to follow up along the four Crane riders rode at a good pace. In an hour's time from when their dust was first seen they was at the foot of the hills where the boys was watching, and at the pace they was riding they would have the steers tracked down in a few hours.

The boys had now lost all hopes of them riders not finding the steers. And there was more than the loss of the steers to think about, for the driven steers would be proof of cattle thieves operating in the country, and as such news was scattered every outfit around would be on the lookout. The boys might not be suspicioned but they'd sure be hindered in trying to get away with any more cattle for some time, because every track of driven cattle would be followed up from then on.

It seemed like there was nothing for the boys to do but wait for the riders to go by, and then they would hightail it out of there during the dark of the night, not for home on the Four-Square range because their horses' tracks could be followed there and that would give them away. They would separate, sort of circle, and would not go back only when sure that nobody was on their trail.

Such was the thoughts running in the boys' minds as they watched the Crane riders, and they'd sort of come to the conclusion that a feller shouldn't have no home when he's doing anything he might have to be on the dodge for. Then there wouldn't be no place where he could be missed from, and he wouldn't have to be so careful about covering his trail because he wouldn't have no perticular place to go to.

But them thoughts was of a sudden left to the breeze as they seen the Crane riders stop their horses on the summit, like as if they was now undecided and wondering about something. Where the riders was, they could see for fifteen miles, acrost a valley to the hills where the steers had been hid, there was a few scattered bunches of cattle in the country. It seemed impossible to the boys watching, but the riders acted like they'd lost the steers' trail. They separated as they rode on again and each man rode towards different bunches of cattle that was in the valley. None rode the direction where the steers was.

Such a change of action sure puzzled the boys. They watched the riders go from one bunch of cattle of another, as if hunting for the steers amongst 'em, and then, when most of the cattle in sight had been looked over they got together again. They stopped their horses once more as if to talk and decide and finally they rode on together, not towards the hills and where the steers was, but down the valley and towards the Crane range.

"Well, I'll be a son of a gun," says Stub.

"Me, too," says Hugh.

The boys could hardly believe their eyes as they seen the riders turn for their home range, and wondering what might of caused 'em to turn they got on their horses and rode to the pass where they had first stopped. There they seen what might of confused 'em, it was the tracks of many driven cattle going all directions from the pass, they was fresh tracks showing that there'd been a round-up in that country only a day or so before. There was fresh tracks of driven cattle stringing along in many places in the valley too.

"But all these tracks wouldn't bother me much if I was trailing the steers," Hugh says. "Them Crane men sure had the direction the steers was being drove, and when they come to these other tracks they could of rode right straight on and picked up the steers' tracks again easy enough."

"Sure," says Stub, with a happy grin, "and that's good proof they didn't suspicion it was their steers they'd been trailing. They just took our trail, only expecting to catch up with some riders who could maybe tell 'em about the steers and to cover the country looking for 'em. I could see that when they come to this summit, and being there was signs that there'd been a round-up they took it for granted that the cattle they trailed was some that'd only strayed from this range and been brought back."

"There must be daggone little cattle stealing going on in this country," Andy chips in, "or they'd suspicioned and followed us up, specially when the tracks was so fresh. I know if my dad had found such tracks anywhere near his range he'd of stuck to it till he'd sure seen whose cattle it was that made 'em."

"Well, we're lucky there," says Stub. "And now, we ain't got nothing but clear sailing ahead and all we got to do is pick up our steers from where we left 'em and shove 'em on for all we're worth."

"Yes. It'll be just about sundown when you boys get to 'em," Hugh says, "and you better get to riding, because they'll be rested up and start feeding out of where you hid 'em." He grinned. "I'll ride back to the family and put Little Joey to praying for your safe return, while I keep the home fires burning."

"But don't forget about the branding fires," says Stub, as him and Andy started to ride away. "There'll be some big calves amongst the Crane herds and we want to keep making sure that we're not the losers while Crane is crowding his cattle on us."

With the shipment of steers, now as good as delivered, they laughed and agreed that that was being well taken care of. They already had a mighty good start.

CHAPTER TWELVE

HUGH DIDN'T SPEND NO TIME with branding fires when he got back to the Four-Square. From the time he hit his range he begin to see Crane cattle, and by the time he got to the ranch he figured that with so many Crane cattle everywhere, outnumbering Four-Square cattle four to one, any strange rider would think sure that this was Crane range.

When he rode to the corrals he seen that both the widow's and Little Joey's horses and saddles was gone, and when he walked up to the house he found it empty. He'd had very little sleep and not much to eat the last few days, and plenty of hard riding. He felt the stove before he started to cook himself something to eat. It was still warm, and being it was now middle afternoon he figured that the widow and her boy had been home for noon. Only out riding a little ways, he thought. He et aplenty to make up for good meals he'd missed, then went to the dugout, heated up some water and proceeded to shave and clean up in general as he hummed a same tune over and over again. It was an Indian war chant, and Hugh was thinking about all the Crane cattle on the Four-Square range as he hummed and went to cleaning up. But his humming of the tune wasn't all war-like, there was a half grin and half happy sound to it, like he was thinking of the spoils of war only, and not at all of losing.

Done with his cleaning up he layed down on his bunk, stretched, and then the tune wasn't heard no more, he'd went to sleep. . . . It was near dark when he was woke by the squeaking sound of a swinging corral

Then went to the dugout and proceeded to shave.

gate. He jumped up, went to the looking glass to comb his hair, and while there tried on a few smiles. He was wearing his best one as he came to the house, and there, just in time to meet the widow and Joey coming from the corral.

There was happy smiles on their faces, too, but they was mostly from the good sight of him. Then as their smiles went away there was troubled looks took their place. Hugh didn't let on he noticed the change and he kept on being cheerful as he started a fire in the stove. But the widow couldn't act so cheerful. She went to fixing the supper, and finally, like as if telling some awful happening, she told him about all the Crane cattle that had been shoved on the Four-Square range while he was gone.

"They've about taken over our range," she says.

Hugh had listened, serious, and when she was thru with the telling he started to grin, as tho it sure was nothing to worry about. That encouraged her some, but she couldn't understand how so many other cattle feeding on their range could be nothing to worry about. To her it meant so much feed taken away from their cattle and that sure was serious. Furthermore, she suspected that Crane outfit shoved their cattle on the Four-Square range for a mean purpose, where their cattle didn't belong, and that sure had set her blood to boiling.

But her talk of what she'd seen and thought didn't bring one frown nor wrinkle of worry to Hugh's face. Finally, and so she wouldn't think he was laughing at her, he started to explain. He didn't exactly stick to the truth as he did, but the widow's mind sure had to be set at ease, and he had to be mighty careful in doing that so she wouldn't know what him and Stub and Andy was up to.

He made her believe that the Four-Square range had plenty enough feed and water for many times the stock that was now on it, that on account of the two springs belonging to Crane for so long, him and the other boys hadn't wanted to rush his cattle away from 'em, and there was other reasons that wasn't so plain to the widow, but was told in such convincing tones that she took 'em for granted.

"We got to be neighborly," he'd said. "Our cattle often run on Crane's range too, you know. And anyway, we'll be arranging things right along now so that by the time winter comes I don't think we'll be seeing any of Crane's cattle on our range, none at all."

Hugh sure meant that last statement. He talked on the subject till he seen the widow feel relieved and cheered up. Even Little Joey who'd hardly said a word, but sure didn't miss one, had lost his peeved look, and by the time the meal was cooked and ready to put on the table there was an all around happy and contented three gathered by a big platter. On the platter was a fine roast surrounded by browned potatoes. That roast was from a fine big calf that Hugh had butchered out of Crane's herds not many days before, and the widow sort of wondered at the grin on his face as he cut tender slices from the roast and placed 'em on the plates.

But she'd wondered so often at some of her pardners' actions and ways, only to find out afterwards she'd had no reason to, that she'd given up thinking or trying to find out about 'em. She'd got to only know that when any one of them or all three was around she felt secure and all at peace.

Like with this last time, she'd felt so helpless and lost and a little scared when the boys was gone and strange cattle crowded the range, but with the first sight of Hugh she'd took on sudden courage and confidence and her worries had evaporated.

The boys had never spoke their past to her, nor where they was from. She'd wondered at that, wondered how they'd got all the money to start the outfit with. She'd never heard of mustang runners to make much money, and she'd met a few. Now, with this last trip, she'd been told they was going to ride other ranges, looking for more cattle to buy, and that would take more money.

At first, while she lived in the dugout, she often wondered herself to sleep about the boys' doings, but she'd never worried nor found a reason to mistrust 'em, and later, after she got to know them better, she found that she'd often wondered only on account of her knowing so little about the doings with range work, and now she was fast getting to where if the boys done things to make her wonder she'd just let it pass as just something she didn't know anything about, and not for her to try and figure out.

She'd never once thought of them being dishonest, for they'd sure proved mighty square to her, and more like three riders sent straight from heaven. Her little Joey sure seemed to think they was, and the way he listened to them, looked at them and tried to copy their every move and action it was plain to see that his big ambition was to some day grow to be like one of them. The widow often noticed that in him, and she couldn't think any one she'd rather see her boy grow up to be like than one of her three pardners, any one of them. She loved all three.

She loved all three as a mother, sister, and pardner and that was a hard combination to beat from her. In them three ways she sometimes dared to be advising and scolding, joking and friendly quarrelling, then ready to fight, win or lose, and give all she owned for them.

She hadn't as yet got to where she could love any one of them with still, maybe, stronger love. At least she didn't think so, but amongst the three she'd got to watching and listening to Hugh a little closer than she did Stub and Andy. She recognized his step a little sooner, seen him and smiled a little quicker when he rode in, and her heart beat just a little faster for him than it did for the other two.

That might of been on account that she'd got to know him long before she did the others. Anyway, Hugh seemed to be a little in the lead in her thoughts, and if such feelings was summed up amongst the boys it would amounted to about the same, for Hugh was always just a little bit more ready to ride back to Four-Square headquarters than Stub and Andy was, and even tho the three might be neck and neck when climbing the porch steps at meal time, Hugh was most always first to get a glimpse of the widow.

The days that followed was very busy ones for Hugh, busy acting to be busy, for even tho he rode day after day and seemed to do his best in shoving Crane cattle back on their range, he wasn't doing half as good a job at that as he could if he really meant it. He didn't shove off no very big bunches, just enough to keep the Crane riders to feeling that he didn't want 'em on his range. He'd sometimes see them riders shoving the cattle in, and he'd only keep out of sight in them times. His blood

would boil but there'd be a grin on his face, and when he would bump
on them riders a purpose once in a while, when they wasn't driving
cattle, he'd act peeved, but only asked 'em to *please* try and keep their
cattle on their range. The boys would only be sorry, there was the excuses
that the Crane outfit was short-handed and that if anything was to be
done about the cattle, for him to see Crane himself, that he was the one
who was responsible. Then they'd rode on, thinking that the Four-Square
was sure a patient and easy going outfit.

There was very little cattle being shoved in on the Four-Square range
now, for that range had all of 'em it could hold and Crane was doing
a good job of overfeeding and crowding it so that in time the boys would
be forced to move their cattle and themselves out of the country. Hugh
kept busy acting as tho trying to shove 'em off, but more busy finding
new and better range for the Four-Square cattle, and in doing that, he
discovered more places where water could be developed and he seen that
in time the Four-Square range could be spread to twice its size. That
would be a good thing to do when they was ready to be rid of Crane's
cattle and when they was well stocked up with their own.

As he'd sometimes talk a little about that to the widow while her
and Little Joey would be riding with him now and again, the widow sort
of doubted him, but it would be only for a very short time, for, with
his confident tone and actions she got to feeling confident too, even if
right then all the range seemed to be Crane range, and she got so she
sometimes even wished, when Hugh killed a fresh beef, that the beef
was one of Crane's instead of their own. Hugh would of more than grinned
if he'd knowed that.

Then, one evening, two tired and dusty riders on two tired and ganted
horses came to the corral and unsaddled. They was Stub and Andy. Little
Joey seen them first, hollered and run out of the house, followed close
by Hugh. The widow got busy putting things back on the stove, for
they'd just got thru with the evening meal.

One evening, two tired and dusty riders on two tired and ganted horses came to the corral and unsaddled.

There was pleased grins on Stub and Andy's tired faces, and Hugh caught the wink from 'em that all had gone well on their trip. They went to the bunk house to clean up some. By then the widow had a good meal ready and the whole family gathered again, two at the table and the others close by. The boys kept their talk neutral and cheerful, but the widow finally had to ask if they'd bought any of the cattle they'd went to see. Stub had to answer that they hadn't as yet on account of hearing of better herds on other ranges, and that he might take a trip that way later on and take a look at 'em.

It wasn't long after supper when the boys hit for the bunk house. The talk got free there and went on in the dark while all three stretched out on their bunks. There's few things that a cowboy appreciates more than to stretch out full length after a long day's ride, even if he's not tired.

"I guess you've noticed," Hugh says, "that we're considerable over-stocked with Crane cattle. . . ."

"Yeh," grunted Stub. "They're so thick that we could hardly make our way thru 'em getting here. They sure must of shoved us most everything they had while we was gone."

"Looks that way to me. I've shoved back a few for bluff, and I've spent no time in putting our iron on some of the big calves I seen, because I figured that's a heap too slow a work for us right now and not worth fooling with."

"Daggone it," Andy grinned from his dark corner, "the way that feller Crane is treating us he's going to make regular cow thieves out of us."

The boys just sort of rested for quite a few days, shoved many bunches of mixed cattle off their range to keep up their bluff and all the while they was spotting where good steers run, but never moved 'em. With the good opportunity shoved onto 'em they'd decided to take advantage of it. They would soon be taking out another bunch, and they was working different this time, for with all the Crane cattle now on their range they didn't go to the trouble of shoving off a bunch every time some steers was picked out. They didn't drive little bunches of steers over the summit to drift into the out of the way country as they had before.

Come a day when only Hugh went out and rode, him and the widow and Little Joey. Hugh rode out to spot the location of where the picked bunches of steers would be, while Stub and Andy rested up and prepared for a long ride that was ahead.

They'd fixed up a couple of bundles of grub and tied 'em behind their saddles, then towards evening they run in some saddle horses and caught two mighty good ones, fresh from a long rest.

The boys had a good sum of money between 'em from the first shipment, and it would of carried 'em for a long spell, but with Crane's aggravating actions and with his sticking temptation right under their noses they sure would take to the temptation and even up on the aggravation.

When night settled on the Four-Square range, the three boys rode out, in a few hours had gathered the steers that Hugh had spotted that day and started 'em on the same long drive the other steers had been trailed on. They didn't expect no more Crane riders on their trail because them riders had once rode that country over and wouldn't likely be back that way unless, as the time before, they got word that some of their cattle had been seen there. It was far out of their territory, and they'd take care that nobody would be seeing this second bunch of cattle on the way out.

It had already been settled that Stub and Andy would again go on with the steers, and Hugh only went as far as the summit bordering the Four-Square range this time. Then there was the usual joking parting words and Hugh rode back. When daybreak come he was on his bunk in the dugout sound asleep and with his spurs on. His pardners would soon be asleep too, soon as they hid the steers amongst the hills, over thirty miles away from the Four-Square.

The widow was a little surprised to see Hugh come to breakfast alone that morning, and when he told her that Stub and Andy had left before daybreak on account of a long ride they'd have to make that day, and out to look for other cattle they might buy, she only remarked that she could as easy as not got breakfast for them if they'd told her. She was past wondering at what queer times them pardners of hers took to riding or how they ever made out with such far-between meals or little grub they'd take when on trips.

Hugh caught a fresh horse and rode out alone that day. Little Joey wanted to go along but he told him that it'd be too long a ride for him and that he wouldn't be back till late. But the ride wouldn't of been too long for Joey, for that boy was getting as hard as nails, and Hugh's reason to leave him home was that he was going to scout around for Crane riders who might pick up his pardners' trails, and he sure wouldn't want Joey with him if he seen any, because he'd have to ride plenty fast again, to warn them as he had before. Of course the boys would sure be on the watch themselves and make sure of their getaways if trouble come, but the sooner the warning the bigger the advantage.

He rode to the pass where he'd left 'em, then up to a tall peak where he could see many miles every way but he seen no riders nowheres in all the country around him, only cattle, mostly all Crane cattle and on the Four-Square range, and with the good bunch of steers that'd been cut out of them it seemed like they'd no more be missed than a blade of grass off the whole range.

The fourth of July was only a week or so away. Stub and Andy got back to the Four-Square, once more very tired and needing rest bad, but there'd been smiles on their faces again as they rode in and another wink to Hugh that all had went well.

Hugh had rode hard while his pardners was gone and, as tho he'd sure enough meant it this time, shoved most of the Crane cattle off the Four-Square range. He expected they'd be shoved back again before long. But now, with range pretty well cleared and the Four-Square cattle all accounted for and doing good, everybody rested up and nothing rushing to do for a spell, Stub and Hugh got to looking at the red four number on the calendar. It only looked like another number to Andy, and the fourth of July just another day.

A few days before that date, Hugh rode out and run in a team, greased up the buggy, hooked 'em onto it and drove up to the porch of the house. And the boys was all surprised, even Little Joey, to see the widow strut out of the house wearing her best dress and her best smile. The dress was the only town dress she had and might of been a few years out of date but she looked mighty fine in it and there was no mistaking the admiring looks in the boys' eyes. Stub and Andy and Little Joey was on their best horses. Hugh was to drive the team, with the widow sitting alongside of him, and as the outfit started out there was a rejoicing feeling in the air, for the fourth of July was sure going to be celebrated by the Four-Square.

The outfit got to town one day ahead of the fourth, but that had been planned on account that all would have to tog up for the event, and the widow could only blink as she was handed a roll of bills to spend for clothes or anything she'd want for herself and Little Joey. She finally got to remark about how many cattle such a roll would buy, but the boys only grinned and Stub said there was plenty more where that come from, and then Hugh added on something about a gold mine somewhere.

There sure was a transformation with the Four-Square folks as they gathered at the hotel that evening. The boys had spent a couple of hours in the barber shop, from the bath rooms at the back to the barber chairs, then they'd went and got all togged up from head to foot in town clothes, all excepting the new hats and boots. But with all the show of togs going on in the big room, the way the widow set off her new outfit made her seem like the only one in that room, and she wasn't wearing no fancy dress either.

Andy and Little Joey was the only two to feel stiff and fidgety in their creased togs. They looked like wolf pups with brass-studded collars around their necks. They wasn't used to such clothes. But Stub and Hugh had wore town clothes many times before during many celebrations of their own making, after shipments of stolen stock, and they set off their creased clothes in pretty fair shape.

The widow'd had the greatest time of any of the outfit that day, and her happy face showed it. There was so many things she'd needed, so many things she wanted that she'd never had, and she spent the whole day going from one store to another, and many packages had piled up in her room before evening come.

CHAPTER TWELVE

After a fancy supper in the dining room of the hotel, the outfit lined out to the opera house. The show was more than enjoyed. It was eleven o'clock when they came out and there was sounds of dancing music from a big hall acrost the street. The outfit wound up there and Andy and Joey stood a little pop-eyed against the wall as they watched the dancing folks, then Hugh and then Stub dancing with the widow.

Joey gave Andy a queer look. "What's everybody doing?" he asks. Andy shrugged his shoulder and grinned. "I don't know," he says. "It looks like they're prancing to music and holding one another so they won't bump."

The town was all decorated with flags and alive with people the next day. There was bands and parades and one place by the court house where people gathered to listen to speeches. The widow and her escort took on everything they could see and hear. Then, as Andy was trailing along with Joey he seen another crowd going in a big lot with a tall board fence around it. There was a few riders there and many horses, and after the speeches was over the whole crowd went that way.

There was a few horse races, then a couple of stout and snorty broncs was snubbed up for bucking horses. It was announced that a twenty-five dollar purse was offered for anybody who could ride one of the horses straight up, without pulling leather or losing a stirrup. Hugh looked at Andy as that was announced and nudged him to go set on him but Andy wasn't looking at the horse he was looking at all the people around that would be watching and that was what scared him. But Stub had held up a hand and run out to the middle of the grounds. He was the first to get to the horse, rode him well and according to rules and run back with the purse money which he handed to Joey. He hadn't even wrinkled his new suit.

Hugh started out when the second horse was announced but he was a little too late, another rider had beat him to the horse.

The boys didn't get to be by themselves much during the celebration, only once in a while when the widow would go to her room to change dresses and look over and admire all the new things she'd bought. Then they'd sort of sneak over to the saloon, take on a few drinks, chew on lemon rind to kill the smell and hightail it back for the hotel lobby. It was at one such time that they run into the superintendent of the big outfit and the boys stayed quite a while longer then. There was good friendly talks and drinks, and when Stub mentioned something about a new wild horse contract again sometime, the superintendent shook hands with him and said there'd be no contract needed, for the boys to go to running the wild ones any time they wanted and that he would agree to the same as before. He winked, meaning that he would again throw in a good range horse for every wild one they caught.

"And any time I can be of any help to you boys," he went on, after taking another drink, "you just let me know. Use my office too whenever you're in town, the boys in there and lawyer Blain will be glad to give you advice or information about land or anything you might want to know."

There was somebody else the boys run into at another time, but not while in the saloon. That somebody else was Crane. The boys acted mighty peeved when they seen him, and he would of gone by after a glance at 'em, but they stopped him. Stub told him that something would sure have to be done about his stock being shoved onto their range, to which Crane played innocent and remarked that the stock only drifted in there of their own accord and from being used to run on that range.

"It don't look that way when we see riders shoving 'em," says Stub.

But the boys didn't do no threatening, they was more for pleading, like they was afraid to make any trouble, and would sure appreciate it if Mister Crane would keep his cattle off their range. Foxy Crane was pleased at their actions and he begin to get bold enough to tell the boys that his cattle had more right on that range than theirs did. The boys acted peeved again at that, but helpless to do anything about it. Crane walked away packing a winner's grin while the boys scowled at him till he disappeared in the crowd, then they done their share of grinning.

"Looks like it worked all right," says Hugh. "He thinks we haven't got guts enough to slap a mosquito, let alone stealing cattle."

With the understanding they'd had with the superintendent of the big outfit, the bluff they'd throwed at Crane, the general fun of the celebration and all, the boys felt that their trip to town had sure been very worth while, even if Stub was a little fidgety once in a while for fear of running into the feller Morris, who knowed so much about him, or some other feller who might know just as much. Hugh sort of kept his eyes peeled too, and Andy was the only one of the three who dared keep his hat back and look the world straight in the eye. Nobody could connect his face with any harm as yet.

The celebration over with, the outfit was glad to get back to the ranch, and, as was expected, the Four-Square range was again covered with Crane cattle. The widow was the only one who didn't seem to like that, but as she got in the house and into her room with all her packages she right away forgot about the Crane cattle as she went to unwrapping and fingering the materials and things she'd bought.

To make good use of their time and take advantage of the good opportunity they had, the boys picked out another fine bunch of Crane steers and delivered 'em to the shipping point. The buyer there was well pleased with getting so many good cattle so regular and in such a safe way. There was no inspection in that state for him to fret about, and the steers being trailed in from another state and such a long ways didn't have to be rebranded, for the Crane brand wasn't known there.

The buyer near doubled his money on every shipment and the boys had a little canvas bag pretty well rounded out with the same stuff. They'd stick the money in the bag like it was only so much paper or metal. It didn't mean much to them as compared with the thrill of getting away with the cattle, evening scores with a trouble maker and laughing at his thinking that he was sure crowding them off their range.

It was getting along late summer. In another month now the fall round-up would be in full swing. There'd be many riders combing all ranges, and the boys wanted to get another good bunch of Crane steers to the shipping point before that time come. For they knowed that at round-up time all the steers they stole would sure be missed, and very likely that they would be suspicioned and watched. They was a little leary and mighty careful in getting that fourth shipment of cattle because it seemed to them that they was making a hole in Crane's herds that was sure beginning to be noticeable. For that reason they made the shipment up of mostly young heifers, they'd be less apt to be missed than steers right then and even tho they would bring less money per head, the boys made that up well by taking on twice as many. They wanted to make this shipment a big one.

The boys acting so patient and easy going or scared to start trouble was all that kept the Crane men from being suspicious of them. The Crane men had been so ordered to keep the Four-Square range crowded to the limit that they never noticed of any cattle missing. If they had they'd figured the boys had only shoved 'em back on Crane's or other surrounding ranges.

Hugh went along for two nights driving with the fourth shipment, that was to make more sure of a good start, and when he turned back for home he didn't ride straight or in any hurry. He could of rode back to the ranch in one day if he'd wanted but just took plenty of time, all the while watching the hills around for any sight of riders who might pick up the trail of the stolen cattle. He camped on the trail one night then stayed and watched on that trail all the next day, and when night come again without him seeing any riders he felt it was all right to ride on home. A stiff wind had been blowing and now what tracks showed of the cattle looked old and dim.

The cattle was delivered and Stub and Andy rode back with another good size roll of bills to stuff into the little canvas bag.

*He camped on the trail one night then stayed
and watched on that trail all the next day.*

In a few days the boys was all rested up from their last trip and now their work was the same as with any hard working and honest cowmen. They got busy and shoved most of the Crane cattle off their range, then outfitted and went to rounding up their own cattle as they had the spring before and branded the calves that had been born since. There'd been no beef cattle in their herds, for they'd bought mostly cows and calves, and no beef stock could be shipped out of them for another year. But it was while Stub and Andy and Hugh was riding by themselves a short while during that round-up that Stub sort of chuckled and remarked:

"Well, we done considerable big shipping this year for not having any beef cattle of our own."

The Crane outfit was rounding up too, branding and cutting out likely steers to ship, and then is when it come to the foreman that there was quite some shortage of steers, and he couldn't gather near enough to make up the count he'd marked down in his tally book. Crane riders was scattered and rode away off their range and the Four-Square range in hunting for the many missing cattle, but there wasn't any trace of them nowhere and none of the neighboring outfits had seen them on their range.

When Crane got word that so many of his steers was missing, couldn't be located, and that it was supposed they'd been stolen, he liked to broke his neck getting out of his office at the bank and to the headquarters of his outfit. He wasn't slow in starting a rumpus there, and he begin to accusing his foreman and riders by saying they'd been asleep on their horses or that wouldn't of happened.

"Yes," says the foreman, all het up, "if you'd kept your long nose behind your desk at the bank and left me to handle what you hired me for that wouldn't of happened. You gave me orders to run all the cattle I could on the Four-Square range. That wasn't only a fool thing to do but also mighty aggravating for that outfit, and us too. You said not to be seen shoving the cattle on their range if we could help it nor to be seen riding there. Consequences is we couldn't keep tab on the cattle, and if there's any cattle missing it's you who's responsible. . . ."

Crane fidgeted furious while his foreman spoke, then he finally got the chance to edge in more words. He remarked that the Four-Square range was more his than anybody else's, then went on to accuse the mustangers of stealing his cattle.

"I've wondered why they seemed so patient and easy going," he says, pacing the floor. "Now I know. They stole me blind while making me believe them to be harmless and got away with many of the same cattle I planned to crowd them out of the country with."

"I'd be careful as to who I'm accusing unless I had some proof," says the foreman, then he grinned sarcastic. "But if they're the ones that got away with your cattle I sure wouldn't blame them. I'd hate to be crowded too."

The argument went on with Crane now sure that the three mustangers was the guilty parties. He not only kept accusing them but threatened to make their country so miserable for 'em that they'd sure be glad to leave. First he'd see if the steers could be traced and the stealing of 'em fastened on the boys. If that couldn't be done he'd scatter to the whole country around that they was cattle thieves anyway and turn the folks against 'em. With their names made bad it would be easy enough to frame up such doings as would mean a prison sentence fastened onto 'em, and get rid of 'em that way.

But there was one plan he'd had which he of a sudden gave up as a mighty bad job and that was to crowd 'em out with shoving his cattle on their range, and before starting back for town, where he would hurry and set the authorities to try and trace his steers, he told his foreman to set his men to get all his cattle off the Four-Square range, remarking they was too handy for the three thieves there. But the foreman only grinned and told him to tend to that himself, that he was thru taking any more of his orders. Then over half of the riders quit too, and that sure upset Crane some more.

But with the few riders that stayed on, the Four-Square range was soon rid clean of Crane cattle. Hugh had got to butcher another beef before that was done, and as him and his two pardners seen the last of the cattle being drove away one day he grinned and remarked, "It looks like Crane finally got hep to something."

CHAPTER THIRTEEN

THE BOYS WAS NOW HARD AT RUNNING MUSTANGS AGAIN. They figured that right then it was a good thing for them to seem busy. Their work of rounding up and moving their cattle to where they'd range best was done, and outside of riding to locate or move them once in a long while there wasn't anything much to do on the Four-Square range, excepting to run mustangs. There was no more Crane cattle to shove off or get away with, and all was now peaceful. The boys would of liked to scouted around and bought more cattle, or hired more prospectors and developed more seepages. They now had plenty of money to do that with, but they didn't want to let anybody know by buying more cattle or developing the range on account that that might raise suspicion as to where they got the money to do that with, and at a time when so many Crane cattle come up missing that wouldn't of been a wise thing to do.

So they went to running mustangs, for quite a few purposes. To have action, to show they was busy at an honest work, a proof they would make some money by the sale of them and a good excuse for when they would want to spend some, also they was ridding their range of them, leaving more feed for their cattle.

They planned on running mustangs all thru the winter and not do any shipping of 'em till spring come, when there would be a better market. And being they figured on working on the big outfit's range as well as their own, the superintendent was glad to going on the deal with 'em, as before, let 'em use the company's range horses to make their paradas out of. And, of course, being the deal was with the company he would see that he got his slice out of it again allowing the boys to add on a company range horse to every wild one they caught, then give them his personal inspection slip.

There wasn't as many mustangs on the Four-Square range that winter as there had been, for with the crowding of the Crane cattle the summer before pretty well cleaned it up of feed. Many of the wild ones had went to other and better ranges, and the boys was getting over half of them from the big outfit's range, and that went well with the agreement they had with the superintendent.

They would run horses for three days or so, take the wild ones caught to the big pasture they'd used the year before, then ride a couple of days tending to their cattle, and on again after more wild ones. With all of that they found all the riding they could wish for, and variety with it, for while running wild horses they'd make their camps in the hills and while riding after their cattle they'd again have the comforts of the bunk house and the company of the widow and Little Joey during good meals while all gathered around the table.

The boys was doing pretty good with their mustang running, and even tho they wasn't doing so good as to make 'em anywheres near rich by spring, they was sure keeping busy and had the neighboring stockmen to noticing they was mighty hard workers. Cold and stormy weather didn't seem to make no difference to them and whenever a neighbor rider spotted 'em they was either fogging wild horses or tending to their cattle. Hard riders minding their own business, and that gave a good impression.

But there was one who couldn't be impressed that way, that one was Crane, and on his account there come two officers to see the boys one day. They come to the house, the widow and Little Joey was there, and while they warmed up by the fireplace and waited they tried their best

There wasn't as many mustangs on the Four-Square
range that winter as there had been.

to get information from her, and even Little Joey, about the boys. But the widow and Little Joey didn't know anything but good to tell about 'em, and the officers seemed satisfied. Everybody they'd seen had said nothing but good about 'em, all but Crane, and when the boys got in from a long ride that evening they soon found out why Crane had been the only one to condemn 'em.

Stub took the lead and told the officers about Crane wanting the springs and range they'd located, and how he tried to crowd and starve them out by shoving all the cattle he could on their range.

"We worked hard to keep his cattle off," says Stub, "and it's news to us that any of 'em has been stole. I expect now he claims we stole 'em, anyway to get us off of here."

"He sure does accuse you boys," says one of the officers, "but I can see why now, and I don't believe any of his stock has been stole. If there was there'd sure be a trace of 'em somewhere. The stock Association's detectives have looked into all shipping and receiving points to within a thousand of miles of here and there's no records of such stock nowhere."

The boys smiled to themselves at that. The shipper they'd sold to sure savvied his business, they thought.

The officers stayed for the night, and when they left the next morning they seemed satisfied that if anybody had stole any cattle from Crane he was accusing the wrong folks.

As winter wore on and the boys kept hard at work they now and again heard rumors of Crane's talks. From one rider and another they'd meet in the hills or at headquarters they got to see that Crane was sure spreading poison. They'd hear how he was accusing them of stealing his cattle. He was also accusing them for other such doing in other countries, even going on to warn every stockman he seen to be sure and keep good watch on their stock while them outlaws was around, and saying that there would be no safety until they was run out of the country.

Come a time when Crane lost all hope of ever getting a trace of his steers or fastening the stealing of 'em onto the boys. But if he lost hope there he sure didn't lose any of getting them out of the country. He went to work all the harder to thinking up of things bad he could spread against 'em, and now them many things he thought of had got to be mostly thru a hate for them. Of course that hate had been stirred thru the loss of his springs and cattle, but that loss had now got to mean little with the thought of satisfaction he'd feel to see them boys somehow get in deep trouble. He'd even thought of hiring gunmen to scare or kill 'em off, but he didn't know of any gunmen he could trust with such a job, they would either give his plotting away for the fun of seeing him get in bad or else would only get the worst of it in a tangle with them mustangers. Crane had now learned that them boys was mighty smooth and sure wasn't lacking in nerve.

So, he put his energy to making up bad things to scatter around against 'em, and in the meanwhile kept his eyes and ears open for bad things he could pin on 'em.

With all bad rumors the boys kept a-hearing, they heard one that upset Stub and Hugh quite a bit. It was that they was wanted for horse and cattle stealing in many other countries, and all that was needed to convict 'em was one person to prove their identity. The person who could do that was known and now being hunted up.

The rider who brought that rumor grinned and remarked that the boys was sure getting popular. They grinned back, but that rider had no more than turned his horse to ride away when they looked at one another, and mighty serious. For they realized how close Crane was shooting at 'em, and during the same second the rider had quit speaking, the name of one person had come to their minds. Morris, . . . that feller from Antelope Basin who had spotted Stub while in town the fall before. Maybe he'd heard the rumors Crane had been handing around and hunted him up, and Crane would of been mighty glad to give him Stub's description. The reward was still waiting too for the man who would lead to his arrest.

There was others besides Morris who might of heard of Crane's talk and who could identify not only Stub but also Hugh and connect 'em with some things they'd done which the sheriff's wanted 'em for. The world is not very big for a man that's wanted by the law, and the boys felt a little nervous at the last rumor they'd heard. Even Andy who so far had kept clear of records was feeling a little nervous.

The boys had been running mustangs that day, and as they rode to their camp in the hills late that evening they talked well on the subject of what the rider had told 'em, and by the time the coffee boiled up they'd come to figure that what they'd heard was only a lucky wild shot from Crane, a closer shot than he could think he had made, for if he'd been anywheres near sure of his talk and if such a feller or fellers as Morris had seen him, he sure wouldn't of wasted no time to brought them to do the identifying and some officers to do the arresting. And instead of hearing only rumors from a rider passing by they'd been facing their enemies and the officers.

Everything was peaceful, and nobody else but the widow and Little Joey was waiting for them at the ranch when they got there a couple of days later and it wasn't many days after that when they forgot the rumor that had so upset 'em. Then, with hearing new rumors which was way off the mark they knowed for sure that Crane had only been guessing and inventing.

The boys' only fear now was of the widow hearing of some of the rumors. They sure didn't want her to think bad of 'em, or again to feel that all the stock, house and work done on the range and which she was sharing in the good of, was from money gathered by stealing. For that reason they sometimes felt like hunting Crane up and twisting his neck so there'd never be another squawk out of him. He'd caused his own trouble, they'd been glad to play square with him if he'd played square with them.

But if the widow heard any of the wild rumors while the boys was away running horses she sure never let on. They figured Little Joey would sure give it away if she had, but there wasn't one chirp from him either, and mother and boy acted the same as always, happy and contented. They always had the same pleased looks when the boys came back from their spells of mustang running. It could easy be seen on their faces how they thought of enjoying the few days ahead together on the range and then gathering at the fireplace at home in evenings. The widow and Joey rode every day the boys would be at the ranch. It took a very bad day to keep them inside then, specially Little Joey.

Little Joey was now growing to be quite a cowboy. His mother had told him that some day she would give him her share in the cattle but that he would have to learn well about them before she would, that he'd have to know them and the range like her pardners did, that he'd have to be able to rope and ride like they did, learn not to whimper when he was cold or hungry or things went wrong.

She didn't have to tell him that because that all was exactly what he wanted to be and do, but her telling made things all the better for him and he was learning faster than she even suspected. And sometimes she also thought that he was learning too fast as he'd be missing at noon and not show up till supper time. He'd be riding all by himself, the boys would be away running mustangs, and he'd be imagining he was boss of the Four-Square while he spotted cattle at one spring and then another, on the flats and in the hills and trying to remember the many cattle by sight. That was too much for him, or most anybody else, but he'd spotted "markers" in most every bunch so he'd recognize the bunch wherever he'd see it again and know what spring they was from and how far they'd drifted. He'd shoved many bunches back when he figured they drifted too far, and while driving 'em he threw many a loop in trying to catch two hind legs. He was getting on to that and he figured to be quite a hand when come time for spring branding.

He throwed many a loop in trying to catch two hind legs.

He was anxious for that time to come, not only to show the boys how well he could rope or what an all around hand he was getting to be, but Andy had promised him a little wild horse to break, all by himself. At that same time, Andy would be breaking some too, after round-up was over, and he'd have a lot of fun. Little Joey could ride good, very good on a gentle horse, but he hadn't rode a bucking horse yet.

As much as Little Joey would of liked to he didn't get to go running wild horses with the boys. But he'd been made near as happy by them telling that they needed a man like him to take care of things at home and on the range.

"You can't always tell when some bad horse or cattle thief might come along and raid the kitchen and then run off with our stock," Hugh had said. "The stock is bound to stray some anyway and we need a man to watch over everything at Headquarters all the time. If you wasn't there one of us would have to be."

That made Little Joey feel mighty big, proud and responsible and he kept an eagle eye on everything wherever he was at, often looking at his shadow while he rode. It looked pretty good size while he was alone.

With the first signs of spring, the boys gathered the mustangs they'd caught. The superintendent was on the job to make a count of them and gave the boys an inspection slip for twice the amount, which amount was soon made up of good range horses. After the horses was delivered to the commission man the boys took on a couple of days of celebrating. They'd worked mighty hard that winter, and anybody who'd followed their trail during that time would of agreed they sure deserved freedom in whatever they done. They fed up on special foods, got a little wild on good whiskey and made the rounds to wherever plenty of fun could be had. By the time the two days was over the boys had sometimes been with the company of the painted ladies at the honkatonks and talked as much at them times that they'd got to believing all they'd said while their rope arms was around their waists. Stub had been a general in some war and now was a retired cattle king. Hugh had started as a bartender and was now a senator, and Andy had been raised in a rattlesnake den and was now the champion rider and roper of the world. He could outride, outlove, and outfight any man. Nobody disputed his word about the riding.

When daylight come into their hotel window on the morning of their third day in town there was a regular passing of a pitcher of water amongst the three. The water seemed hot, but as they shook their heads after drinking it they got to feeling pretty well as they had during the two days before.

But there was a lot of work to be done. A wagon-load of grub would have to be got soon, it would be round-up time again and there was already big calves that should be branded even before then. It was after a few eye openers and breakfast that Stub left his two pardners in the restaurant, remarking that he'd have to buy a few things and would be back and ready to ride out of town in less than an hour.

Soon as he got out of the restaurant he hot-footed for the bank where he asked to see Mister Crane on very important business. He acted so pleasant and peaceful that Crane figured he maybe was anxious to make some deal to turn the springs over to him, and then all would quit the country. With that thought in mind he even smiled and invited Stub in his office. But he'd no more than closed the door when he felt, too late, that he sure hadn't been wise in doing that, for Stub's pleasant and peaceful look had changed to that of a snarling gray wolf. Crane wasn't exactly scared at first because he felt he could take care of himself, but he didn't know Stub as yet.

He got to know him plenty quick, for Stub didn't waste no breath or many words, only to let him know why he was going to give him the whipping of his life.

Stub tried to make that as quiet as possible but chairs and desk got in the way, and wanting to make a standing up fight so he could do his punishing on Crane to a turn he didn't think of a holler from him. And there was no holler from him, not till that feller figured he was about to be tore to pieces by them bony fists of Stub's. But Stub had done him to a turn by then and sort of changed his complexion, and when he did holler it was with the sound a drowning man would give. Another blow and he sprawled on the fine rug on the floor.

Stub didn't get back to his pardners in an hour, as he'd said. He faced the Justice that day. Crane appeared against him, his appearance wasn't pretty, and the judge decided right there and then to give Stub thirty days in jail. But he didn't pronounce the sentence, just made it appear to Crane that that's what he would get, and maybe a fine too. Crane walked out feeling happy but his face couldn't show no expression to that effect, and when the Justice made sure he was gone he made Stub tell his story over again. He listened well, grinned a little, and when Stub was thru he says, "This is the second time one of you boys have got into trouble. We want to keep law and order, but I've got to admit that you've been right both times." He smiled, and went on, "For the good of the cause I know you'll be happy to contribute twenty-five dollars, and I will let you go, providing you hit out of town within an hour. You're supposed to be in jail for thirty days, and don't forget that."

With that day's happening it was sundown by the time Stub was free to go to his two fretting pardners, and when he told 'em how he come to misjudge time by so many hours they figured it was a wonder he didn't misjudge by days instead. In less than *three* hours later they all rode out of town, happy. The shipping and celebration had been mighty successful and now they could go to riding with light hearts.

But the boys knowed better than to think that the whipping Stub gave Crane would tame him, but they had that much satisfaction, out of his hide. They wasn't surprised when they heard more rumors, rumors that didn't amount to much, and they had to laugh at one, that Stub was now in jail on suspicion of cattle stealing. The rider who brought that rumor also had to laugh as he told it to Stub who right then was very much on horseback and riding his range.

A wagon-load of grub was brought out of town and when it was put away it was decided that a good chuck-box would be put on the end of that wagon. Then, with skillets and dutch ovens in the wagon box there'd also be plenty of room for grub, bed rolls, tents, rope cable for corral, and all other things that was needed. It would be a regular round-up wagon like is used with regular cow outfits, for, now the Four-Square *was* a regular cow outfit.

The chuck box, jockey boxes, water barrel and all was fastened onto the wagon. The whole gathering of Four-Square folks was putting the finishing touches on the wagon one evening and joking amongst one another as to who was going to give up his horse to drive it when a rider come into sight. . . . That rider had been one of Crane's men, one who'd quit Crane during the rumpus with him the fall before, and after he was told to turn his horse loose, get himself something to eat, and then joined the three mustangers in the bunk house, he said something about wanting a job. He seemed like an answer as to who was going to drive that wagon.

But there wasn't much time used to driving the wagon, only when moving camp every couple of days, the rest of the time the new rider made himself mighty useful on a horse. He couldn't ride the rough ones like the three mustangers could. He was quite a bit older than them and got over being reckless, but if he couldn't ride a rough horse he sure made up for that on any long rides on gentler ones, as an all around cowman, a wizard with rope and stock and range.

He wasn't many days with the folks on the round-up when all felt they'd been with him for years and sort of wondered how come he hadn't been with 'em before that time. The widow took to him like she might of took to her dad, Little Joey would of called him grandpa if he'd knowed what the word meant, and the three mustangers felt sort of happy as he'd talk to 'em and call 'em "Son."

CHAPTER THIRTEEN

Ben Dowling was the rider's name, and he was with the Four-Square outfit only a couple of weeks when he sort of took it under his wing and begin to give orders to all, even the widow. By the time a month went by he sort of owned the outfit and nobody tried to make him think he didn't own at least part of it. He took it to hand to see that an iron wasn't burned too deep or blotched up, that ear-marks was cut clean, and in all ways, with the cattle, range, springs on down to the chickens he kept tab and put in his words as to this and that. The widow would mark some things down in the book, Joey got to watching his saddle blanket so it wouldn't wrinkle and make a sore back and the three mustangers listened to his "mark my words," grinning at his orders and rode to their work, feeling that gold was plain dirt alongside of him.

The round-up and branding over with and spring work all done, the boys didn't just sit around to whittling on sticks. Andy run in a few young horses that'd been picked out of the wild ones and started breaking them, there was a little wild one for Little Joey in that bunch too.

It was now well over a month since the last celebration, and Stub went to town again, not to celebrate but to get a load of lumber and a couple of carpenters, also a China cook. A cook shack was built in a hurry and the Chinaman went to work wrassling pots and pans there. The widow didn't at first take to the idea of a Chinaman doing the cooking instead of her, but she was finally made to laugh about that and she seen where her pardners was right again, there was more to cook for now and she got to realizing that that had been quite a job. She was now more free to ride and do other things she liked.

The cook shack was no more than finished and the Chinaman trained to Ben's orders when Stub and Hugh decided to take a long trip in scouting for cattle to buy. With Andy and Ben on the place they felt that things would be well looked after while they was gone, even to Crane's rumors or what else he might try.

It may be wondered why the boys would want to be buying cattle when they was so good at stealing them. . . . Stolen cattle would mean that the brands would have to be changed so they could be kept on their new range, there'd be the danger of the owners tracing them, detecting the original brands and the cattle would be living proof of their theft, for an original brand can be read for a long time after another brand is put over it.

It was altogether another thing with stealing cattle as the boys had, and shipping them. The cattle was soon in other hands, shipped many states away and soon slaughtered, and the evidence of the theft was made into shoe or saddle leather by the tanners before it was found out.

By stocking up their range with boughten cattle they would not only prove a clean record of 'em but a clean record of themselves in the country, and they wouldn't have to be looking over their shoulders at anybody being on the trail of 'em, or have any fear of sheriffs and warrants.

The Four-Square range was again in fine shape. Most of the mustangs had been caught or run off of it, Crane cattle wasn't shoved in on it no more, and the boys seen that it would take care of many times the cattle they now had on it. They had clear control of that range, they would get cattle with a clean bill of sale of 'em, and now that Crane wasn't bothering any more, only with his fool rumors, they sort of forgot about him and prepared to work, with only fine intentions of keeping clear of all trouble and to leading honest lives, all, outside of butchering a Crane beef once in a while for their own use, or putting their brands on big calves that neighboring outfits sometimes overlooked.

With all such good intentions in mind, Stub and Hugh filled up two kyaks (pack boxes) with enough grub to do for a couple of weeks, made up a bed roll and all was set to put on a pack horse. It was evening, and early the next morning they would be starting out on a cattle buying trip.

They was happy and felt at peace with the world when morning come and they started out on their trip, but their peaceful feeling turned to boiling war spirit when, as they stopped to a neighboring outfit's cow camp that night they was told another of Crane's made up rumors, a very different kind of rumor and one which, as the boys thought it over, sure called for action.

The trip and peaceful feeling was forgotten, and they rode back to the Four-Square, where by candle light in the bunk house that night they gathered with Andy and Ben, and all stomped the floor as they chewed up on and digested that rumor. Old Ben was for oiling up his gun and taking personal care of Mister Crane, but Stub and Hugh was for handing him more lasting punishment, and Andy was for everything that was started, if started soon enough.

Crane's latest rumor was plenty of cause to stir such a commotion as it had. The boys had only laughed at the other rumors but with this new one they wasn't the only ones aimed at, it was aimed mostly at the widow. The talk had been spread that she was of the kind who was mighty free with men and would live with any who had the price, plain scum and fitting only with such as the renegades that was her pardners.

The boys had been for hanging Crane up to a high limb when they first heard that rumor, but they finally cooled down and got to thinking that such actions would only go towards proving that what all he'd said might be true, and the talk would still live on after the buzzards had picked his bones clean. As it was now, nobody seemed to believe his talks, and that eased their feelings some. They went to doing some cold hard planning and come a time when the four decided to act on a scheme that was very likely to make Crane hunt a hole and wish he'd said nothing but good about the Four-Square folks.

It would take some time to go thru with the scheme they had in mind. It would be very risky too and would call for plenty of hard riding, but, if all went well, they would stop Crane's aggravations for good, and the risk they would be taking would only make things more interesting. There is no fun riding a rocking chair when your heart is set to riding an ornery bucking horse, one you want to tame and match skill against.

Stub and Hugh prepared for another trip, not a cattle buying nor a cattle stealing trip this time. Andy went along with them, as far as town, and there the three mustangers went to the big outfit's offices, got the attorney to prepare papers to the effect that Missus McKay would be sole owner of all the Four-Square holdings, rights and stock. The three signed the papers in front of a notary, then Andy took charge of 'em. He rode back to the ranch and his two pardners rode on.

After a few days' ride, Stub and Hugh come to where their trails forked. They rolled a cigarette while they talked some more on their scheme, then one took one trail going one way and the other took the other trail going another way. The three mustangers was now scattered three ways, but all working for one cause, with one thought, and they was as much together on that as if they'd been riding side by side.

CHAPTER FOURTEEN

IT WAS A STILL AND HOT SUMMER DAY on the Four-Square range, but nobody was idle there. The widow was mending some socks in the shade of the porch, Little Joey, riding his half broke horse, and Andy, on one of the same kind, only bigger and ornerier, was on a circle in keeping tab of the cattle. None was missing, for the Four-Square range was now the best in the surrounding country, and their main trouble was to keep stray cattle off of it. A few miles away from them was Ben, he had a big yearling tied down and muttering to himself, as he "run" (branded) the Four-Square iron on its slick hide, that the Crane outfit had sure got careless since "Gimlet" Garrity quit. Gimlet had quit at the time Crane started the rumpus when so many steers come up missing the fall before, and the yearling Ben was running the Four-Square iron on was, or had been, a Crane yearling.

Ben made sure the iron read well, then took his "Piggin String" (hogtie rope) off and let the yearling loose. He'd got on his horse, coiled up his rope and started to ride on, looking for another victim, when he seen a tall thin strand of dust hitting for the sky. It was a few miles away, but the day being so still the dust went high, like looking for relief from the heat. Ben's good range eyes soon made out two riders under that dust, riding slow enough, and going straight towards the Four-Square Headquarters.

He kept out of sight till the riders disappeared in that direction and then he maneuvered to ride so as not to be seen, and still be at the ranch

He'd got on his horse, coiled up his rope and started to ride on.

about the time they got there. There was no telling, he thought, as to what infernal things Crane might cook up, and he was always on the watchout for anything he might start.

So, he was prepared for anything but the good sight of the two riders unsaddling by the corrals, for they was none others than Stub and Hugh. A crop of dobie caked whiskers covered their faces, they'd shrunk in weight, so had their horses, but they was home again and the cracks in their sunburnt faces all led to smiles. They'd rode hard but there'd been no disappointments in their long trip.

CHAPTER FOURTEEN

Andy and Joey rode in some time later, after Stub and Hugh had got out from behind their mask of caked whiskers. The Four-Square folks was all together again. The talk was homey and cheerful as all gathered around the table for the evening meal, then to the porch of the house for a few hours. The widow seemed happiest of all, her whole "family" was with her once more, and as the boys talked she didn't get no hint of what they kept hid under their cheerful words.

It was late in the evening, the widow and Little Joey had gone to their rooms, to bed and to sleep. It looked like the boys was sound asleep too, for the bunk house was dark. But they was a long ways from asleep. All was stretched on their bunks, talking on their scheme and laying more plans.

It was along with them plans that Ben rode away from the Four-Square one day, straight to see the foreman of the Crane outfit. Some things, all important to the scheme had been talked about with him before and decided on, and Ben only acted as sort of messenger. He rode back to the Four-Square with a smile.

The summer passed without the boys buying any more cattle, as they had intended, and they seemed satisfied to just stay with the little bunch they had, take care of them and go to running mustangs when they could. It was a very peaceful summer, there was visitings from neighboring outfits' riders and all sure acted as neighbors should, all excepting Crane who still hadn't let up inventing and scattering all the bad he could about the mustangers and "their woman."

Many neighbors, who by now knowed the boys and the widow well, often asked why they didn't do something to stop him, that they'd be glad to help string him up or any such like. The boys hardly ever answered to them questions, they only smiled a little.

It was fall, and near round-up time when Crane got word from his foreman, and *he* didn't smile when he read the short note that'd been brought to him. It read that many cattle had disappeared and him and his riders had rode day and night but hadn't been able to find any trace of where they went to. It was thought that there was thieves at work, but no strange or suspicious acting riders had been seen, day or night.

Crane burnt the roads to the ranch again and stirred up another rumpus, accusing his men of being asleep in the saddle, accusing everybody, and mostly the Four-Square folks. He felt a little relieved, after he had all his words out, that his foreman and riders didn't quit as the other ones had. They'd stood up for their rights, just right, and then asked his advice as to what could be done. Crane didn't see the foreman's wink at the riders.

"I'm going to have this stealing stopped," says Crane, "and I'll have the law on the trail of who is doing it."

"But the law can't see any further in the dark than we can," says the foreman, "and it don't know our country as well. You can send as many law-men as you want, we'll be glad to help 'em and they'll relieve us some so we can catch up with some little sleep before the fall works start."

Crane went back to town, and it wasn't long after that when stock detectives and all kinds of detectives sort of swarmed around in and on the high points of the Crane and Four-Square range. They done a heap of hard riding and detecting, day and night. Then, to do some detecting from the "inside" a few tried to get jobs with both the Crane and Four-Square outfits, but the Crane foreman only said that he already had more men than the payroll allowed him, and the Four-Square complained and wished they had more cattle so they would have enough to do for their own selves.

Riders seemed to be everywhere, good stock association men. They investigated and detected for all their worth, but only found from all their work that the Crane men done plenty of riding and only for the interest of their outfit, none ever come up missing to draw suspicion. And as for the Four-Square folks they sure seemed Four-Square, for they got it from the neighboring outfits that the mustangers had been very much on their own range, riding after their own cattle and running mustangs. They could of been found home every night.

Crane burnt the
roads to the ranch.

Another thing, which sort of shook the law-men in their investigating, was that Crane seemed to be the only one to be making any holler or missing any cattle, and that from all neighboring cattlemen they got proof after proof that Crane had long tried in many ways to get rid of the Four-Square folks, mighty fine folks, they said, and for the reason that he wanted their range. He'd overcrowded it with his cattle and tried to starve their cattle off. The whole country knowed that, and when the superintendent of the big outfit verified all, added on how well he knowed the mustangers and would vouch for their character, finally advising that all eyes should be kept on Crane instead, also chipping in a few tips about him that might be interesting to law men, the investigating riders sort of begin to disappear, till by the time the fall round-up was in full swing there was none around to be seen, day or night.

Crane swore and fretted and paced the floor of his office, and when one investigator after another, thru the tips from the superintendent of the big outfit, begin to appear and get inquisitive he not only swore and fretted but he got sort of nervous.

All the while things kept a being peaceful on the Crane range, the foreman had sent in his note about the cattle stealing, he'd kept his job after that and tended to his business, with his and his rider's eyes closed to everything but what they was supposed to see.

Any outside rider would of figured the Crane men as good hard riding cowboys, the same as with any good cow outfit.

The Crane men was good hard riding cowboys, but with plenty of outlaw spirit in 'em, and they liked their little jokes, such as they was having with Crane. The foreman had picked them out from plain hard riding cowboys and *there* was a difference that Crane couldn't see.

The foreman and his riders was all with the scheme the three mustangers had mapped out. The foreman had had plenty of time to pick his riders for that purpose, and while doing that is when Stub and Hugh had went to their territories and picked good cattle thieves, fellers they knowed well and who often had wanted to go pardners with 'em, in anything. Them fellers had been hard to locate and that's why Stub and Hugh had been long in their trip, but the ones they'd located and decided to use with their scheme was good men for that game, and there was over a dozen of 'em stole another few horses from the country they left as they started for the country they was told to come to. They come by twos and threes, and like the mustangers, leaving bad names behind 'em, but not like the mustangers, not caring much if they made good their new names. The only thing they watched out for was that nobody picked up their trail on the way to the mustangers' country, and not to be caught on anything they done after they got there, at least not till the job was done, the job that Stub and Hugh had lined out to 'em.

Stub and Hugh had made that job so it would be mighty easy and profitable for them. With Ben's help they'd first got to know that Crane's foreman didn't give a daggone for Crane and that he'd close his eyes on any sign of stock missing if by doing that he would get a share of the proceeds. He had a family to support. . . . The share had been agreed on and the foreman grinned and then agreed to close his eyes while he rode. He was then advised to pick riders who'd do the same and they would get some share too, then they could go on riding the same as ever, and keep up a bluff that all done their best as to Crane's interest.

When the cattle thieves came, by twos and threes, either Stub or Hugh rode with 'em for a day or two, showed 'em Crane's range and cattle and told 'em to get to work and use their own judgment as to ways of getting the cattle out of the country and shipping points across the line into another State where there was no inspection. They was warned not to take too many bunches to any one shipping point and was also relieved of any fear of the Crane riders being on their trail. That had been all fixed. The only thing they'd have to watch would be inquisitive riders along the trail, maybe stock detectives who'd sure be apt to cause trouble or give word to other authorities or Crane himself. They would want to be as careful as if they was stealing in their own risky ways, and that way they'd be a heap safer all around.

That was easy for the cattle thieves Stub and Hugh had picked out. They'd had plenty enough experience so as not to get careless and they would be all of careful, with taking not too big a bunches of cattle at a time, not too often, and scatter the shipping of them to different points. Everybody went on to their work happy, while Crane paced the floor of his office, getting more and more fidgety.

With all the scary questions Crane had had to answer to investigating men packing books, and other investigating men packing badges, for some weeks he wasn't all in good humor or peaceful or rested when one of his riders dropped into his office (Crane looked to see that the door was open. He hadn't forgot Stub's visit.) and handed him a note to the effect that many more cattle was missing, that all had rode night and day trying to find them but with no results. It was suspicioned that the cattle had been stolen.

"And," the rider says, "there's been some men looking over some of your cattle too and wondered about the brands on them."

Crane's actions was very different than before when he got such a note as the foreman sent him. He didn't show no symptoms of wanting to burn the road for the ranch. Maybe what the rider said about men looking over some of his brands sort of stopped him. Anyway, all he done was to just face a blank wall for a spell and tinker with a pencil. Finally he turned to the rider and asks, "Why didn't the foreman come in himself to tell me this?" And the rider says, very serious, that the foreman couldn't leave right now, not with the cattle stealing going on and with the old brands being wondered about.

If Crane paced the floor before, he about raced on it after the rider left. He only gave the rider word that he'd look into the stealing right away and for him to hit back for the ranch. Then before the rider went out the door he asked what brand of his it was that had caused wondering, and when the rider told him he thought of only one man who would know about it, that was the superintendent of the big outfit. . . .

The Crane men kept a-riding and not seeing, the cattle thieves kept a-stealing and not being seen, and the Four-Square folks just rode, happy and on their home range. Only once in a while would Stub and Hugh disappear for a few days, keeping tab with their friends, and cattle thieves.

Winter was coming on and the Crane herds was shrinking to where it was figured there'd soon be more Crane riders than cattle. Then later on, a day along about Christmas time, the foreman himself rode to town to see Crane. Crane was staring at some figures on a paper pad, he turned it over as his foreman appeared, and when he asked him what made him come in he was told there was only a few hundred cattle left on his range, and that most of the riders had to be let go.

"With the way this stealing is going on," says the foreman, "you won't have no cattle nor no outfit at all and there's no use of me keeping riders when I have no use for them. I come personal to tell you this."

The foreman felt pretty pleased with everything on general as he walked out of Crane's office. He'd himself got a good hunk of money out of Crane's cattle, a man which he figured was lower than a skunk's tracks, and he'd had a great pleasure in getting that money and working with the three mustangers. It all might of been crooked, but also more square, to his spirit, than crooked. He knowed right even when it would be called wrong, and his conscience was all smiles.

And to any who might wonder, nobody could say that he didn't keep Crane posted as to the cattle being stolen. He'd done that well and at just the right time, for the cattle thieves. He grinned at the thought as he rode back to the ranch.

With all of Crane's worries, investigations and things tightening up on him at the bank, with all that was surrounding and closing in on him there, he got to watching for a way out. Then there was that brand on his cattle, what few he had left. That brand was *living evidence* against him, stolen cattle from other ranges, none that he'd stole himself but which he'd had stolen for him. He'd have a hard time to explain that. And now that his outfit was nothing more than a shadow, he got to do some hard figuring, like a trapped cayote, on how to save his hide. A cayote would chew his leg out of the trap if kept in it too long. . . .

It was during the Christmas holidays, everybody in town was feasting on turkey and spreading cheer, everybody, seemed like, but Crane. Crane was facing a cold wind acrost open country and heading for his ranch. He drove slow, doing a heap of thinking, and he didn't start no rumpus with his foreman and riders when he got there, instead he wanted their help, specially the foreman's.

He asked the foreman to his office of the ranch house and there he talked to him in confidence.

"I'm licked," he says, "and I've got to get out of the country on the quiet. I want to sell my outfit and I don't want to advertise that in town or anywhere. Will you help me and find somebody who would want to buy it, on the quiet, till I at least get out of the country?"

"I'll sure be glad to do all I can to help you out," says the foreman, and he meant that.

That's how come that a few days later, Stub came into Crane's office again. Crane was for closing the door and not letting him in, but he finally understood the look in Stub's eyes, invited him in and closed the door. Some dickering was done quiet and the two come to a price on the ranch, then Stub went to Blain at the big outfit's office, and had him look into things as to deeds and mortgages. The deeds was found clear, a notary was hunted up, and then Stub and Crane gathered to Blain's office. All was fixed up there. The deeds of the Crane ranch, holdings and stock was turned over to Stub, which was right away transferred to the widow's name, Stub handed Crane the money and the deal was over. The Crane outfit now belonged to the Four-Square outfit.

Stub didn't waste no time to get back to what had been Crane's range headquarters, for he was in a hurry to stop his friends the cattle thieves from running off any more cattle, but he didn't have to worry there, for the foreman had already took care of that. Most of the cattle thieves had gone on to other territories, leaving grateful words for the three mustangers, also a share of the proceeds from the cattle which hadn't been asked for. That was a case of honor amongst thieves, where thieves went that honor one better.

Only two of the cattle thieves was at Crane's headquarters when Stub rode in. They'd stayed only to deliver the other cattle thieves' messages, also the share of the cattle sale proceeds. With the messages from all they would like to help again any time the mustangers worked up another scheme.

After the two cattle thieves rode away, Stub sort of shook his head and wondered how many honest men was as square and free hearted in their dealing as they was.

He walked into Crane's old ranch office and there he found the foreman putting some figures down on paper.

"I'm just marking down how many cattle and horses there is here," he says. "I guess I'm thru with my job now, and you'll want some tally of the stock."

Stub grinned. "You're not thru with this job unless you want to be," he says. "I'd like to have you keep on handling this outfit for us."

That was more than agreeable with the foreman. "I'd sure like to be with you folks," he says. He stuck out his hand and went on, "I'd be a regular cow foreman for you and you can sure depend on me to work for your interest."

"You've proved that," says Stub.

Well now, the Four-Square spread was quite a spread, with quite a few cattle and with range enough for many times what was running on it. The Crane herds would have to be built up again, and there was plenty of room for improvement with the Four-Square original herds too. That was easy to see and decide on, and soon as there'd be signs of spring, Hugh and Andy would go on a scouting trip where they could buy good cattle at a fair price.

All was at peace with the Four-Square and Crane range. There'd been no more rumors from Crane, not till one day, and then that rumor was *about* instead of from him. It wasn't only a rumor but it was spread in the papers, of his disappearing, and with most of the bank's money. There was a big reward posted for him.

That was a lot of news for the country around, but to them who knowed him they wasn't at all surprising news, and when they come to think about it they figured for sure now that all Crane had said about the Four-Square folks was not only lies and to get them out of the country, but them Four-Square folks also sure must of had something on him. It more than looked that way, for now they had his outfit and he'd quit the country.

When spring come, Hugh and Andy went on their cattle buying trip, leaving the others to take care of the branding, and by middle summer two long herds was drove onto the Crane range, one was scattered there and the other was split in two, and one-half scattered on the Four-Square. There was plenty of cattle now to keep quite a few riders busy, the Crane foreman was happy with his job and men, old Ben was happy with doing his bossing on the Four-Square, the widow was happy and kept pretty busy handling the books and marking down all cattle, expenses and such, Little Joey was also happy in trying to be everywhere at once, riding and roping, and the three mustangers was happy as the rest. They was feeling like big cowmen now. The only thing was, everything had got so peaceful, everything going so well that it seemed their work was done. Everybody on the outfit had took charge with all heart interest, if they thought of anything to be done it was already done before they could mention it. They was just riding around like lords and seemed like not allowed to do anything. They wouldn't of been surprised to see their horses groomed, saddled for them some morning, have their coffee served in bed and find their boots shined.

It was great to see all the cattle and the range, all theirs and with not a string on their holdings by no one. It was mighty fine home and range and a living of plenty, but that spoiled some things. There was no fun in branding somebody else's cattle any more, nor even butchering a neighbor's beef, they had too many cattle of their own. And there'd be no fun in stealing any more bunches of cattle, for there was no reason, they had plenty of money and there was nobody to aggravate 'em for any such work. They sometimes even wished Crane was back on the job.

Stub was the most contended. Hugh was some contended too, when the widow was riding by his side, and Andy contended himself with breaking horses or running wild ones. There was one thing they would often do, running wild ones, but the fun would stop at the end of the chase, for they didn't need no mustangs and they didn't care to ship 'em any more.

They was glad when fall round-up come.

They was glad when fall round-up come. The hard riding, with all the "family" together, and the other riders, chased away the restless feeling that had begin to take holt of 'em. Counting the widow and Little Joey, there was twelve riders with the round-up wagon that fall, then there was a regular round-up cook too, and a horse wrangler. There was two wagons to haul the grub, water and bedding, a "cavvy" of a hundred saddle horses, and as that outfit strung out across the big flats it looked like a sure-enough round-up outfit. At least, the widow and Little Joey sure thought so.

With all the range they now had, the mustangers didn't see where it was at all necessary, as they had thought at first, to develop any more water or pipe the water from the springs to where better feed might be. There was now plenty of feed everywhere to very easy take care of all the stock they had, all the stock they would want to own, and they didn't care to spread to any bigger outfit than what it was. For the size it was a heap more than plenty to take care of the four pardners of the Four-Square.

Round-up over with, the boys was sort of lost as to what to do. There was plenty of riding of course but their riders seemed to be handling that very well and, anyhow, there wasn't so much thrill as they thought there would be with riding after their own cattle, and they now realized that the getting of 'em was a heap more thrilling than the owning.

Even Stub had got to feeling that the getting was a heap more interesting than the having. To sort of break the spell, the mustangers and the widow and Little Joey went to town for a few days. The widow had great fun buying things again, but with her and Little Joey, the boys was sort of held down in their ways of celebrating. Then again, the folks around town had got to hear much about the three mustangers, how they was responsible for the crook Crane to be found out and him leaving the country, they was looked at as big and prosperous cattlemen, was respected as such and the boys felt handicapped there again in their celebrating, for everybody would have their eyes on 'em and they couldn't at all be free in their actions. They even had to give their opinion as to who they thought was likely candidates for this and that office, and such like, and the judge and sheriff even bowed to 'em when they'd pass 'em on the street.

They felt near at their old ease when, back at the ranch, a heavy storm come and filled every dobie tank and cow track full of water, the cattle scattered all directions to new feed, for there was water everywhere, and when the storm waters dried up and cattle had strayed far from their range is when they was some contented again, with their riders and finding all the cattle that had strayed away.

A little more interest was stirred up when Andy one day spotted a cream colored mustang, near white, with jet black mane and tail, it was a stud too and of good size and build or he wouldn't of looked at it the second time. It was a mighty pretty animal but too oddly marked and noticeable for Andy to want him for himself. Such odd marked horses and so easy to be seen and recognized again don't blend well with the country and any horse thief or cattle rustler keeps shy of them. The outlaw rider will always pick on a straight-color horse, no pintos, no blacks nor whites, but dark buckskins, dirty-grays, mouse-colored, bays, sorels and such like.

Of course Andy wasn't no outlaw rider no more, he was a very respected citizen in the country, like his two pardners, Stub and Hugh, but he couldn't outlive his thirty years of outlaw raising and practice in a year or two, and his raising wouldn't as yet allow him to care for any horse of color or markings that was "give-aways." He wanted to catch that horse for Joey.

That horse was new to the country. Neighboring riders said they'd heard of him, that many had tried to catch him and that the way he come to this country was because he'd been chased too much in others. That made the catching of him more interesting, and the three mustangers planned to relay on him and "put a twine on him" (rope him) before he run on to other ranges.

The boys run the stud one day to find out which way he would circle, left him alone a couple of days and then took their stations ten miles or more apart. The stud, being mighty wise, didn't keep to his circle and he got clean away from 'em. They run him another day and found that that horse couldn't be depended on to run any certain direction, then they got leary that he would quit the country.

They left him alone for a day or so, the stud was getting sore footed, and more tender on 'em if left alone and not heated up. Then on another day's run, the boys not taking any certain place to relay from, it happened to be Stub's luck to have the chance to spread his loop on him. The horse had been run close to sixty miles that day.

The catching of that horse was another feather to the mustangers' bonnets, and the neighboring riders coiled their ropes up to their saddle, with remarks that there was no use trying to catch any wild horse them mustangers wanted.

But with Stub catching the stud that sort of left Andy out as to who he wanted to give him to. Stub was neutral, and then Hugh comes along with the remark that the stud would sure make a fine horse for the widow. Stub and Andy grinned and, well, Andy figured, Little Joey would have plenty of chances at many other good horses.

Hugh took it to hand to break the horse himself, laughing at Andy that he wanted to be sure the horse was broke right, and as the widow kept a-seeing Hugh riding him time after time, she wondered at the pretty sight of that horse and how Hugh was taking so much pains with him.

The horse was learning fast and fine. Hugh had took the buck out of him at the first few saddlings, and by the time spring was in the air the horse was gentle as a gentle kitten and wise to rope and rein. Then, one clear spring day, Hugh put the widow's saddle on him and brought him up to the porch of the house.

It would be a couple of weeks now, and time for spring round-up. With spring breezes, the boys had got pretty restless. They would be glad when round-up started. But that work would only last for a few weeks and then there was a whole summer facing them, a summer of restlessness and aching for action besides the riding after their cattle and such like work. Their riders could do that well without 'em.

They'd thought of that quite a few times, all three of them, but none had dared give a hint to one another of any rambling hankering for fear that such hankerings wouldn't go well with one and the other, after all had worked, planned and stole so hard to make home range and outfit where they wouldn't have to dodge from as they had in other territories. It was great to have that secure feeling but that had sort of wore out on 'em, and not a one dared say anything, not even after one noticed the other two's jingling spur rowels while their bodies was still, and noticed his own spur rowels jingling too.

Such was the strength of the three mustangers for one another. Then one day there come a sudden relief.

A rider from the big outfit bumped into Ben. He had a very important message he wanted to deliver to Stub, and Ben took the written message, saying he would sure take care of it. Ben read the message and he scouted the country, where he figured they'd went. He found the three together, off their horses and making marks with brush twigs on the dobie ground as to how one brand could be changed into another without even the owners of the original suspicioning.

Ben's dust at a distance, and then his worried look gave them a hunch that all wasn't well but they sort of welcomed that as Stub was handed the message. Stub read it and passed it on to his two pardners, and Ben was surprised as he watched the expressions on the three faces that none showed a flicker of excitement.

The message was from the superintendent of the big outfit and it read that a feller by the name of Morris had come onto his range looking for cattle to buy, that while going thru he'd seen a black, blazed face horse in the big outfit's pastures which he recognized as belonging to one of the outfits he was buying cattle for and one of the many that had been stolen from them. He was sure, because he'd rode that horse himself. He'd asked as to who the horse and the others he recognized belonged to and before the superintendent got wise to the talk, Morris had been talking to the ranch bookkeeper. The bookkeeper had given away the names and descriptions of the men, the three mustangers, and of course, Stub's description. Then Morris had started for town in a hurry, remarking that the three mustangers was wanted, not only for one but for many cases of horse and cattle stealing. The superintendent wrote that he seen that no riders was near to be deputized and Morris had went to get officers to do the arresting.

The boys handled the message for a while, recollecting Morris, and thinking of the new evidence he'd found, and at the same time a little fearful as to how one and the other would take the message. Each one was waiting for the other to show a sign to the effect of it, while in their hearts they all felt the thrill of being on the dodge again. The thrill come, not to be against the law but to be in action again, in the action they was used to.

Stub crumpled the superintendent's note, lit a match to it, watched it burn and then mashed the ashes in the dobie dirt with a boot heel.

"Well," he says, "it looks like it's our move, and we're all in for it this time."

Ben couldn't figure the boys out. "Who in samhill can prove you stole them horses," he says to all three.

Stub grinned. "There's other things besides that that can be proved," he says, and Hugh agreed that there was.

There was some more that Ben couldn't figure out. Like for instance, the boys didn't jump on their horses to make fast getaways, or showed any fear of officers soon to be on their trail. They rode back to the ranch, light as spring breezes, and after they got there they only went to the bunk house and stretched out. It was evening, but evening or no evening the mustangers sure wasn't acting as men with the law on their trail.

The boys layed in the bunk house one whole night. Ben done the less of the sleeping, and before daybreak he was up watching the skyline for officers.

To the widow, everything was all cheerful when the boys came to breakfast. She wondered, as the meal was over, how Hugh took her hand and pressed it, Stub and Andy done the same, placed good arms on Little Joey's shoulder and told the widow they was going for another trip, a long one.

With the message from the superintendent of the big outfit and the good reason showed to them why they'd better be riding, the boys sort of lost the hankering they'd had to be on the drift again. Wherever they looked it was theirs, the hills, the cattle and the horses. And, with all their restlessness, Stub got to realizing mighty strong that it was quite a spread him and his pardners had got together. Hugh felt near the same and would of liked to presented the widow with a few more good saddle horses, and Andy wanted to finish the horses he'd started to break, while Little Joey watched him.

But, before noon they'd gathered a string of fresh horses and run them into the corral, good fresh horses and the best in the country. Out of them the three mustangers caught the three best ones and saddled 'em. Bundles of dry grub was tied behind three saddles. Ben was told as to the handling of the outfit, that all of it was to Mrs. McKay's name, and his eyes was moist as he shook hands with the three mustangers. But moist as his eyes was he was the first to see a dust on the skyline, and half a dozen riders under it, the officers.

"Ben," says Stub, as him and Hugh and Andy got on their horses, "we're going to leave a dust too. Point it out to them."

"Yes," says Hugh. "We don't want them to stop here."

Andy added on a word for Joey, and the three mustangers begin to ride, on three fresh horses.